Shirley Day

ATTERCOPPE

ATTERCOPPE

SHIRLEY DAY

ATTERCOPPE

SHIRLEY DAY

Dedicated to the kids for letting me get on with it, and my husband for telling me about the dream.

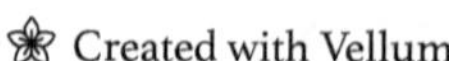 Created with Vellum

1

CAR TROUBLE

The rain pounds on the metal roof, frenetic as a troupe of angry monkeys as my fingers fumble with the catch on the glove compartment. My phone hasn't got a connection. The satnav on the car's bust. He took the wrong turn in the road, but it's me who'll end up having to pay.

'There's a map here somewhere.' My voice sounds too small, apologetic. I hate it when my words do that. It irritates the shit out of him too, but that's out of my control. The night is dark. We're lost, and the man next to me, sitting in the driver's seat, is an out-and-out grade-A nutter. This I know for a fact because I've been "married" to him for the past eight years. A large, awkward slice of my life, seeing as I'm only twenty-three.

Even in the darkness, I'm all too aware that the raging storm is not just on the outside of the car. My husband has his own angry cloud circling above his head. He's not speaking. He doesn't need to; the silence that surrounds him is as messed up as a wire scrubbing brush stuck in an electrical socket.

My fingers feel fat, inept, as they continue to press the knackered catch on the glove box. He should have hired something more modern—the car's a wreck. He likes to travel incognito and unflashy, but this pile of scrapyard jiggery-pokery is getting us nowhere fast. I rattle at the catch. Why won't the damn thing open? Then I stop. A cold wave of terror passing over me. Actually, I don't want it open.

'I think it's locked.' My voice has lost its little girl squeak of panic. Instead, I manage to keep it quiet, natural—not too studied.

'Locked!' He growls.

'Jammed. Jammed,' I correct myself quickly, needing to get some kind of control back. Maybe I am young, but I'm the voice of trust. People take everything that comes out of my mouth as God's honest truth. Most people. Most likely, I could feed the Dalai Lama a lie without him noticing the tiniest dull in my aura. Jayden, my piece-of-shit husband, is sadly a different story. He's got a fib detector embedded between his white luminous ears and permanently set to on. So, treading carefully is the name of the game. Taking a deep breath, I try to centre the "story". It's an old trick. The first rule a telesales con artist gets to learn—you need to get the story working for you.

'Pretty sure I can remember what the satnav said before it died.' I'm leaning heavily on a diversion tactic: if a situation is not working, point it in a different direction. Only Jayden is also right up to speed on every trick in the manual; he wrote it. Besides, I'm not so cool in the flesh as when hiding faceless at the end of a telephone signal. Which is a problem since no one is answering their phones anymore. But that's another story.

For now, a little luck and bluster are what's called for.

This current situation could easily all go belly up and ballistic. My "loving" husband could lean over and attempt to open the glove compartment. It's locked, but he's a walking bundle of muscle and fist. If Jayden goes towards the glove box, there's no point in me blocking it. He'll enjoy the fact that he has to push me aside. Also, if I block him, he'll be on the lookout for something odd. Keeping it contrived yet casual, I lean back in my seat just as he leans forward across me. My fast-pumping, over-large heart appears to have crawled up through my windpipe; I can barely breathe.

'I'll take the car back on Monday, get a refund for the satnav.' *Helpful* is always a good trait. It opens people up, normally. Only tonight, for Jayden, with the hammering rain and the wall-to-wall dark wallpaper of trees we've found ourselves jammed in, *helpful* has the opposite effect, fuelling his irritation. Instead of reaching for the glove box, those fat, fag-smelling fingers fiddle angrily with the satnav itself. So angrily, he pulls the damn thing out of the dash. Its wires dangle down by the dark well of the gear stick with all the spark of a dead jellyfish. It'll be him who'll have to argue for the money back on the car now: there's damage, and that's always a tricky one to walk away from. At a slight five foot six, I don't have the frame for intimidation-bargaining. That will have to be Jayden's job. In reality, keeping my wits about me has to be my current focus—protecting myself, which also includes avoiding him going into the glove box.

'Honestly, Jay.' My voice sounds light but not flippant. Helpful, but not sycophantic. In short—neutral. Because anyone who's ever had the shit kicked out of them knows that fear is an invitation. 'We need to go back down this road through the woods, to the right, then out onto the A12.'

'Damn.' His heavy, bloated fingers strike the steering wheel.

I let the sound of his anger echo through the car for a moment. A dim beam from our headlights is being thrown back from the trees, illuminating the little blue-ink cross tattoo on Jayden's white, hairy index finger. Funny a man like him ending up with the symbol of forgiveness etched onto his skin. It's not exactly his style. But there's no time for ruminating on theology. We need to get the wheels of the blessed car moving forward because if he's driving, he's going to have to concentrate on something other than me.

'Stupid bitch.'

It's not the words that are worrying. It's the tone of his voice, which appears to be going in slo-mo. Always a bad sign. The body's fight-or-flight index slows the world down so that you can hatch up your escape plan. Something I don't have. For me, it's already too late. I turn towards him, cowering in my seat. Pressing my back as far as it will go into the hard, plastic car door behind me, pressing till the sharp handle pushes through my wide, black puffa. Jayden's face glares at me, over-large, moving into my space, set into some kind of hideous Goyan mask of anger. His eyes, burning dark pricks of irritation. His jaw locked. Those over-white teeth glinting, barred in a calcium grill of hate.

There's a short, sharp slam to the back of my head. My body jerks forward as a splitting pain engulfs me, a sear of hot, white light flooding my brain. Somewhere, he's talking, spewing out insults and reprimands. The words are unclear because the ringing in my ears is far too loud. I'm almost inside the sound, if that's possible. Gripping the dash, taking a moment to get my breath, to re-anchor myself in the world of the living as I discover, no, it's not the sound I'm inside: it's hell. My body caves as my arms sprawl across the dashboard, floundering. My limbs have zero volition of their own. They wibble like they haven't even got any bone. I need to get out. If I want to survive, it's now or never.

Somewhere I sense he's moving again, not towards me, thank God. It must have been a one-hit deal, not the bumper package. My immediate goal is to remain injured and invisible until I can muster enough energy to make it worth the run. There's no point in running unless it'll get me clear of his blows.

Jayden's turning the key in the ignition. The engine coughs. The bunch of metal tongues clatter and chatter as he swirls them again and again. Turning too hard, too often. His left foot pressing down so sharply into the footwell that it could easily go through the floor. If he doesn't break through the metal and give the clutch a breather, the engine will flood. The rain hammers even harder. The car spluttering as though drowning. I allow my fingers to touch my forehead, exploring the damage, pulling my hands away when a line of pain courses angrily through me. A warning. There's a cut somewhere. In the dim yellow glow reflected from the headlights, I can see trails of bright red blood on my fingertips.

The driver's door opens. The soundtrack outside is of a curtain of rain seeping through the ringing and raw pain of my own private universe, the persistent hush sounding curiously reassuring, like a lullaby.

The light through the windscreen suddenly falls into darkness. At first, I think I've passed out, but then the pain reminds me that having passed out is not a possibility. He must be looking at the engine—the hooked-up bonnet is throwing the interior of the car into darkness. Idiot. The silent insult gives me a pinch of satisfaction. Jayden wouldn't know how to fix a lawnmower. It doesn't matter. What matters is that suddenly, there is time, time without scrutiny.

Grabbing my bag, I unzip the hidden pocket in the lining, pulling out a small cluster of spare keys, allowing myself just one second to glance up at the bonnet for good measure. He's still behind it. His shadowy form glimpsed through the gaps. Relief washes over me as I slip the miniature square-ended key into the plastic lock, and the glove compartment opens. Feeling past the crumpled paper of the map, reaching for the felt grey wallet inside, my fingers fix on its thick textured weave. Freedom. The thought is so delicious it floods through me top to toe with a warm wash of hope. There's a plastic bag in there too. It rustles as the felt purse moves past it. Useful. Putting the wallet in the carrier bag to protect it, I wedge them both into the inner pocket of my coat and ease the glove compartment closed. Taking a deep breath, placing one hand on the door handle, I allow myself just one last moment to fill my lungs—this is it.

Pressing down hard, I push the door open and jump out, moving quickly to the front of the car. Knocking the bonnet support and ramming the lid down hard as I can muster on Jayden's large ugly head. His body buckles as he groans and swears. Those wide stocky legs of his wriggling, comic book funny in the absence of his torso, but this is not the place for amusement. I'm poking the hornet's nest. This injury has to be meaningful. I press down harder before swinging the bonnet back up. His face turns slowly towards me. His curly dark hair strung lanky from the rain around his high cheekbones.

There's a red, angry burn on the side of his temple. The pupils of his sharp blue eyes are swollen. White, golf-ball wide, surprised, yet already filled with hate. A cotton-thin thread of blood trickles down the line of one cheek. Vermillion like his temper. His mouth opens in a shout. He draws back a little, readying his entire weight for its lurch towards me, but I'm too quick. With all my might, I whack the bonnet down again. This time leaning on top of it, every inch of my being bouncing my buttocks against the metal hood.

Jayden's angry muffled screams come from inside the engine. I wonder if I've got another slam dunk in me? Another opportunity to enjoy the righteous indignation on his face. Maybe not. His arms are octopusing out backwards from under the bonnet, trying to catch at my legs, my body, anything that can haul me to him. Only I'm careful not to get too close. No, another slam dunk would be asking for trouble. Instead, giving it everything I've got, I kick his right leg. He hollers, the sound strong and angry, but his leg buckles. That's enough. That has to be enough.

Turning towards the road, my heart sinks. It's stretching out, a long wet snake, ahead of me. Cutting its straight, hard path through the wood. He'll find me in an instant if I stick to the tarmac; mow me down with a look of manic delight on his blood-smeared, engine-burnt face. I twist my body towards the cover of the trees; that's where I need to be, hidden, and I run.

2

HIT

I hear him growling from the road behind me. Angry words barked into the night, rabid dog style. His roar seems close despite the distance I keep putting between us. He has a presence, my husband, one that extends so much further than his own personal space. That's why the fit had always worked so seamlessly. He has the muscle, and me, I'm that little slip of a nobody that can pass for a person's daughter or niece or that nice girl next door that everyone used to know. The one they forgot the moment they stopped seeing her. Tonight, I need to play on that "invisibility". Finally, make it work for me, blend in.

Stumbling forward through the trees, my foot catches on a root, a branch? It's unclear; in the dark, I can barely see. My boot sticks, and I'm thrown off balance, falling forward into the damp mossy undergrowth. The smell of wet autumn leaves fills my nostrils as my face comes down smack on the soft, decayed layers of the forest floor.

'Bitch,' he shouts from somewhere behind me. The sound pulling a shiver down my spine.

From my hiding place in the tangled undergrowth, I

glance back. My breath coming so fast it's in danger of bringing vomit with it every time it bursts from my fragile body in watery gulps. In the fractured light from the road, through the crosshatch of trees, Jayden's shadow is moving ape-like. Forwards, backwards, pacing the length of the silhouetted car. His wide arms rising and falling in rage.

Reaching out for the nearest tree, rather than standing upright, I pull myself through the mud on my stomach like a slithering worm. Once behind the wide trunk, I feel a little comfort, as though this small envelope of forest is shrouding me in an invisibility cloak, and I press my face into the wet bark, drinking in the dank smell of lichen and moss as I crouch in the darkness, hidden. The intermittent shouts of anger emanating from the road make me feel like a hunted animal crouching in its burrow. Waiting for a dog to stick its snout towards me in my hole and drag me with sharp teeth back out into the world. And yet, for a moment, I feel safe, surrounded by the thick air. The smell of it, dense with vegetation, mud and mineral-laden rain. The smell so thick that it seems almost physical. As though a tangible barrier exists between that beast of a man and myself. The wood is protecting me.

My heart continues to thump as the ape-man paces backwards and forwards, in the spotlight now. The rain soaking into him. His Jesus hair, those dark brown locks he's so proud of, are flattened tight and straight, clinging to his thick skull. Luckily, there's barely any moon, and the head-lights from the car are pointing idly along the road: the wrong direction. It's me who is getting the show, not him. My heart beats so loud in my ears that I can't hear every-thing he's growling out into the night, just snatches. It doesn't matter. He's braying for blood.

There are two things, I remind myself as I clutch the

tree, digging my nails into the soft, rain-sodden trunk. Two things I need to remember: keep quiet (definitely) and keep moving. Only I can't do that. I'm too scared. Paralysed. Clinging to my tree, I sink my nails even deeper into the wet wrinkled bark, anchoring myself to the spot. I can't move. I can't run. Tears roll down my cheeks.

AFTER WHAT SEEMS LIKE FOREVER, the car engine fires. The wheels begin to turn, spraying up a squelch of mud in their wake. Jayden won't stop looking for me, but he's on the tarmac. Avoid the road, and I should be fine. Maybe not fine, but if this were a game, I might make it to the next level. Pulling my nails from the bark and circling the trunk between both hands, I hoist myself to my feet. This isn't a game, though. Maybe there's a smattering of similarities; the idea that life has levels of survival. I've spent most of my natural slinking along at level one. I could have died there too, but this evening I'd shot my head above the parapet. The longer I survived, the better chance there was of me breaking free.

As I untangled my ankles from the cluster of ivy I'd gathered on my slide through the mud, the vines cut into my palms. It would be easier to stay, to sink down on this spot and give up the ghost. It's October, so there isn't much leaf cover dressing the wood. Come morning, he'd spot me easily. That can't happen. I glance furtively around. The stark bones of trees span out either side of me, a myriad of imaginary paths winding their way in all directions. Which is the right one? All the adrenalin that had been pushing me forward has vanished. Lethargy falls on my shoulders like a heavy woollen blanket. The rain drips down my face, running in streams across my body, finding its way into my coat. I'm just going to go forward. If I run around in circles, so be it, but I'm going to move one step at a time in the direction I landed. There is no alternative. And so, with heavy feet, I run.

I'm not actually any good at running, especially when my head feels as though it's been split in two by an axe. Realistically, I should have been practising: sprinting to the shops when he wanted milk or fags. This was always going to happen at some point. I'm twenty-three; my body should be able to cope with a jog through the woods, but this is not a jog, and it doesn't take long for my limbs to scream out, reluctant and worn. You need to breathe if you run, and I'm far too panicked for breathing. Every breath I pull into my body is all over the place, choked with sobs and wracked with poor-mes, which have to stop. *Poor me* never got anyone anywhere. Establishing a rhythm is important. I can do this. It's not a sprint. This is for the long haul. One, two. I count. Then again. One, two. As the mud slips and slides out from under my boots. One, two. The brambles tangle at my legs, trying their damnedest to trip me up as I sprint through trees and fields, and more trees and more fields, and so much mud. One, two. This time I don't fall.

IT'S STILL DARK when I come to the end of the wood. Stumbling out onto another wet strip of tarmac, I feel an instant surge of panic. The trees, even without their leaves, had protected me. When I had come to a field, I'd stayed beside the woods. Now, this sudden exposure feels all wrong. I shouldn't be here. He'll find me. He's on the road. I need to stick to the...white scouring light engulfs me. A harsh squeal of rubber filling the air. This is it. I half lunge to the side, attempting to get back into the wood, but something hard clips my leg. My body seems to leap up without me before, winded, I fall face down onto the wet ground.

The vehicle screeches to a final halt. Instinctively, my hands flounder their way protectively towards my head, hoping the *punishment* will be quick.

Somewhere on the road, a car door opens, creaking on its hinges. The sound etching itself towards me, shrill above the incessant clatter of the rain. Despite an overwhelming sense of dread, I'm surprised he doesn't slam the metal door hard behind him. He must be saving his energy for me. The engine is still on. Over its dull low groan, I hear the weary tread of a man.

'Oh, good God, no.'

Not my man. Relief courses through every vein in my body as a limp, apologetic hand tugs feebly at my arm.

'Miss. Miss? Are you alright?'

It's not him.

3

———

ARRIVAL

Out on the road, we hadn't spoken much. Open your mouth on the tarmac tonight, and there had been a strong chance you'd end up dead from drowning. The man had been at my elbow, all apologies, helping me to my feet and limping with me to the passenger door. I'd thought there had been someone in the back of the car as we rounded the bulk of the old Volvo, but when I got inside, there was no one. The door rattled closed like a hard shaken bag of bones as the old guy pushed the metal panel shut on me.

If I'd thought Jayden's hire car had been pre-industrial revolution, this was in a whole different league. All sharp edges, rectangles, and corners, as though its angular body had been designed by a madman with a ruler. I collapse back into my seat. Ahead of me, the headlights dip as the bent man walks across their beam. He's tall and thin, bent by age, twisted as an old coat hanger. I'd have made a stab at mid-seventies, though he could be older. When people run over sixty-five, I find ageing them problematic. Even drenched by rain, his hair is completely white, cut short with that monk's

balding bit in the middle. I shift in my seat, suddenly uncomfortable. The car smells odd—old cabbage odd. There's a
thick fur of dust in the cup-holder and even on the dash. It's
unlikely the thing's had a clean since it rolled off the
assembly line, so the cabbagey smell is not so surprising.

The old guy opens the driver's door, bending himself at
the waist and turning his body out into the night so his
backside falls into his seat, accompanied by an involuntary
grunt. His crinkled hands are shaking as he turns to face the
front and takes the wheel. I buckle my belt as the man eases
his foot down on the accelerator, reversing out of the pool of
mud he'd washed up in and setting us back on the dark
road. I wasn't sure he'd apologised for almost taking me out?
Then again, I wasn't completely sure it was his fault.

'Where are you going?' His voice is gruff, as though he
doesn't have much of a call to use it.

The engine is on, emitting a low, rattling rumble. We
both stare ahead at the wet tarmac and the sheeting rain.
He's feeling embarrassed, in my debt. For my part, I'm in too
many types of pain to know what my current emotional
state is.

'I...I need a hotel. B&B. Somewhere cheap.'

The old guy says nothing, doesn't even bother to nod his
head in acknowledgement, just sets the tyres running again.

AT FIRST, I'd been relieved for the lift, not a whole heap
interested in where we were heading, but, after around
twenty minutes of silence, paranoia kicks in. It's black
outside, trees everywhere, rain washing the windscreen.
There hasn't been another single sign of life on this ink-
black road. I glance over at him, his hands still jittering as

they thread the wheel forwards and backwards. The car has a problem with the steering; it doesn't do straight, continually needing to be pulled back into line. Only that's not what's worrying me. I have no doubt we'll get to wherever he's heading, but this man could be anyone.

'Where are you taking me?'

His mouth moves, but over the rattle of the engine, it's difficult to hear the exact words.

He's spitting out some kind of name. Anglo-Saxon, uncomfortable: too many consonants in all the wrong places. Bloody difficult to commit to memory; with all its Ts and Ps, it sounds as if he's swallowing teeth. I don't know where it is. Nowhere I've heard of before. None of that's a bad thing; someplace off the map is exactly what I'm after. Provided coat hanger man will leave me in peace when we get there.

EVENTUALLY, the car pulls up on a street cut with dark shadows outside a gabled medieval building that's hunched and darkened, crouching in the rain, distrustful as a reptile. There's nothing opposite the building, just a low wall and a street lamp.

'Here,' he says.

I stare at the place, not exactly sure what it is: pub, inn, B&B?

The rain is still pelting down, rattling on the car like a legion full of persistent fingers. Without the noise of the engine, the sound is worse, seeming to poke into my brain. Riffling my thoughts. The old guy creaks himself out of the vehicle. Ambling across the headlights again before opening my door for me. Opening it wide this time despite the rain, as if to prove this seriously is the end of the line. I don't even know his name.

THE INN SMELLS of damp varnished wood, heady and oppressive. The reception desk has a bell, a hand-sized curved bronze dome and a wide, lined book, open and at the ready. There's also a little bench seat pushed back along one wall, sporting a tongue of faded red cushion. Too tight and narrow for sitting on, a decorative welcome rather than anything genuine.

After a quick beat on the bell, the old guy calls gruffly into the bowels of the building, 'Out front.'

I stare into the passageways, expecting someone to materialise. No one does. Turning to ask the old man if everything is okay, I realise he's gone. The smell, too, the cabbagey smell. He's taken that with him. So, it's not all bad then.

'Room?'

I turn back sharply to see some girl, barely out of school, standing behind the book, a cheap pen twirling awkwardly between her large fingers. As though she's been practising the twirl but hasn't quite got it mastered yet.

I nod.

She's a squat-looking thing. Her black shirt and skirt flecked with white bobbles that most likely she won't have a clue how to get off, or maybe she hasn't noticed. Her hair is a textbook case of mousey brown, with a thick, clubbed fringe falling over her eyes heavy as a fire curtain. Even though we're around the same height, she holds her head at an angle so that when she looks at me, she's always looking up through the blunt edges of hair, which gives her a sneering, untrusting appearance.

She's not a big talker, not free with the smiles and the welcomes, but she books me in for the night. Payment being deferred till check-out. I figure she's a few sandwiches, sausage rolls and a sherry trifle short of a picnic. The type who prefers to grunt rather than talk. When I ask her about the Wi-Fi, she just blanks me. An approach which is not exactly on any customer training handbook, even if the Wi-Fi is crap. I get the feeling she got the job because she was available, not because she had any special talent, which figures. If you're hanging around in a place like this after puberty, there's probably a good reason.

Safely ensconced in my room, I paper the walls with the sodden notes from my felt grey purse, sticking the wet bills on the lumpy, cream-coloured plaster above the radiator to dry out. Then I go for a shower. It's the *right* kind of water pouring out from the showerhead—warm. When I do eventually extract myself from the cubicle, the towels that are hanging ready and waiting in neat rectangles on the heated towel rail are soft. They smell of flowers. All of this is nice. They're softer than the ones we have back home. The en suite's not up to much though; a tinge of orange mould lurking in the corners of the grouting, and the basin creaks when I lean on its edge.

Thankfully, the toilet has that telltale blue wash of squirted cleaner piped around it and smells of bleach rather than urine. The actual room is the same kind of story—old but clean. Although, it's probably best not to look too hard into the corners. Dark wooden beams strut across the ceiling at awkward angles. I must be up in the gables. There's an underlying musty smell, with a high note of canned spray polish. More aluminium can than scent. Not great, but an improvement on the old-cabbage aroma from the old guy and his car.

I root through every blessed drawer, searching for a hairdryer. Reluctantly inhaling forgotten pockets of air that have been trapped for years inside shaky rectangles of wood, trying to keep each bone-brittle old drawer lined up and on its runners. I shouldn't have bothered. Not one of them holds a dryer or a code to the Wi-Fi.

Still wrapped in my large white towel, I flop down on the bed; it sinks below me with around twenty years of memories. This place is one of those should-have-been-retired inns, pubs and hotels. The type you avoid. The type that thinks *makeover* refers to a doily under a tea set. There is, in fact, a doily under the tea set and a few cartons of UHT milk. The room, the entire building, smells of old people and even older wood. It smells of coffins nailed up tight and forgotten. The air is so cloying that despite the storm, I get to my feet once again, cross to the wonky sash window and try to wedge it open.

Surprise, surprise: the thing is stuck, bloated with decades of swallowed dampness. When I bolted, I'd left my cigarettes in the car. I don't even want a fag; I just want to stop this place from invading my nostrils. Maybe I can scrounge one in the bar. If not, I'll have to spend the next eight hours inhaling all that mustiness: all that trapped old person, woodlice and dust. Thank Christ, I won't be staying long. There's a knock at the door. A hesitant rap.

'Yes?' I call out. It's not Jayden; he wouldn't knock.

'Dry clothes for you,' comes a small voice.

The landlady had promised me something when she saw the state I was in. She'd been really helpful, way nicer than the receptionist. Which was a surprise because I'd been a mess when I stumbled through the door. My boots had more mud stuck tight to the soles than an Essex farm-yard after a rainstorm. Which was pretty much what I'd been through. Times fifty. Actually, more like times a hundred.

I don't know how long I'd run through the woods. It had seemed as if I'd run for hours. I'd run until every inch of me had been wet and caked in mud, as though I'd climbed myself out of some primordial slime.

So when I arrived at this place, the woman in charge had said to leave my boots in the porch, stuffed with newspaper. Leaning forlorn as a drunk at a Christmas party against a radiator: a last-ditch attempt to dry out the innards. Then, straight off, she'd promised me something warm to wear. Something from lost property. I didn't care as long as it was dry.

Pulling open the door, the landing outside is already empty. The girl who called through the wood must have other things on, or maybe she's off for the night. Either way, for once, she was moving fast. I pick up the bundle. A mackerel-grey top, a black hoodie, a pair of sludge-green cords: men's, most likely, going by the square cut.

I wouldn't say any of it fitted, but I'm not really in a position to complain. The landlady woman had said she'd put my old clothes in the machine. I'd have them back in the morning.

Once dressed, I stare at my dishevelled face in the mirror and realise there's a problem with the human condition: as one need satisfies itself—I am clean, I am mostly dry and have somewhere safe and warm for the night—another need crops up. Hunger gnaws away at me from the inside. No surprise. If I'd been wearing one of those step counters, it would have worked its way off the scale. Refuelling has to be my next port of call. A couple of bags of nuts will work.

So far, I've avoided using my cards. Cash is always better if you don't want to be traced. I grab a wet twenty from where it's fallen off the wall. Plastic never sticks for long. The twenty should do me though. I have no intention of staying downstairs long, just get what I need, then straight up to bed, out of sight.

4

BAR-ROOM GOSSIP

My feet crush cat-burglar style over the dull-red carpet. Its fibres squirming, thick as crystallised moss under my splayed toes. House hospitality obviously didn't run to shoes. It's still raining outside. I'm not sure how that is meteorologically possible unless you happened to find yourself inside an Old Testament story. Glancing out of the large, blackened window at the end of the landing, I can see trails of silver liquid sliding over the dark glass like electric worms. Another peal of thunder punches the night. It doesn't matter because whatever the weather throws at this small piece of nowhere, come morning, I'm out. For tonight, I'm thankful for the warmth of the place and barefoot will do.

Besides, barefoot isn't all bad. Barefoot means quiet, and quiet suits me. The last thing I want right now is any kind of scream for attention. Not so for the carpet. I cannot believe anyone in their right mind would choose something so loud. Maybe they got some kind of bulk order deal. That would work.

There are acres of the stuff, and every inch is shouting

full volume as it stretches itself brazenly across the wide landing before slipping down the staircase slack as a tart's furred tongue. All the while sporting that same insane pattern, the kind of design you sometimes catch sight of in one of those land-that-time-forgot curry joints. A bit Wes Anderson if you squint, only the wrong *bit* of Wes Anderson and the squint would have to be semi-blinding. We had patterned carpets back home, and they have a plus side; a bold design hides a multitude of sins. A quick once-over with the hoover, and all is forgotten. Kind of. Sometimes. Maybe that was the idea here: a roadside doss-house like this, sins covered over, is kind of part and parcel of the entrance fee.

I pick my way down the stairs, catching the soft sound of voices from the bar below. One male, one female. The man has an odd croak at the end of each sentence as though he's swallowed a frog. I'm willing to bet it's the old guy who picked me up. There's that same Estuary taint, the one that holds on to the end of each word, hitting the consonants as though it's trying to headbutt the living daylight out of the things.

'Fright of my life,' he's saying, crucifying the 't'. 'Just flew out of the darkness. One minute it was endless black rain, then that face, melting like lard across the windscreen.'

'Stan!' The woman's voice is softer, rounded and gentle, with more than a touch of *amused* about it. 'Poor thing. Lard! Besides, seemed to me the fright went both ways.'

I hear the clink of a heavy glass set down on the counter. So heavy it must be one of those old-fashioned pint mugs, the type with the weighted base and ear-jug handles. The sort of glass that means someone's stopping for the night.

'Maybe I did give her a scare. But I tell you, Maggie, I could have done without it today.'

'To be honest,' the woman's words jostle, her breath coming unevenly; *Maggie* must be wiping down the bar as she talks. More a case of enjoying the catharsis of work rather than being too busy to stop—I'd only clocked three people since I'd arrived. She couldn't exactly be rushed off her feet. 'You ask me,' she continues, 'it didn't seem as if that young woman fancied being there either.'

She's got that right.

'This blessed storm.' There's a note of accusation in her tone, as though some weird entity has brought the storm down on all of us out of spite. To back her up, the thunder gives another long, low grumble.

Though I notice there's a bit of extra time creeping in now. The spacing between those acid indigestion God gurgles is widening out; the storm must be moving on. It's done its worst, played its tricks. Hurled the old guy and me together—an odd couple if ever there was. Now the elements have other lives to meddle with.

'I wasn't expecting to pull out the heroics,' the old guy mutters from the bar.

The woman suppresses a snort. 'Really, Stan? Thought you were ever ready with the old cape and jet pack?'

His tongue hits the roof of his mouth in a tut, as though he can't be bothered to pick the joke up and sprint away with it. 'It's been a long day, Maggie. Not one part of it would I want to be doing again.'

Him and me both.

'Well, you did right, Stan—bringing her in. No one should be out on a night like this.'

Another peal of thunder, but more muffled; the storm is fast-footing it off across the horizon. I'd love to be following. All in good time. I stand at the bottom of the staircase, hand resting on the more-chip-than-paint wooden banister, not quite ready to enter the *story*. Wondering what turn it might take without me adding my eight stone of weight. I'd always found listening was a habit worth cultivating. I've spent most of my adult life with my ears pinned back and open, spinning throwaway comments into something I could build on. Only the conversation from the bar seems to have petered out. It looks as though the oldies have no intention of playing ball. A clock ticks into the silence somewhere, marking a little time off before the conversation splutters up again.

'Seriously though, last thing I needed after the funeral,' the man called Stan says.

Funeral. This is news to me. He hadn't mentioned it in the car. Maybe because it all felt a bit too close to the bone. As though Stan was making a habit of playing footloose and fancy with fate—he'd almost wound himself up with two funerals in one day. Had he been driving too fast? I wasn't sure. How can you tell when all around you, the world's collapsed neutron-star-black into nothing? Speed needs something to peg itself up against. All I knew for sure was that old Stan and his clapped-out Volvo appeared on the scene back-to-the-future DeLorean style—hurled right at me. When I saw those headlights that close, I thought I was a goner. Come to think of it, the night still has a few hours left. There's a strong possibility that I can get myself finished off before dawn.

At the bottom of the stairs, the bar gets itself trapped in the far wall—reflected by a large rectangular mirror. I can see the old folks in the pub clearly as if I was looking through one of those old-fashioned serving hatches. The woman, 'Maggie', stands behind the counter. I'd seen her briefly when I arrived. Not the vacant girl who took my booking. This was the older woman, the one who had taken my boots and dropped them in the porch to dry. The landlady.

She must be about my mum's age. Fifties, I'd have said. Her hair greying, hoisted back carelessly in a tortoiseshell clip, and a few months short of a toner. A familiar type—a little too much meat sticking to the bones. No doubt, from the smell trapped inside the place, she'd have found herself in a fixed fight trying to shift those pounds; the inn? Hotel? Pub? Must have built its reputation on morning fry-ups. The stench of fat is stuck so deep in its marrow that every breath I take feels as though I'm digesting eggs, bacon, fried bread, and a sea of beans. Even the air could serve a person enough calories to push their daily intake into the problem zone. So yeah, she was on the chubby side. Then again, what do people want out of age?

Unless you're some top TV star, looking good after forty comes calling is pretty much beyond possible. So why not settle? Most of those skinny older women, they fall short of *fashion statement smart*. They just look mean and scrawny. Maybe a bit of fat added to the bones is the best way to launch yourself into those middle years: kindly, warm, generous. As opposed to brittle, boney and showing the world your skeletal tent poles. Not such a tough choice.

I glance down at my pale hand on the banister, more claw than palm. I could do with a few fry-ups myself. Besides, I realise when I stare back into the mirror the woman behind the bar is looking at the old guy as if she cares rather than being concerned about her Botox sliding off under her skin or her blow-dry curling at the wrong three-sixty degrees. I haven't seen people looking as if they cared in a long while. Where I come from, they've stopped being interested, and I feel something stirring inside me, a kind of ache which has nothing to do with my empty belly and its quest for a bag of dry-roasted nuts. I'd like to have people who cared.

'I'm sorry, Stan,' she says, and you can tell from the soft tones she's using that she genuinely is. 'I know this morning was tough. Davey was a good friend.'

I wouldn't normally have been interested; before tonight, I'd never met this *Stan* guy; only, it was odd because we'd sat next to each other in his clapped-out estate car for almost thirty minutes, and not once did he mention his 'tough' morning, a funeral, or anyone called Davey.

In the mirror, I can see Stan shaking his head as though the whole day's been a damn sight too heavy for sitting on anyone's shoulders. Then he stops, sighs and tilts that jug-ear glass pragmatically towards his lips.

'To Davey.'

'Davey,' Maggie mumbles.

'Only one good thing about it.'

She shoots the old guy a question with her eyes.

'I'll never have to do that again.'

When reflected-Stan puts the glass back down on the bar, it's drained empty. Not bad going for a geriatric. Though it could be worrying if he's got plans to wedge himself back behind the wheel. Luckily the landlady's on it.

'Tell you what, Stan, I'll give you another, on the house, if...' She pauses, twinkling those tired old blue eyes, playing with him. 'If...you promise you'll walk home.' Her eyes narrow when she delivers her ultimatum.

I get the feeling she's good at this, dishing out the cane with the carrot. Working behind a bar gives you a lot of practice on that front. Managing the punters is where the art lies, not pulling the pints. Anyone can pull a pint.

Sure enough, the old guy sighs as if it's a relief being brought into line, handing over the reins of your life—*she knows what's best.* He puts his keys down on the bar, and quick as if she's under a contract sealed in blood, Maggie refills his glass.

'She was lucky you weren't going fast, our little stranger.'

I smile. I've never been called that before.

'I was fast enough. Straight out of the darkness she was. One minute nothing, then...'

'I know. You said, *lump of lard.*' Once again, the woman called Maggie sounds amused.

The full glass scuffs back across the countertop, and the conversation stops just long enough for Stan to take a hearty slurp, complete with sound effects.

5

ENTERING THE STORY

'I still reckon she needs to go to the hospital.' Maggie's voice has a concerned edge. 'I know she told you she didn't want to, Stan, but sometimes people get concussed. They can go around looking fine, then...'

I stare up at my face in the mirror. I'm angled just at the edge of the frame. The mirror's a kind of *check-before-you-go-on-stage* type affair. You can see what you look like and who your audience is.

Don't forget your face? That was one of my mum's lines. Stupid. No one forgets their face. Only she'd be screaming ad-dabs now because the image that stares back at me is one sad specimen. The check-before-you-go mirror is most definitely telling me, *head back upstairs, fix yourself up.* Tonight, not even youth can keep me afloat on the looks front. My hair, wet from the shower, hangs in damp black tubes around my shoulders, straggly as the short-arse tails of a family of rodents, but hunger drives me forward.

'I'm not concussed.' I poke my head around the doorway. The room is dimly lit, empty apart from the landlady and Stan. Which is odd because I could have sworn there'd been a couple of people sitting huddled in the shadows. I must have got that wrong. The corners of the room are empty; I'm still a bit on edge.

'Oh, sweetheart.' Maggie's voice is warm and open, as though she's known me all my life.

She eases herself from the working side of the bar for a moment in order to slip one large, chubby, flour- and rose-water-smelling arm across my shoulders.

'It's okay.' I step away. I function better without sympathy, and I'm not used to people touching me. Not with kindness, at least.

'Course.' Maggie pulls herself back. She doesn't seem offended, even though she has every right to be; my bite was far too quick, too sharp. But no, this woman is a pro. She must have spent years dealing with every shape of humanity that a bar-room can throw at a person. She lets me go effortlessly as if to say—everything is fine. She's just giving me a bit of space to breathe into, and this is all peachy-keen and absolutely normal.

'You hungry?' she asks with a little smile and another one of those eye twinkles. 'I put a bowl of stew on for you and Stan.'

Stew means spoon. Spoon means eating slowly and questions. It was nuts I was after. Something I could squirrel back to my room and flip-top into my mouth. 'No, I...?'

'Maggie's stew's the best.' Stan cuts my mumbling in half.

Maggie smiles. 'I don't know about that, Stan, but after the shock you've both had, a bit of something warm inside those stomachs wouldn't go amiss. No charge,' she adds quickly, and I wonder if she's been making assumptions.

Do I look like the sort of person whose pockets are running on empty? It's not good to look like that. You look like that, and people start asking questions. I push my bare feet closer to the bar stool as Maggie bustles off towards the kitchen, leaving me to feel awkward; Stan's not much of a talker, and we'd already had the half hour in the car together, trundling through the wet Essex flats. I wasn't sure we could go another round on the conversation front. The clock ticks into the silence as Stan steels himself a few moments with his pint before shifting awkwardly and deciding he probably should make an effort.

'Maggie's a great cook.' He turns his face towards me, eyeing me wearily.

I get another whiff of whatever it is that Stan smells of. Rotting vegetation? But only a whiff. He must have left most of it in the car. I pinch my nostrils tight from the inside.

'You brushed up alright then.'

I glance down at my clothes, way too baggy.

'Yeah,' I say. Only I don't believe the part about brushing up. *Clean and dry* doesn't stop me from looking a sight worse than moribund.

'There you go.' Maggie again. Two steaming bowls in her hands and a big smile across her face.

'Honestly, I'm not that hungr...' But my God, the smell! Thick gravy and veg sending out every kind of homely that I haven't had in years.

She slides the plates effortlessly across the bar. 'There. I had Dawn put all your old clothes in the dryer before she went home.'

Dawn?

'She checked you in.'

Dawn. The irony isn't lost on me; nothing will be dawning on that one anytime soon, but I just nod and smile.

'I'll put your things outside your room when they're done. You'll feel better after a bite of something to eat.'

She adds a couple of bread rolls, neatly delivered on side plates. The rolls are still warm. I don't even bother to butter mine. My mouth is melting. Saying nothing, I just eat. I have been running on empty, literally. All through the woods and over the mud, miles and miles of flat Essex slop, grabbing at my heels as if it was alive and wanting to drag me down. The spoon can barely go fast enough, and the warmth spreading across my tongue feels fifty shades of fantastic.

'And a drink?' Maggie asks, her voice bright. 'On the house.'

'You'll be going bankrupt if you're not careful,' Stan chimes grimly.

It strikes me that Stan's the sort of guy who likes the tone of his voice set to *prophet of doom*.

Maggie eyes him shrewdly. 'Courtesy never bankrupted anyone.'

The woman is homely as a welcome mat.

It doesn't matter. I can't spend too much time sitting on show. 'I don't really drin...'

But she's uncorked the bottle. I can smell it from two metres and counting. That red wine is hitting my senses, smart and sure. Just one will be fine. The rain lashes at the windows. For the moment, I'm safe.

'Are you positive you don't want to go to the hospital?' Maggie pours a glass, her eyes never stopping looking concerned. Genuinely concerned. If this is just pub banter, the breweries should bottle it and dish it out to every publican on the planet.

Then again, she has got a point; my head hurts like buggery. She's probably right about the bit I overheard—the concussed thing—but I seriously don't feel like heading back outside. The night is persistent as a giant wet dog biting into the old place. I'm not keen on going anywhere that doesn't have a roof till this shitstorm's sailed away. 'I'm fine.'

She scrutinises me for a moment. Taking time to drink me in. 'That's a nasty bruise on your head.'

Sadly, I don't have to ask which bruise she's talking about. I know exactly where it is. It's singing its own private full-on string symphony of pain. I reach one hand up to the side of my forehead, feeling at the edge of my hairline. I wince as the skin screams hot under my fingertips. Not that anyone would notice the wince. I'm good at keeping signs of hurt on the inside. I stop pressing the damn thing and try to grab a better look in the mirror, the one that runs down behind the optics. Even in the bar-room gloom, I can see the dark shadow of a bruise flowering.

'I had it before I bumped into Stan.' That, at least, is the truth and yet as the words slip from my mouth, I can't help but remember a hard fist smacking my head forward and my brain rattling inside my cranium, brittle as one of those Mexican jumping beans. I slug down a large gulp of my red. Shit, I'm in trouble. I stare out of the window. Hopefully, he won't be able to find me here. I don't even know where the fuck *here* is, so how is he going to keep up? The wind howls outside, desperate as a pack of dogs hard on the scent, but that's stupid; it's just the wind. People can't sniff other people out. It's not as though he's the giant in Jack and the Bean, bloody *Fee Fi Fo*, Stalk. A shiver rips down my spine quick as an ice cube slipped under the collar of your shirt as a prank.

When I come back to the moment, I know in an instant that they've been shooting glances at each other: Maggie and Stan, bouncing their looks as though we're at the men's finals on a Wimbledon court, and they're eyeing the action.

'My car broke down. I hit my head on the...the bonnet. It

was up in the air and then crack.' I give them all the gestures. Act it out so there can be no doubt.

'On the A12?' Stan slips in.

Why do men always think in terms of roads?

I shrug. 'I ended up in the woods; must have walked a long way.'

I can still hear my breath as I ran, my breath coming fast and furious in my ears. Only now, it's different. Now it's screaming at me—*liar, liar.*

Stan clears his throat. 'And you left the car in a lay-by?'

Next, he'll be bringing out a bloody ordinance survey.

Luckily, Maggie must have caught the rise of my shoulders as the liar's look of panic crosses my face because she reaches out over the bar and gently touches his elbow.

'It's okay, Stan. The car will wait. Main thing is, you're both safe.'

Safe. And with that, the door rattles open in a gust of angry wind, and my heart leaps through my throat, threatening to bring the stew up with it. I grab the butter knife, the one lying beside the ruins of my bread roll and turn towards the door, ready. It's not what I expected, though. At first, I'm not sure that what is standing there is so much better. Even so, I loosen my grip on the knife; everyone knows knives are a weapon, even something rounded and only good for sliding through butter. Carrying any kind of weapon can get you slammed up. Especially when standing framed in the open doorway, soaked by the storm, is just the ticket—a weather-beaten police officer.

'Maggie, sorry. Came as soon as I could.'

'Oh, Phil, you're fine.' Maggie barely looks at him. She's already clearing away the plates, taking the knife gently from my fingers as if I hadn't just grabbed it Mulan-style. 'Eve, this is PC Green.'

For a moment, I can't for the life of me think who Eve is, then I realise, Eve—that would be me. Luckily, I have enough cash to pay for the room, and if I need to use my card, the E will still work if I hold a thumb over my surname. When you're going to lie big, it's best to sail as close to the wind of truth as you dare. I'd learnt a few useful things since I'd been married.

'What a night.' PC Green shakes the rain from his black waterproof.

I'd have him at mid-forties, maybe younger. He's got a full head of short dark hair, spiked up as though it's gelled where he's just run his fingers through. Only that's probably the rainwater holding it vertically. His age is hard to place because he's so wet that his face looks more like it's covered with melting plastic than skin.

He brushes the rain from his hands. 'Sounds like wolves outside.'

'What?' Stan looks blank for a moment as though he's just remembered something weird, a different conversation that he's pulling out of some long-lost time-space continuum.

'The wind,' PC Green explains, giving Stan a curious look. 'Howling loud as banshees and wolves.'

Then suddenly, everything shifts. Stan does the oddest thing, which is even stranger because I'm hardly in a position to go saying other people are behaving oddly. Only there's just something weird about the way the old guy moves, as if somewhere, someone must be tap dancing on his grave. Full-on dancing with an orchestra. Riverdance, possibly. Everything about Stan suddenly looks scared shitless, and broken. It makes the hairs on the back of my neck spike as the old guy pulls himself up from his stool and walks, jerky as a sleepwalker, over to the window. The window that's showing nothing: a black panel of dark night. You can't even see the street outside, yet still, Stan stares out into the blackness. It's creepy. Unnerving.

I feel the bones of the medieval inn closing in on me, and the corner, the one where I felt the people were when I first came through the door, well, I could swear the lights dip darker over there, the shadows becoming a little thicker. Although I barely have time to wallow in the attention shift because PC Green, I suddenly notice, is not looking at Stan. PC Green is pulling up the stool next to me and doing a quick forensics with his eyes. The once-over might be kindly, but I'm in no mood to be giving anyone the benefit of the doubt. I'm willing to bet PC Green doesn't miss a beat. I will seriously have to be out of this place first thing tomorrow.

'I hear you've had quite a night, Eve?' His sharp green eyes flick over my face.

Nodding widely, I try to catch my breath, find my voice, and cement a story. I'm so not interested in Stan anymore. I need to keep my wits about me. 'My car broke down.' I reach a hand up to the bruise on my forehead, the one Green is looking at so intently. 'Tried to fix it.' I manage a stupid-me, girl-on-her-own, fixing-a-car shrug. Although I'm not convinced PC Green buys it. He's not the type to go for any pre-millennium Penelope Pitstop damsel-in-distress crap. No doubt he prides himself on being the kind of copper that never swallows anything whole, not even a spoonful of Maggie's stew.

'I'm exhausted,' I sigh. Pulling myself up from my stool. 'I should...'

He nods. 'Course you are. Where did you leave the car?' PC Green's taking out his mobile. 'I can get it phoned in.'

'It's okay,' I bristle, then try to make out like I didn't just bristle by doing some kind of odd one-handed brush down the side of my sludge-green trousers, or at least the trousers I happen to be wearing courtesy of Maggie and her lost property box. 'It was a lay-by.' I'm struggling, wanting to avoid questions. I certainly don't want nosey parker police squads trying to locate my car. They won't find it. 'My husband. He can get it tomorrow.'

PC Green glances at my fingers. No ring. I pull my left hand back from where I'd left it so naïvely on the dark shiny wood of the bar. 'Actually, I was with him. We had an argument. He was trying to fix the...'

I can feel Maggie leaning in a little, not with her body, nothing so tactless, but leaning right in with her wide open, ever-caring ears.

'To fix the car,' I bluster. 'He was trying to fix the car. Shouldn't have walked off, but I was so mad, I just stormed away.'

PC Green nods as if to say *and why wouldn't you, in the middle of nowhere, in a rainstorm and not knowing where you were going.*

'I've called him.' Why can't I shut up! 'He'll come get me tomorrow.'

PC Green nods again, but his copper eyes aren't saying *end of story.*

'He...Stupid argument...I...' *Shut up! Shut Up!* I think because I need to give them less, not more. Then, the worst thing, tears start pricking my eyes. I'm drowning, till...

'Fuck!' Stan's voice echoes out sharply into the room. Ripped from his mouth in a note of sheer terror.

'Stan?' PC Green's on his feet, moving towards the window where Stan's staggering back from the cold dark glass. Literally staggering, as if he's pissed, or having a cardiac, or someone's just thumped him hard in the chest.

Which is kind of great because suddenly no one's interested in me anymore.

Stealing a moment, I wipe the flustered expression from my face, dry my eyes and get myself sorted. I shouldn't be sitting here. The stew and bread rolls routine lulled me into a false sense of security, but this is not my world. It's not safe. I push myself away from the bar. I seriously should have been upstairs with a packet of nuts.

'Think I'll just...' But no one is interested. Stan's face is so much whiter than lard. There's not even a word or a fat for the kind of pallor his features have gone.

'I saw something.' He's shaking. 'Something's out there.'

PC Green peers through the wide windows into the darkness.

I hang back, having no intention of going anywhere near that window or that door, but Maggie's wandering over towards it as well, drawn like a somnambulist. Soon they're all standing lined up and staring out into the night as if it holds all the answers. Staring into the deep, dark void. Can they see anything? To me everything is looking still and silent and empty. Suddenly, the door rattles on its hinges. Rattles ridiculously loud, and we all jump as if we're stringed puppets jerked unwittingly into action.

'It's just the wind,' Maggie says, clutching her chest in relief, but she looks shaken. With good reason. That hadn't been just a normal passing-breeze rattle; it was as though someone had just tried to batter the door down.

A sheet of water belts the windows as if thrown wholesale from a large bucket. Instantly, Maggie, Stan, and even PC Green, they all start back from the glass. Not even a badge can protect Green from this *whatever* is brewing up outside. But the panic is gone in an instant. Green's body loosens.

He shakes his head, amused at the overreaction. 'Storm Walter.' He smirks as if he's feeling foolish. 'Walter?' He shakes his head again. 'How do they think up those names?'

Maggie's hand reaches out gently for Stan's shoulder. 'Stan. It's alright. There's nothing out there, only the night, and...' she smiles kindly, her tone light when she speaks again. 'Like Phil said, it's just old Storm Walter.'

Stan lets out his breath in true mouth-breather fashion —heavy. Only, curiously, there's no relief there. His eyes keep twitching from side to side as if he's trying to collect his thoughts. As though somewhere in that knock-around-empty brain of his, there's something, something very important that he needs to put together; two bits of the same puzzle that desperately need linking but keep slipping out of his grasp, out of his conscious mind.

'Stan?' Maggie's voice is full of genuine concern.

I wonder if she's ever thought a bad thought about anyone in her entire life. Probably not. Besides, whatever she's doing works; her concern prompts Stan to pull himself back to human. He shakes his head a little as he tries to get a grip.

'It was just Davey said...' Stan mumbles.

Maggie and PC Green shoot each other a look, one that has me absolutely lost.

'Davey?' I ask. Secretly pleased to get the conversation away from me.

'Stan and Davey were close.' Maggie lets a small, sad smile creep up over her lips.

'Best friends, all our lives.' Stan sits himself down heavily on the bar stool, leaning his elbows on the long wooden plinth of bar as though he wants to plant himself there, grow into it.

'Davey passed.' Maggie locks me with her eyes. 'Funeral was today, so Stan...'

And suddenly, settling back onto my stool, I see how I can make this work: *old guy, shouldn't be driving, poor eyesight.* He's seeing things for Christ's sake, *emotionally traumatised after the death of his lifelong friend.* I feel the bruise on my forehead. Why had I said all that crap about the car bonnet? I guess I can backtrack. People's memories are all over the place, especially after a shock.

'Right before he died...' Stan interrupts my train of thought. 'Davey told me the strangest thing.'

PC Green rests a reassuring hand on Stan's shoulder. 'He went quick, Stan.'

Only Stan's not after reassurance; he's shaking his head. 'He'd been having this dream, see. Couple of months. Bad dream. I knew he was having it, only he never...'

I seriously can't be doing with dreams. It's late. 'Ow.' They all turn to look at me. Not exactly something I would normally want, but since I can see now how I can pull this balls-up into something positive with only a few minor tweaks, attention is what I'm after. Rocking my body gently, I sway my stool, hoping I'm not actually going to have to fall off the damn thing. I've been battered and bruised enough for one evening. Thankfully, my luck's holding tight because as the front legs of my stool lift into the air, for once, an officer of the law happens to be in the exact right place at the right time. PC Green, without a second thought, like the true hero he is qualified to be, comes through. Strong arms encircle my shoulders, holding me up as the front legs of my stool work their way firmly back down to the floor.

Maggie reaches a concerned arm out towards me. 'Phil, I think she's got to go to the hospital. That bruise on her head...'

And just like that, they're talking about me as though I'm not there. I'm more than happy. Let them make the decisions. It always works better if no one can see you pushing on the levers.

I let go of a barely audible protest. 'No, I...'

'Alright,' says Green, as the wind rattles the window-panes again.

Bugger. I lost that one a bit too quick. We need to go to the hospital now. I'm about to moan a bit more; ideally, a medical once-over on the night of the *incident* would be best. Luckily, before one more sound has to slip through my mouth, Maggie comes up with a way better plan.

'Doctor Dancey, then. Take her to see Stuart.'

PC Green nods. 'Good idea, Maggie.' He turns back towards me. 'The doctor's just down the road. Won't take a minute.'

'No...' But this last protest is deliberately half-hearted and framed with a wince.

'Come on. You'll be back and tucked up in bed in half an hour. Stan?' PC Green turns towards the old guy. 'I can drop you on my way.'

Out of the corner of my eye, I see Stan's fingers grip the bar so tight you'd need a crowbar to prise him off.

Maggie shakes her head. 'Don't worry, Phil. I think Stan needs a spot more company tonight. No doubt we'll still be here when you two get back.' She turns her attention to the old guy. 'Another drink, Stan?'

Stan doesn't say no.

'And...Eve, love, just grab my coat, sweetheart.'

Again, that name. I'm going to have to get used to it.

Maggie looks at me kindly, her eyes tilted up—she's already pulling Stan's pint. 'All your stuff is in the dryer. My coat's on the peg by the door, so help yourself.'

I get to my feet and realise, straight off, there's a problem. 'My shoes.'

Maggie laughs. 'Erin won't go thanking me if I let you walk into her place with no shoe leather.'

Erin? I'm lost, but Maggie's not backtracking for explanations.

Instead, she glances at my feet. 'I'm a six and a half.'

'Six,' I say, looking down at my luminous white splayed toes.

'That'll work.' She kicks off her shoes, leaving them for me to step into and pushes them with her toe, the customer side of the bar.

I hesitate. Is she sure? Why is this woman so sweet? A sizable chunk of me wishes she wasn't because Maggie being so nice is only going to make the next step in the game a little harder.

The wind rattles once again outside. Maggie shoots an anxious look towards the door. Her pint almost pulled. 'Go on, you two. Soonest gone, soonest back.'

6

———

DANCEY

For the second time in one seemingly endless night, an unforgiving beam of white light scours my retinas, sharp and angry as a mug of bleach swilling down a plug hole. 'I was up on the curb, walking,' I hear myself saying as instinctively I pull my head back. 'I guess I was walking towards town.'

'You were a long way out?' I can't see PC Green, only his shadow, thrown up horror-style on the wall in front of me. Despite the lack of detail, I can imagine the look on his face: intent as a micro-biologist.

'I didn't realise how far out I was. I knew we hadn't passed a town for a while, so I figured…'

Simple, simple. I need to pull myself back to the facts, well, at least my *facts*. This is not a geography lesson. I should have said I came out of the woods, but that just sounds odd. Walking on the road seemed more normal.

The point is that someone, Stan, mowed me down. That's what I need to keep hold of. 'I'd had an argument with my husband,' I say, adding a note of breathlessness. 'Stupidly I got out of the car. I was just walking. I'd been at it for a good while. Then the car came out of nowhere. It was a narrow road, but I think the vehicle was over my side?'

I add the question mark, my voice tapering upwards at the end. How the hell would they know? It was only me, Stan and the car on the scene, but it's good to let people conjure up their own answers. Give them enough rope; that was one of my mum's favourites.

The beam of light pulls away. The space directly in front of me now filled with a wrinkled just-the-right-side-of-dead face. The owner is well over sixty. His skin loose enough to have been chewed and regurgitated through life a dozen times—Doctor Dancey or Stuart. Though I'm sticking with the doctor part: professional all the way.

'And you said the car went up on the curb?' he asks.

Actually, that's not what I said at all. I said I was on the curb when Stan's four wheels came clowning out of nowhere, but the mistake is useful, so I don't correct it. 'I just remember the lights swerving towards me, and then...'

'Do you want tea?' Mrs Dancey—the *Erin* I'd heard about earlier from Maggie, the one who wouldn't appreciate me traipsing barefoot through her house—is asking. She's standing in the doorway, wrapped in a brushed-cotton, pink dressing gown. Erin's a good fifteen years younger than her husband. I guess that comes with him being a doctor; she's nabbed herself a safe bet. She's still young enough to be making an effort; we've caught her on the hop. A headscarf wrapped tightly over a hive of rollers and a look of deep-dyed concern crisscrossing her clean, makeup-free face. I notice that Erin's brought the tea tray anyway. I wouldn't be surprised if the kettle were on the moment we arrived through the door. It's coming up for midnight, but there's a plate of shortbread biscuits riding next to a white china pot. Homemade, probably, the shapes mismatched. PC Green sticks out one hand and tucks in.

'Maybe just a tea,' I say, not because I'm thirsty. I never drink tea. My mother used to tease me about it. She said I had a phobia. That I was actually afraid the leaves might escape from the pot and map out my future: a bad future, one would suppose. Only that mumbo jumbo's all bollocks. Despite my upbringing, or maybe because of it, I don't truck with superstition. The *not drinking tea* is partly an aesthetic thing; it always looks like dishwater to me and pretty much tastes the same way. Odd taste buds, maybe, but I cannot see the attraction.

Tonight though, I'll hold my nose and neck it down. As always, there's a reason—accepting a small offering will make this woman, Erin, like me better. Odd that. Take a tad of hospitality from a person, and they can't help liking you better for it. There's probably some basic human instinct underneath it, some kind of primal bonding unwritten rule. Despite the smiles, the person offering most likely feels that as soon as you accept the tea, the open door, the proffered seat, return the smile, a connection is made, and you're in their debt. Selling your soul for a knockdown price. I'm not the type to go selling my soul cheap, and I'm certainly not up for new friends. No. Just the sympathy vote. That's the ticket. Accepting the tea will win me that.

Erin, I think to myself as I reach for the cup. She must be Irish. Canny buggers, the Irish. Hopefully, it's way past her bedtime, and despite the pop-up hot drinks concession, she's running on automatic.

'There's no concussion,' the doctor announces to the room. 'But that bruise is only just beginning to shout.'

Erin peers at my skin, before nodding, satisfied. 'I've got some arnica upstairs.'

Dancey shrugs as if to say it can't hurt, and his wife scuttles away into the off-stage shadows of the house.

'And you've spoken to Stan?' Doctor Dancey flicks off his little light and stashes it back in his black bag, switching his attention effortlessly to the "guilty" party—Stan. The old guy in the Volvo, driving way too fast after burying his life-long friend. I'm the victim here.

'He'd...' PC Green lowers his voice a little, '...been drinking by the time I'd got to the pub.'

Dancey raises one large, bushy eyebrow.

'This was after he'd been driving. Only a couple.' PC Green clears his throat awkwardly. 'He'd had a shock, and what with the funeral.'

'Not the point.' The doctor pauses just long enough to take a sip of his tea. 'Stan was in here earlier. Let's just say alcohol's probably not the best indulgence at the moment.'

I'm a bit lost, but only for a second—medication. The old guy must be taking something. Something newly prescribed that very day. *Can cause drowsiness.* Bet it's got that written in Helvetica somewhere on the neat, brown, child-locked bottle. Stan, bless him, could be turning out to be my ticket to Easy Street.

PC Green raps his fingers against his cup. 'Davey was a shock.'

I'm beginning to feel like a spare part on an Ikea assembly line. I'm not interested in Davey. It's Stan we need to get back to.

Thankfully, the good doctor seems to be on the same page. 'Davey was seventy-six.' Dancey sounds weary. 'People don't live forever.'

I'm guessing from Doc Dancey's rounded shoulders and world-worn attitude that this is a story he's facing all too often—a quaint old town, not a whiff of gainful employment. An ageing population zombying into the future, surviving despite clogged arteries and midnight feasts on shortbread. Everyone wants to live forever these days, but the doctor knows full well it's not going to happen. That doesn't make it an easy task, though, being the one who has to spread the news.

'Arnica.' Erin reappears, brandishing a small silver tube.

'Darling, would you mind taking Eve into the other room? I think the fire's still on enough to kick back into life.'

Erin nods and is about to usher me out, but before she manages the manoeuvre, I slide my phone to record, stashing it under the ample pink cushions on the couch that I'd been sitting on. Whatever they're going to say about Stan, I want to be in on the action. Although, the other room sounds good to me. Naturally, I don't like being too close to the law. They may not have superpowers; they can't look into your brain and unpick your thoughts, but I've always felt it's best not to underestimate anyone in uniform. They're tenacious, trained bloodhounds, and unless they're of the *easy-life, retiring-next-week* variety, the uniformed are most certainly people worth giving a wide berth to.

'I know this is going to sound strange,' Doctor Dancey mumbles as I pick my way out of the room, 'but Stan was concerned about something, something odd that Davey had said.'

Whatever it was, I lose the thread as I round the high-glossed white door-frame into the other room.

'THERE.' Erin stokes the fire with a poker, letting sparks fly out of a grate that I could have sworn had well and truly snuffed it. She's a dab hand at this. No doubt I'm not the only lost soul that's ended up on her doorstep after pub hours.

'And I'll get you a rug.'

I go to protest, but she doesn't wait. She's off.

The Dancey sitting room is straight out of Knitted Weekly. I have no idea if there is a magazine called Knitted Weekly, but from all the throws, the covers, and the coordinated cushions adorning the doctor's sitting room, Old Erin could be editor-in-chief. I'd like to say it's garish, with its vomit of dull yellows and greens. The ever-ready cynical part of me would dearly love to take satisfaction in the room's vacuous stupidity—all that twisted wool a testament to time being wasted and woven away, just going to show how mindless some people's lives are. And yet...this place with its scented diffuser, and the dry wood sending earthy-smelling coils of smoke into the air, it all feels like home; that is, like how a home should be, and more than half of me wishes it was mine.

'Not a night to be out wandering the lanes?' She's back with the rug, crocheted, of course, and unfurls it across my legs.

'Thanks.' I adjust the neatly crafted woollen chains over my knees, fighting an intense desire to stick my fingers through those intricately spaced holes and wiggle. I don't. She's watching. 'Teaches me to argue with my husband,' I bumble. 'Car broke down and...you know what it's like.'

Only she probably doesn't.

'I'm blaming him for not checking it out. He's blaming me for not knowing the first thing about how to get it started again.'

She eyes me curiously. 'He must be worried now?'

'I phoned him from my room at Maggie's. He's fine.' There's an odd pause. 'We apologised. You know how it is.'

Why do I keep trying to bring her in? 'All heat of the moment stuff,' I explain. There's another pause. 'He'll grab me tomorrow.'

'So, you walked away from your husband, and then you met Stan?'

'Well, not straight after. I'd walked quite a way.'

Not walked. I'd run. I'd sprinted. I'd scrambled off the road and through the woods and over marshy fields. Only she doesn't need to know any of that.

'It would have been fine, but...seriously, one minute Stan wasn't there the next...'

She nods her head slowly. 'He was climbing the curb?'

There's an odd edge to her voice. I don't follow at first, then realise, damn—curbs are for pavements. There were no pavements, not where Stan and I crossed paths. 'Verge. Sorry, just...it's been a long night.'

She fixes me with her green eyes, but the warmth has gone from them. Erin might have a default setting of smiles and shortbread, but as soon as those eyes start boring, I get the feeling she's a long way from being a pushover.

'Stan's a good man.' She brushes her palms over her dressing gown as though she's got something on it, only she hasn't. It's immaculate. 'He knows those lanes like the back of his hands. Drives them every day, a little too slow,' she flicks her hard eyes back towards me, '...most would say.'

'I, well, I...'

'And you called your husband from your room at Maggie's?'

I can tell from the intense expression Erin's giving me that something about my story is not stacking up, but I'm too far in for an easy reverse out, so I nod.

'Which is truly remarkable,' she pulls in her cheeks, as though savouring a lemon, 'seeing as the mobile network's down.' There's a brief pause, one in which she elbows me a little more time to allow this last nugget of truth to soak in. 'Maggie telephoned us from the landline.'

I say nothing. Anything that comes out of my mouth stands a good chance of digging me in deeper. Then again, I could have called from my room. My mouth drops open, the words up close behind, but Erin's too quick.

'Maggie called us from the landline in the bar. I can't remember the last time any of the landlines in the bedrooms at The Wreckers worked.'

'Wreckers?'

'Maggie's place. The Wreckers. That's what it's called.' She sighs before giving me a long hard stare, but not like she's oh so clever and caught me out, more as if she's sad for me, genuinely sad about whatever it is that I'm up to. 'I think you'll be alright by the fire.'

I nod. I guess I will.

Then she rummages in her dressing gown pockets and pulls out my phone.

I say nothing. For a moment, neither of us does, before she hands it over to me.

'I switched it off for you.'

I reach out to take it, but Erin doesn't let it go. No, she holds on to the edge of it like a warning.

'Didn't want your battery to go flat.'

'Thanks,' I say, but I don't mean it.

She releases the device. 'Not a problem.' She smiles. She doesn't mean that either—not the words, not the smile, not any of it. Erin fixes me again with those green eyes. 'And that bruise of yours, well, I don't suppose that will go giving you any trouble come morning.'

. . .

THE WIND'S dropped by the time we pull towards The Wreckers. There's a sign swinging from a black iron bracket fixed to the wall, hanging between two first-floor windows. I hadn't noticed it when I'd arrived with Stan. Now, I can't believe that I could have missed it. As PC Green slides the car towards the curb, the headlights catch the sign in their beam, sure as a spotlight. The painted rectangle shows a masted ship, its sails torn. The skeleton bones of two towering spars clawing helplessly at a stormy, dark sky as the vessel leans across its fixed, painted board, raked at an impossible angle. Frosted waves lap up around the ship's bow like a pack of dogs, their eager tongues lolling, excited for the kill. The scene is lit solely by a jaundiced moon cutting a fickle escape path across a stormy sea. In reality, there is no moon. Not even a sickly one. The night is dark, cloudy and wet.

'Erin's a bit of a star.' Green pulls on the handbrake. 'Every committee in town, she's on it.'

A busybody, I think. She probably has a freezer packed full of food for all occasions: neatly labelled, tupperwared and portioned for every flavour of disaster.

'Her and Maggie are the backbones of this place.'

I say nothing.

He glances over at me, slumped in my seat. I suddenly feel very heavy, as though that old Essex mud has finally caught up with me and is sealing me into place. I can't be bothered to extract myself from the warm car, even though the lights from The Wreckers are currently blazing as proudly as if nobody's ever heard of the climate crisis or conserving energy. I swear they weren't on that bright when we left. None of that is, of course, my business, but even with all that bright brilliance, nothing is making me want to leave my seat. The pavement between the car and the entrance to the pub is dark and wet as a cold seal, and behind that large rattling front door to the inn will be sweet-as-pie Maggie, with her concerned face and forty questions.

I wish I could just teleport myself inside, so I was upstairs in my woodworm-smelling room and under my sheets. The next fifteen minutes between door, Maggie, and bed are not important. The trip to the doctor was a waste of time. I can see that. Erin, I could probably have worked my way around. It's a known fact that people in shock muddle events in their stories, and anyone not holding one foot in the grave would tape-record a conversation if they felt an insurance claim was on the horizon. Taping a conversation is hardly evidence that I was up to no good. So, Erin disapproved? Had her doubts? Big deal. That wasn't what was weighing me down.

In truth, I wasn't so sure I could make this scam fly anyway. Even if Stan confessed that he'd been pissed out of his head, taking prescription drugs that caused drowsiness and had actively aimed the car right at me just for the hell of it. Even with all of that, I am currently running on empty. It's time to face reality—with my hubby on the warpath, most of my network will be burnt. *My network*? Who am I kidding? It was always only ever his network. Nobody gives a toss about me, which is why I'm currently living under-cover as some girl called Eve, whatever the fuck my surname is even supposed to be. I need to get out tomorrow, disappear without a trace.

'THINK it was worth checking you over.' PC Green raps a quick trill on the steering wheel, driving my attention back to the here and now. 'Doctor says you should be fine by the morning.'

'Yeah, thanks,' I say. I need to get moving before I grow into my seat. Slipping out of my belt, I glance up at the pub again with its bar-room lights star-spangled-bannering out. I'm guessing Stan's still in there, earwigging poor old Maggie. She'll have turned the lights up high as the grid will allow to try and prise the old guy from his seat. Only probably that's not working; he'll be growing roots and have no intention of moving on. I seriously can't be bothered with more chit-chat this evening. I'm dog-tired and not interested in any of these people. I intend to cut through that bar as fast as possible. The damp old room, with its smattering of bathroom mould that I've got waiting upstairs, is suddenly seeming oh so attractive.

I turn my attention to PC Green. He's looking tired too. He might be on night shift, but that doesn't mean he's not itching to get back to the station and fall asleep over his desk. Or maybe that's not his style. Maybe this evening, he was planning on throwing himself deep into some of the nine hundred pages of *Anna Karenina*. Maybe that's his thing. I always wanted to work night shifts. Thought it would be fun to be reading a book when the world around me slept; be paid for doing it too. I'd have kept the book in a drawer so nobody knew I had it and taken it out when everything went quiet. When I knew there would be no danger of being interrupted. I figure people who do night shifts, they must have a drawer full of personal stuff. One drawer of everything that matters to them: a book, a packet of biscuits, a photo of someone they love. I never had that kind of a job, that kind of drawer or even that sort of someone who could smile out of a photo at me.

'Hmm,' I grunt. When you get to thinking like that, it seriously is time for bed. I turn to Phil. 'Thanks for taking me. I...'

Suddenly there's a rapping sound. We both stare out of the car. Beyond the dark strip of wet pavement, framed in the window of The Wreckers, is Maggie. Her face pale. A phone tucked under her chin. I wonder if her patience has finally worn through—she wants to get me in, hand Stan over to my driver for a neat on-the-way-home deposit, and lock the door. Then I realise, with a sense of relief, Maggie's not looking at me. She's looking at PC Green. She's tapping on the window of the pub, looking straight at him with a sense of urgency, as though willing him to come in.

'Okay.' He releases his belt from its hold. 'Looks like I'm walking you to the door.'

I haul my reluctant body from its seat. A slug of ice-cold air catches me in the throat as I open the slab of metal between me and the outside. I seriously have had enough of this.

Once standing street-side, the wind charges at me, tearing at my hair and flapping the edges of Maggie's borrowed coat, making it fly out like rogue tent flaps. I grab at everything, flailing like a seagull thrown a chip as I try to fix it all in place. Fingers clutching at loose fabric, I slam the car door behind me and, head down, strike out towards the warmth of the inn.

The pavement's still wet from the last downpour. Mounds of leaves cower in damp half-lit corners against the pub's unflinching walls or stray, slug-like, across the slate-dark walkway. I hear Green's door slam shut somewhere behind me, but I don't wait to see him lock up. I hurry towards the black door of The Wreckers. I need to get in, get warm, and get to bed.

Only something slides under my right foot.

It's as if a creature is caught beneath my shoe and the hard pavement. A snake? I shiver. My instep lifts slightly, raised up by something living? I feel its edges, its outline, beneath the sole of one borrowed plastic shoe. A shoe which suddenly feels too flimsy: not enough of a barrier. Not a snake. No. Couldn't be. But it's as though I'm stepping on a hosepipe. Only this, whatever this is, is three times as wide and slithers out from under me, long, slimy and pulsing. An eel? I gasp. A thick channel of icy air rushing mercilessly into my mouth. Ripping out a small, involuntary scream from my ribs as my foot slides from under me, and my backside hurtles towards a rock-hard floor.

'Eve?'

This time I wasn't so lucky—no one breaks my fall. Green's voice comes from far away as my already bruised body slams onto the wet, hard ground. No sooner do I make contact than I draw up my hands in horror. Scared I'll touch it, whatever *it* is. Every inch of my skin crawling with disgust; there had been something alive and slithering under my foot!

'Eve?' Green's voice becomes a little louder as he rounds the bonnet of the car.

But I'm not interested; the contents of my stomach curdle. Repulsion wraps around me like a wet blanket, touching every inch of my being. I just stood on something living, something that slid like a snake! Only surely it was too wide. I stare around me into the darkness, into the sodden clumps of leaves cowering in the corners where the pavement meets the inflexible walls of The Wreckers. Running my eyes hastily over the fractured reflections of light and shadows. Bile rises in my throat, and my mouth runs dry all at the same time because I must be going mad —I see something. I can actually see something with my own wide-staring eyes—the damp heaps of leaves ripple, ripple as if a large creature is sliding away, amphibious in its stealth. A moving form, unseen—hidden beneath the autumn brown mouldering heaps.

'You okay?' PC Green reaches down for me.

I feel the warmth of his fingers on my shoulder, even through my coat, and I realise I've gone deathly cold. Every inch of body heat has vacated. Pushed by fear and repulsion from my body. My teeth clank together, jarring as bare bones in the absence of muscle, nothing to absorb the shock. Uncontrolled.

'Did you...?' I stutter, barely able to get my breath.

'Those leaves can be damn slippy.' There's not a note of panic in his voice. 'Are you okay? You went over kind of hard.'

I say nothing, total confusion filling my brain. It's as if PC Plod and I are both living in different worlds.

'Yeah,' I mutter, meaning nothing.

'You sure you're okay?' Phil pulls me gently to my feet.

I glance down. There are a few clumps of leaves scattered across the wet pavement. They must have been under my shoe. It's true. I could have slipped. Then again, that doesn't explain what happened; I felt movement. I felt a coil of something alive under my...

There's another bang on the window. Maggie's pale concerned face stares out.

'Come on.' PC Green corrals me forward. 'Let's get you out of this. You've had enough for one night.'

I don't argue. The last place I want to be is out here tonight. My mind's playing tricks on me. I know that must be all that it is. Maybe the visit to the doctor had been a good thing. If he hadn't given me the once-over and pronounced me with a clean bill of health, I'd seriously be questioning my sanity. I'm just tired. Imagining things. I let PC Green usher me quickly forward towards the inn.

. . .

'PHIL'S JUST GOT BACK.' Maggie's speaking into the phone as we come through the rattling, black-lacquered door to The Wreckers.

'Maggie?' Phil asks, knowing something's up.

'Talk later.' She puts the receiver back on its hook. 'What happened?' She shoots me an anxious look.

'I just...slipped,' I say sheepishly, uncomfortable about perpetuating this current disaster-prone image of myself. I seriously can't remember the last time I fell flat on my backside before tonight. 'The dead leaves. It was slippy out there.'

She manages a resigned smile. 'I told Dawn to sweep them today, but I guess this wind.'

It's most likely more a case of Dawn not being arsed to clear away anything she'd swept, but I keep quiet. I don't know Dawn. Being useless and being lazy are not necessarily the same thing.

The TV is on over the bar. The sound turned down. There's no Stan, but it's even more obvious from the inside of the pub that the lights are blazing full blast, as though The Wreckers is expecting a coach party.

PC Green eyes Maggie cautiously. 'Are you okay?'

Ironically, she hoists one eyebrow. 'Not exactly. This storm.' Maggie glances anxiously out through the darkened windows. 'It's giving me the jitters.' She lets loose a deep sigh, pulling one hand through her hair, trying to post loose strands back into the tortoiseshell clip that sits low at the back of her head. 'Stan left around twenty minutes ago. I was just waiting down here for you to come back and...'

'And?' PC Green asks.

'It's all so daft.' She toys with the edge of a dishcloth,

as though embarrassed. 'I was cleaning down the optics, and I got this...I got the strangest feeling.' Her brow furrows. 'It was as though I was being watched. I glanced up in the mirror, and I swear to God, Phil, I saw people.' She shivers.

PC Green scans the empty pub.

'No, no,' she says, her voice breathless. 'That's wrong, not really people. It was more shapes.'

Now we are all staring at the benches surrounding the bar, the hard, cushioned edges of wood that circle us like some kind of jury's den.

'Stupid,' Maggie shrugs, trying to chase out the uncomfortable chill that's crept in with her words hoping to drag us all, with a hint of self-deprecating irony, back to reality.

We must look like a bunch of muppets, standing there staring into what little there is left of the shadows expecting to see a cluster of people that we somehow failed to notice when we'd come in through the front door.

'Like I said, stupid.' Maggie smiles. 'So, I switch on all the lights, every single last one.'

She's not joking. Not one corner of The Wreckers has managed to keep hold of a penny pinch of darkness or, for that matter, a degree of modesty—the extensive cobweb situation is on full view.

'I've been managing this place for twenty years, Phil. Over, probably, and I know what people say, yet never in my life have I been spooked, only...' She dries, unable to explain the full creep show experience she's just been through. 'But then...' Maggie pauses, reluctant to go on, reluctant to be drawn towards the precipice of this event that doesn't stack up. 'Then it just got worse because...' She looks directly at PC Green. 'You know how this place always makes more noise than a wooden ship on a windy sea. Listen to it hard, and I swear even on a quiet day, you can hear every minute this place has ever lived through.'

PC Green smiles and nods—what's the surprise; old buildings creak.

'So, I switch on the box to get a bit more normality back into the room, and then this...' Maggie waves one long, cardiganed arm towards the TV.

PC Green and I both stare up at the box of blue flickering light. A *breaking news* headline strip is looping continually at the bottom of the screen. "*Variant*," I notice. "*Contagious*," it says.

Maggie sighs. 'I thought we'd done all *this*.'

PC Green pushes passed me, moving towards the live-and-streaming image so he can get a better look as Maggie grabs the remote from the bar, turning the sound back up. The clipped, mid-sentence tones of the news presenter filling the room.

'What scientists are now calling the Astrapi variant because of its ability to strike like lightning. This latest variant appears to be not only highly contagious but currently shows little evidence of responding to any of the current vaccines.'

A picture flashes up on the screen. It looks like all the other images we've, quite honestly, had our fill of by now; some kind of Corona trumpeting moon affair; the legend "*Astrapi variant*" emblazoned across it; as though it's a beauty queen at a pageant. The soundbite continues with barely a pause for breath, focusing back on the newsreader's sincere face. 'Medical professionals are warning, Astrapi could strike with more severity than the four other major variants encountered so far.'

Instinctively, we all take a step away from each other, yet

closer to that TV, as if the news is pulling us in, sure as a magnet.

'So far, there have only been a handful of cases confined to East Anglia.' The clipped British voice continues seamlessly as the smart woman's immaculate blonde, blow-dried head is replaced with live footage—pictures of the army driving up in trucks, blocking off roads. Stopping cars and turning them back. Planes at Stansted lined up on the runway, grounded. There are a lot of people wearing masks. A lot of people in white protective suits.

'Not again.' PC Green sinks down onto a bar stool.

'It's only just broken. I called Julia to tell her. She's working in Colchester tomorrow. Thought it might be best to stay put.'

It's not clear who Julia is, but this doesn't seem important now.

'Okay.' PC Green runs a hand through his hair. It's no longer wet. No longer spiked up. Instead, it flops a little boyishly around his face, too tired to bother with structure. 'I better go back to the station. It's going to be a long night. I'll email Erin, ask her to put an announcement on the parish website.'

'You think anyone will read it?'

He shrugs. 'Chances are they'll hear the news tomorrow when they get up. People will have to make their own decisions as to the risks they want to take.'

'I stockpiled masks for the shop,' Maggie blusters, her mind buzzing through some kind of mental checklist of practicalities. 'I can get those down to the store tomorrow.'

PC Green nods. 'We've been here before.'

Maggie raises her eyes heavenward. 'Oh yeah. Two steps forward, three steps back. It's the *lightning-fast* part I'm worrying about.'

'You know what they're like with their names. There were a whole lot of *coulds* and *mights* in that news item. Let's not worry till we get the facts.'

Maggie stares back up at the TV. 'You think life will ever be normal again, Phil?' She sounds bereft.

But me, I feel nothing. I'm halfway between bored and exhausted. I've heard this riff so many times now.

'Stan left okay?' PC Green pulls himself back off his stool.

In true human being fashion, they've moved on from the disaster. Until it strikes someone standing next to you, no one is interested. Not really, besides, the virus is the least of my worries, and Phil and Maggie are back on the day-to-day. They don't need me.

'Like I said, he left about twenty minutes ago. He'll have no idea about any of this, but...'

'Every time you think it's over.' Green sighs.

We're back on the pandemic. A brief nod to it. They're becoming a cliché. 'Sorry,' I cut in. It's as if they've forgotten I'm here. They both turn to me, almost surprised to see me. 'I just wanted to say thank you. For everything. I'm going to be off early tomorrow, so...'

They look at me, eyes a little wider, as though I've just beamed down from Mars.

'You're not going anywhere till you've tested.' PC Green doesn't sound exactly harsh. More pragmatic and inflexible. There's a protocol he'll be working through. One which I seriously don't want to get caught up in.

'Sorry, But I...' I can't stay here. One planet-shaped virus is not going to stop my husband. Not even if it's planet-shaped and planet-wide. He's a scarier option than six months in intensive care. Besides, the bugger never gets sick. If there's one person not getting this virus, it'll be Jayden.

Stick around, let him find me, and intensive care is going to seem like a package holiday. I need to keep on the move.

My face must have paled to lifeless because suddenly Maggie's concern is no longer the global pandemic or Stan but solely centred on me.

'Oh, Eve love, don't worry. You know what these things are like. They're never as bad as the experts think. It's just because it's new. They have to be cautious. You'll be out of here in two days tops.'

I feel a swell of panic taking hold of me. I can't stay here for two days. Two days is enough time to scour every town between here and Colchester. If he finds me...

'Don't you worry about the money,' Maggie says gently. 'If you are worried about the money. We can sort something out. I can always do with a helping hand.' Her voice, despite the late hour and the panic and the fact I've buggered up her night, is still full of warmth.

'I...' I have no idea what to say. I have no idea what to do. Luckily, yet again, Maggie comes to the rescue.

'Now, the most important thing for you, young lady, is to get some sleep. I'll get Dawn to bring you up a lateral flow test tomorrow. Leave it outside your door with your clothes. They'll be out of the dryer. Now,' she pushes a tumbler of water across the bar, 'take this with you, and straight up.'

I don't argue. I grab the water and head towards the stairs. Behind me, I can hear Phil tying up the loose ends of the evening.

'So how was Stan when he left?'

'Hmm, okay.' Maggie draws the words out. 'I guess. Only...he told me the oddest thing.' Her voice trails away a little at the end.

PC Green, ever helpful, jumps in to finish her sentence with reassurance. 'He'd had a hard day, Maggie.'

'Yes, but this was...' Her voice fades a little before delivery as though, whatever it is, she's reluctant to air it, to give it life. Then again, I can hardly hear Maggie anymore because they're talking quietly, and the boards on the stairs groan with every step I take. She was right about the old place making noises.

'Don't you go worrying on Stan,' PC Green announces brightly. Loudly. 'I'll check on him, myself tomorrow.'

And that was it. I don't want to hear anymore anyway. I'm going to wipe that recording from the doctor's off my phone. I wish I'd never gone to see him. I could have been tucked up in bed hours ago, oblivious to the virus. I'm dog-tired. Besides, it's not just Maggie who's been imagining things, I remind myself. I'd been convinced I'd stepped on something weird, mistaken a roll of leaves for some kind of nightmare under my poor tired foot. I want my bed. Any bed.

7

THE WRECKERS

'I've put it outside.'

I wake to an irritating, barely there tap-tapping on my door, accompanied by the hesitant voice of dippy Dawn.

My head hurts. 'Sorry?' I blurt through a mouth so dry it feels as if I've been swallowing hairy caterpillars for the past eight hours.

'Maggie texted me last night,' Dawn half-whispers through the wood. 'Told me to put a test outside the room with your dry clothes, and then get you breakfast.'

Test?

'This Astrapi thing's a nightmare,' she chimes. Walking herself through a phrase that's becoming too well worn to be either interesting or worrying, as everything starts flooding back to me, the news item, the headline banner set to repeat, the army machoing around under their masks.

'I mean, Maggie's alright,' Dawn rushes to reassure. 'She's not positive or nothing. She just had a late night. Apparently.'

'Right.' Hadn't we all. Although the late night was partly

my fault. Maybe all my fault. I guess on the positive side, it meant Maggie had known about the outbreak from the very first news flash. Although perhaps that kind of news is the kind you can do without. The first time the virus hit, I'd watched the briefings religiously. Six o'clock every evening, I'd be there. It seemed as though the whole country was doing the same. A good few years on, and we're all of us jaded. It rarely makes the headlines anymore. Most people are more than happy to let the bad news catch up with them. Because it does, eventually, and what's another column of digits added to the infinity-style figures the government keeps pumping out.

Besides, the bad news tends to yo-yo. It's always some new variant pitted against some old vaccine. It takes a couple of weeks for the truth to settle, for the people in the labs to work out if it is a new problem or some kind of vague representation of the last instalment. Nobody panics anymore. When there are bodies turned away from the hospitals when the oxygen runs out. When, and if, a person's loved one gets hauled away by faceless people in white suits. You can panic then. I don't have any loved ones.

In fact, I'd have been relieved to see my husband being pulled off on a stretcher, but then our marriage is not what anyone in their right mind would call conventional, and besides, he's got the tenacity of Rasputin. Maybe I've got a bit of that too. If there is another variant on the rampage, I'm vaxed, boosted and have bizarrely avoided all other strains. My head may be hurting, but it has its own sweet reason for that. A punch from a fourteen-stone idiot will give most people a headache. And my mouth might well be dry, but again, that's not due to any virus. I ran a long way last night, and one glass of wine in the bar with a chaser of tea at the doctor's is hardly going to knock the edge off any kind of dehydration.

I take a swig of the water that Maggie had handed to me before I went up to bed. The woman thought of everything; the dry throat is sorted, enough anyway. I'll be fine. I let the blankets slip from my body and wish I hadn't. My bed-warmed skin prickles in the room's damp air, and I pull the blankets back up again. In the gloom of morning, my room at The Wreckers looks even less inviting than it did in the ever-indulgent darkness of night.

The sandstone-coloured carpet barely reaches the walls, and the wooden ceiling beams appear angular and awkward, still sporting the tar-black paint that's been out of fashion for years, along with many cobwebs. The colour is all last-century-wrong, and I'm not even buying that every one of those black spiney spindles of support cutting through the ceiling has a purpose. I wonder if they've been put there simply to reassure the occupant that something is, most probably, holding the roof up.

Personally, I'm not convinced. Some of them stop short of the wall they're supposed to be bridging. The place is a mess. It defies all conceptions of architectural harmony. Not only are most of the beams useless, but they also have the impression of being shifty—the kind of thick-angled spokes that threaten to shift location if a person fails to keep an eye out and joyfully clip the unwary guest hard around the head. This place is crying out for a makeover. Though probably it's gone beyond that. The best bet would be to knock the entire matchstick palace that is The Wreckers down and start over.

'I'm supposed to do you a cooked brekky.'

Dawn must still be outside the door.

'Great,' I say. The effect of Maggie's late-night stew has

burnt itself from the sides of my stomach. Yet again, I'm starving.

'It's in the price. You paid for it.'

I haven't *paid* anything. I glance over at my cash, plastered patiently on the window ledge above the radiator. It's not been dented yet. My tummy grumbles expectantly, and I wish Dawn would just get on with the food prep.

'I said, *great*.' I hit the last word, hoping it will put a little fire under Dawn's feet. The girl is more snail than human. Staring at my pale face in the large, age-speckled mirror hanging over the dressing table, I realise that I'm maybe not in any position to go throwing stones. I look a sight, and the doctor was right; that bruise on my head has begun to shout.

'Only...'

I start. Dawn is still there! I thought she surely must have slipped off to the kitchen. She's becoming tiresome. Everybody hates a lurker. Besides, that full English is getting no nearer.

'Only I'm not that good at cooking,' she mumbles. 'I always worry about the bacon because of the worms. Sausages are the same, and my eggs never really...'

Whatever Dawn's eggs never really do or don't seems beyond words or human understanding because she trails off, leaving the idea of a global egg disaster hanging. Surely there's nothing too seriously incompetent you can do with an egg? Even if you break the thing, you can just scramble it up in a pan. An egg is never far from a success story. But...I think of Dawn, her rounded apologetic shoulders, her meek-as-a-mouse personality. That hair! Even mine has more shape, and I cut it myself. If she's plucked up enough courage to give me a warning about the eggs, it's probably best not to put her to the test.

'Can you do toast?' I shout back.

Silence. Then, 'To be perfectly honest, the toaster's a bit of a bugger. It's not like a domestic toaster. It's like a chef's toaster. They're different. A lot bigger. I'd say you'd be safer with cornflakes. Or you could always wait for Maggie. She won't be that long.' Pause. 'I expect.'

'I'll go for the cornflakes.' I need to be back on the road.

'Good idea.' There's heartfelt relief in Dawn's voice. 'You get yourself washed, and I'll have that cereal out on the table in a flash.'

Maybe it's for the best, I think as I throw the covers from my legs, steeling myself for the cold. I can down the corn-flakes in two seconds flat. If Maggie's not around, I might even be able to slip out without paying the bill. I know it's a cheap trick after all her kindness, and my money situation might look healthy enough, piled up and drying out, but it won't last long. I hadn't been able to pull anything out of the account. So I'd been squirrelling cash away from the house-keeping. Four hundred and eighty pounds, to be precise. It had taken me eight months. I had wanted to wait till I got to a thousand, but as it turned out, I wasn't given that option. I hadn't banked on doing a runner last night.

Only, he didn't take me on trips anywhere. I'd felt suspicious. So I'd brought my cash along as a *just in case*. Four hundred and eighty pounds would be enough to get me started. Luckily, I don't have many needs. I can live cheap, but winter's coming, and I have no intention of ending up on the streets. I could try to pick up with some of the Trav-ellers Mum and I used to live with. I haven't been in touch for years, but they're the kind of community who remember. Then again, that could be a bad thing. I wasn't sure exactly what terms Mum had vacated on. Most probably, it had been with her stuffing her pockets. She had a big Afghan coat at the time, which I knew for a fact had a false lining. She'd been wearing it the morning we left, even though it wasn't cold.

I'D BEEN TWELVE. All in all, it had been idyllic that summer; some of my best childhood memories are about the camp. I'd been happy. Then, out of the blue, early one morning, Mum had leaned over my sleeping body, nudged my shoulder and shushed into my ear. The door on the caravan had been easy to open. In the winter, it would have been a different story. Come November, the thing was permanently stiff with ice and closed tight shut. But in the summer, it was loose from the constant comings and goings. I remember the whole thing really well because the escape seemed like some kind of magic trick. The dew had made the grass wet, and it tickled my bare feet as we slouched past the cluster of caravans, making sure to go the long way around to avoid the chickens and the dogs. Mum hadn't let me put my trainers on till we cleared the vans; putting on shoes would apparently have taken too much time. We were just up and out. I didn't want to go at first. She kept tugging at my thin bandy arms, her nails on my skin sharp, so I knew they were there if needed. I was in no doubt about the score. She sharpened the buggers daily. So I didn't say anything. There was no point. She wasn't the kind of mother who listened anyway. I tried to pitch the whole thing to myself as an adventure. It kind of worked at the beginning.

As we stood on the empty B road, her thumb pointing up towards a sky that was just beginning to turn from dark to rose, I'd taken a good hard look at this woman, my mother, who every few years kept moving me on. Her dark hair flowed loose over her shoulders like some goddess from an Arthurian legend. She was stunning, having the power to turn heads whenever she walked into a room. I so wanted to look like her, but my hair was never as dark, and my skin seemed more prone to dirty olive than lily white. I was desperate for her to love me, though, to have one kind word from those thin painted lips. She was pretty on the outside, my mother, at least when she was younger.

As she grew older, she turned into folds of bone and skin and twisted bitterness, and I stopped being desperate for the few kind words she'd manage to throw at me occasionally like dog biscuits. She never meant them anyway. Yet that morning, standing there in her hippy coat with her pale skin and rose lips and that hair flaring out around her, she looked like some mystical warrior queen.

The story she spun me was simple. She'd told me she'd got wind that the council was moving the Travellers on; the police were going to be involved. 'We' didn't want that, she said. My school record wasn't good. They'd take me away. I always got the feeling there was more to the story, like maybe she was running from unpaid bills and government bureaucracy. Like maybe the running had nothing whatsoever to do with school and me. Like maybe she only took me along because she thought somewhere down the line, I might prove useful.

She could tell that morning that I didn't want to go. She used that name for me, the one that drove me up the wall. She called me Grumpy because she said I reminded her of that dwarf, the difficult one. She'd taken my face in her long pale hands, looked me straight in the eye and said, '*Don't you worry, little Grumpy. We'll catch up with Grant and the others further on down the road.*'

I was in awe of my mother, but I loved Grant. The thought that we would be meeting up later made it easier. I should have known it was a lie, but I chose to swallow it whole. By the time we got picked up by a farmer in a red four-wheel drive, the morning had come out in all its summer colours—powder blue sky, rooted by the vivid greens of the fields. And I'd built a whole daydream for myself, a happy time when we'd all be united, and whatever Mum had in those large coat pockets of hers would have saved the day. She'd be keeping it for all of us. Hiding it from the authorities, who were even now about to raid the camp.

There'd be singing when we all met again, and camp-fires and warm hugs from people who had become like the grandparents I'd never had. Elders who could reprimand if a pinch from a mother got too sharp. Most of all, there would be Grant. My mum's "man friend" at the time. I liked him more than anyone I've ever met in my entire life with his gentle giant hands that he spoke with and bramble beard that never hid his smile. He got me books from the library, and even though there was barely enough space in that caravan to swing a chicken (his joke), we found some-where we could hide the books from Mum. Mum never liked books. She said they encouraged people to dream, and that was bad because a girl like me, a grumpy old dwarf of a thing, shouldn't have dreams.

That morning, standing on the road, my mother cupping my face in her hands, that was the last time she ever mentioned Grant or the Travellers. We never went back or met up further down the road. Her Afghan coat got lighter at the next town we hit, and for at least a week, my mother was smiling, and there were drinks in the pub every night. As an adult, it's obvious. Mum stole stuff and pawned it when we reached the next stopping place. There was no going back for her.

And me? Would they let me back now? Mum had been the adult. She had to take the responsibility. They'd know that. I'd only been twelve at the time. There was a possibility that Grant might take me in. We got on so well. He'd been abandoned as a kid. His parents just moved on and left him at the camp. The camp simply absorbed him. He'd been born deaf. Maybe that's why his parents left; they thought it was too much trouble. They couldn't have been more wrong. Grant was an absolute gem of a person. Living in a caravan should have been a low point in my life, but in fact, it was the safest I ever felt. So that could be a possibility now.

Staring once again in the mirror at The Wreckers, my whole big, bright balloon of hope bursts. Who am I kidding? That was more than ten years ago. Grant must have been at least forty-five. He'd be shacked up with someone else by now or dead. Travellers have a hard life. He was probably dead, and even if he wasn't, arriving beside his axle, dragging trouble in the shape of my husband behind me, was no way to return.

I glance at the clothes Maggie gave me last night. They're folded on the chair by the en suite. The sludge-green cords and the oversized hoody. They weren't what anyone would have chosen, but they are warm and dry, and with only one set of anything to my name, it might be best to keep a hold of Maggie's cast-offs. A second set of clothes is not going to hurt. So, on the bright side—this morning, I find myself alive, dry, a little richer than I was last night and with the promise of breakfast. If I avoid paying the bill, I'll be quids in.

Wandering towards the curtains and parting them a

little in the middle, I get a better picture of where I've landed. Who would have thought? Sure, the road is out there, waiting. Just an empty strip of it. The same road we came in on last night, but this morning, despite the gloom, through the narrow crack in the curtain, I start to understand the lay of the land. Just the other side of the road is a thin pavement, edged with a long, low wall a couple of feet high. Pretty unremarkable, but the wall separates the pavement from something I had in no way expected—a crinkled wash of glistening flat mud.

There's a gloss of brown ooze falling away from the road and the pub for as far as the eye can see. The bed of an estuary cut through with thin trails of water. It seems strange somehow as if some larger-than-life force has magicked it there for me fresh this morning. The mud seeps into a trickle of tea-brown water, which in turn washes out onto the horizon, merging into a long grey slab of mackerel sky. This place really is the ends of the earth.

WHEN I STEP, showered and dressed, out onto the dusty upstairs landing, I see the lateral flow test packet propped up against the wall in the hallway. It's lying neatly across my folded dry clothes. I can't be bothered with any of that now. I haven't been in contact with anyone recently apart from my arsehole of a husband and the impromptu carnival from last night—Maggie, Phil, Stan, Doctor Dancey and wife. Okay, so that is a lot of people, but I have the feeling none of them get out much. So the chances of contagion are pretty slim. Besides, I'm feeling fine. Dropping the unopened test kit and the stash of clothes back in my room, I head off to find that cereal.

· · ·

'THERE YOU GO.' Dawn slides a china bowl full to the brim with golden orange flakes in front of me. She's managed to knock me up a mug of coffee too. So far, she's doing okay. Though I have my doubts that all those clamouring leaves of flaked corn are going to stay in the bowl, not once I've poured on the milk and stuck in a spoon.

Also, this is not a dining room. This is just the same bar from last night, a chair drawn up to a table and set self-consciously in the middle of the carpeted floor. I have no idea why Dawn's set the table centrally rather than just leaving it where it was, hugging the walls like the others, but I reckon it's probably best not to draw attention to it. Dawn's the nervous type. Any comment or criticism is likely to cause a meltdown. It could be worse. She could have stuck a little candle on the varnished wooden top and a single rose in a jar. Nothing would surprise me.

'Oh, that's a nasty bruise.' There's a sympathetic wince in Dawn's voice as if she can almost feel my head slamming against the dashboard, my husband's rough hands clutched at the back of my neck, his fingers tethered tight with my hair. So tight, my scalp pulled into peaks, but I'm not one for sympathy or explanations.

I reach instinctively towards my forehead, tugging at my hide-behind long fringe so it falls neatly across most of the damage. 'Looks worse than it is,' I lie.

She nods dismissively. I get the feeling she's lost interest. 'You don't mind if I do the laundry in here, do you?' She huffs with all the finesse of a middle-aged washer woman as she empties the laundry basket that she's been carrying across the long, varnished bar. Sheets tumble out, gathering in knotty lumps across the wood.

'No. You're fine.' I couldn't care less, but it seems an odd place to sort washing. If that bar isn't spotless, the sheets will pick up any dollop of lager going and carry the crust of it with the linen to bed. I've been cleaning for Jayden since the very start of our "marriage". He was not a tolerant man on the domestic front. Which means I'm a bit OCD as far as cleanliness goes. Luckily, Dawn and her laundry skills are none of my business. I'm just thankful it won't be me lying on those sheets.

I pour the milk over the cornflakes, and up they rise, sure as a grounded galleon when the tide rushes back in. Thankfully they don't spill over. I don't like cornflakes much. They remind me of flattened popcorn. I love popcorn, but there's a time and a place, and also that attractive 3D shape, which is not happening in my breakfast bowl.

'Only the lights better in here,' Dawn continues, 'so...'

I don't know where Dawn would be comparing the bar to, but the daylight spilling in through the large medieval windows of The Wreckers is pretty poor. Maybe she normally processes the laundry in a coal cellar?

'Do you know what time the buses go?' I ask, loading my spoon and angling it towards my mouth.

'Hmm.' She folds a pillowcase neatly into six.

That last turn is so obviously one turn too many, but again, I say nothing.

'Normally twenty past the hour, depending on the tide.'

I'm not sure if I heard her right. Did she say tide? That seems odd. Maybe she said ride? Maybe?

'Only they could be working on a reduced service today,' she rattles on, surprisingly talkative after her sullen indifference of last night. It's as though she knows me now, so feels entitled to blabber. 'Reduced because of the virus an' all.' Suddenly she stops folding and fixes me with her vacant blue eyes. 'You did your test?'

I nod. A nod is not a lie. It could be an involuntary

twitch—another of my mum's golden nuggets of wisdom. The woman should have written a book, *How to Parent Using Bullshit and a Broom Handle.*

Oblivious, Dawn smiles, relieved. 'Only, you know—you coming in from outside and everything. Just wanted to be sure. Last time the virus got bad, the parish council cut the island off.'

I'm not sure I'm following. 'Island?'

'Attercoppe's a tidal island. It would be a normal island, only we've got the causeway now.'

Attercoppe, that must have been the name Stan was spitting out last night—the place he was taking me.

'Only one road in, one road out, so isolating the village is easy-peasy. It's not even really that tidal anymore because of the mudflats. We must be the only place in the world that's getting bigger. Silting up, that's what Maggie says. Silting up so much that one day the mud'll just stop us all in our tracks.'

I remembered the acres of wet brown slop that I'd seen from my window, slithering away towards infinity.

'But we've still only got one way in, one way out. Can't go over the mud. It's actually seriously dangerous. Most years, somebody loses a dog. But in cases like this, virus cases, we can just pull up the drawbridge.' She laughs. 'Not that we have an actual bridge. You just got to put someone on the road in a police vehicle. They did that during the Black Death. Not the police vehicle, just probably some farmer with a pitchfork.' She laughs, picking up another sheet and folding it. 'Worked though. None of them died. Well, not that time anyway.'

I stop shovelling my cornflakes. 'Sorry?'

Dawn smiles sheepishly. 'I don't really know anything

about any of that Black Death stuff, bit before my time. It's just like…local stories.'

I'm not a whole heap interested in history. It's the geography that I'm trying to get my head around. 'What, so this place is an island?'

Now it's Dawn's turn to look at me like my brain's working in slo-mo.

'Not all the time, 'cus of the causeway. So now it's just when we have a high tide.' She raises her eyes heavenward, relishing this brief moment of superiority. No doubt, she doesn't get this kind of one-upmanship treat too often. 'I'll take these up to Maggie.' She nods towards the folded sheets. 'You just leave everything there. I'll clear it when I get back down.'

I stare at my cornflakes. The bottom layer has already turned to squelch in the bowl. I can pick something up on the road. I'll grab my things, then be off. If the buses come every twenty minutes and the tides are in my favour, I should be able to get out of here pretty quick. I guess if the tide did cut me off, my hubby wouldn't be able to get in either. Although the thought of him waiting at the end of the causeway for me gives me one hell of an uncomfortable feeling, the kind of feeling a pheasant must get when it's squatting in a gorse bush and spots some guy in a wax jacket loading up a gun.

BACK IN THE quiet of my room, I give my teeth a quick once-over with the disposable toothbrush someone left for me when I arrived. I don't have much stuff, just my coat and my bag. I'll take the toothbrush. There were a few chargers in the room too. I guess they have to put them in here, what with the phone situation. I decide to nab the one that's currently charging my own phone. No one will miss it. In places like this, everyone expects you to nick the towels, the toothpaste, the ketchup. Chargers will be no different. It's built into the rate. Not that I intend to pay. I like Maggie, seriously I do, and I would pay if I could, only I can't. If I hurry, I can be out of here before Maggie's got herself to the front desk. Pushing my fingers down the back of the bed to unplug the cable, I suddenly freeze as a scream rips through the building. Dawn?

Running towards the scream is instinctive. If I had an ounce of self-preservation, I would have been running in the opposite direction, but I can't do that. I could so easily be the person emptying their lungs in terror. Someone is in trouble. Before my brain has time to rationalise what I'm doing or why, or even if it's a good idea, I am sprinting through the building, back across the landing and down a long, dark corridor.

I can see Dawn ahead of me, standing in front of an open door, her legs wrapped in a sea of dropped linen. Her mouth open in horror.

'Dawn?'

The girl's body seems paralysed as she continues to stare at something just out of my sight, something through the open door.

'Dawn?'

She doesn't turn towards me. Doesn't take her eyes off the *something* inside that room. Instead, where the words should be, Dawn lets slip a guttural groan. Her bottom lip trembles, and she slumps boneless as a rag doll against the door-frame and begins to sink.

'Dawn.' I draw up beside her, pushing my arm under her elbow to give her support. 'What...?'

She gasps, trying to get her breath back, but not for one

moment does she look at me. I follow her gaze and suddenly my own knees give. Through the door is a small bedsit. Different from my hotel room, more personal. Someone lives here. All of that's fine, would be fine, but lying on the floor, wedged between the edge of the bed and the wall, marble-hard eyes staring at the ceiling, hands clutched across her chest as if thrown there in terror, is Maggie.

'No, no, no...' Dawn whimpers.

'Call an ambulance.'

'No. No.' Dawn continues to sob. Her body helpless as a wet dishrag.

'Dawn,' I pull her face around to mine, 'you need to call an ambulance. Go downstairs and phone.'

I stumble into the room and drop to my knees beside Maggie's large, cold body. Blind panic hitting me as I realise I don't have a clue as to what I should be doing. There's a whimper from behind. I glance over my shoulder. Dawn is still leaning against the door-frame, wide-eyed and mumbling.

'Dawn. Phone,' I shout. Pulling Maggie's arm into my own. It's still warm. Still supple. That's good. That has to be good. I'm pretty sure people go cold and stiff when they're dead. I feel for a pulse, wishing I knew how I should be doing this. Is it wrist or neck? I can't find anything anywhere. 'Dawn. Phone,' I shout again.

'No,' Dawn shrieks. 'No. I can't. I can't.'

My God, the girl is useless. My fingers grasp Maggie's. Gently holding her hand, I press down into the soft part between her wrist and her palm. I can't feel a pulse, but that means nothing. I could easily be pressing in the wrong place. A pulse is a tricky thing to get a hold of if you're not in the know. Laying her arm gently down again, I feel for my own pulse, just trying to figure out where you're supposed to place your fingers. I can't find mine either. I can still hear Dawn whimpering in the background. What the hell is wrong with her; all she has to do is make a call.

I grope in the pockets of my trousers for my own phone. I am out of my league here. One first aid course when I was ten at a local swimming pool is hardly going to save the day. My fingers clutch frantically at my back pockets, and my heart sinks. These are not my jeans. I'm wearing the sludge cords. Stupidly I'd left my phone in my room. I'd been going to unplug it when I heard the scream.

'Dawn, where's your mobile.'

She jitters, her eyes roving wildly.

'Dawn?'

'I...Downstairs. Down...I can't.' Her knees give once again.

This is useless. 'Okay, wait here.' I'm not sure if I'm talking to Dawn or Maggie at this point. Yet, Dawn picks it up.

'No!' She looks at me with a face of full-on horror, glancing wildly over at poor Maggie's lifeless body. 'I don't want to be on my own. Not here. This place...' Wild-eyed, she glances around her.

Seriously! 'My phone's in my room,' I explain. 'I need to get my phone because I have to call an ambulance.'

I cannot believe I'm having to explain any of this! Isn't it obvious? We need to hand Maggie on to someone, anyone, who's been trained specifically in this kind of shit-hits-the-fan scenario. Pushing out through the door, I knock Dawn's shoulder as I go. How does an individual get to be so large and yet so incredibly clueless?

'I'm coming with you,' Dawn says, pulling herself back to her feet and through the door-frame after me as if proving she can walk. 'I'm not staying here. This place gives me the creeps.'

So that was it. That was what all the folding the laundry in the bar was about. Dawns's got a thing about The Wreckers. But now? This is so irritating, so unnecessary. Dawn will only slow me down. Sadly, I can't see a way of getting out of it. There's not a hope in hell of the girl leaving my side. She's spooked herself, and no amount of sensible is going to get her back doing anything even remotely useful.

I leave the door to Maggie's room open; when the paramedics get here, they can just steam right on in. With me supporting Dawn, we limp back to my room. It feels as if I'm caught in some kind of bizarre three-legged race. I want to rip off the rag holding us together and run for the hills, but I remember the stew and the warmth of Maggie's words. I might have intended to do a runner without paying, but I get the feeling Maggie would have understood. The woman was a star. This is different. I can't let her down now. I've met so few people like her in my life; sometimes, you have to do the right thing. No, that's wrong, I realise—sometimes you want to.

In my room, Dawn sinks down onto my bed, snivelling. I grab my phone, pull out the charging cable, and start to dial as I head to the en suite. I need to grab Dawn a few squares of loo roll for her nose. I can't do with the snotty nose and the possibly dead woman. The nose is one horror too far. I press 999 and ask for an ambulance, feeling my heart stop racing just a little as an absurdly calm woman's voice comes over the line. She asks me if Maggie is still conscious? That's a no. Is she breathing? I should have checked, just to make certain. I tell the woman I'm not sure. I'm not sure of anything. The only thing I do know is that they need to come quick. This is an emergency. Every time I offer more detail, Dawn lets out a little sob. The absent woman with the calm phone voice tells me to stay where I am. They're handing me over to someone who can talk me through CPR.

'They'll be here soon,' I tell Dawn.

'Can I go home?'

I seriously do not want to be left holding this can of worms. 'I don't think that's a good idea.' I fix her with a hard, unflinching stare, the kind you might give to a child.

She looks at me with her vacant blue eyes set to puppy dog. 'The hotel's empty. No other guests. Just you. There's no need for me to stay,' she whines.

I'm not liking any of this, but I need to tread carefully. 'I'm on hold,' I say simply. Trying to keep my voice calm. 'They're going to talk me through CPR. What time does your shift stop?'

'Five thirty,' she says. Realising she's tied into place by the rota.

I nod. 'Well then.' Luckily, I sound way more authoritative than I'm feeling.

'Hello, Miss?' comes a voice from the end of the phone.

We need to get back to Maggie. 'Yes. I'm here.'

Suddenly Dawn's eyes pop in pure horror, and that large bloodless mouth of hers hangs open on its hinge. I sigh loudly. I can't cope with any more dramatics. I hope to God that Dawn's current reaction is not because she's just seen a spider. Nothing would surprise me.

'Are you with the patient now?' comes the woman from the end of the line. The contrast seems too cruel—how did I get myself stuck with Dawn, the joker?

'No, no, I'm in...'

I look behind me, following the line of Dawn's gaze. Then I see it—propped up beside the wall, just inside the door, sitting on my pile of clean clothes is the test. My test. My unopened test.

'Shit.' Dawn jumps up from the bed.

'Ma'am?' says the voice at the end of the line.

'Yes, I'm still here.'

I go towards Dawn, reaching out a hand reassuringly— I'm fine. I don't feel sick. Only Dawn is in no mood. No rota is going to tie this girl in place. She hunkers down into her body like a rugby player about to go in for a tackle. Suddenly, she's looking more bull and bolshy than I would have believed was humanly possible for a short square thing like Dawn. The change puts me out of step, off my guard for one moment too long, as uncoiling her shoulder, Dawn flies into me with the most incredible force. Whacking me so hard, I tumble back against the wall, just missing one of those sharply angled beams. Hitting my head, instead, against the partition wall as I go down. The phone flying up and out of my hand.

'You didn't test!' Dawn screams with all the finesse of a banshee.

'I felt,' I stumble over my words. 'I feel fine.' Slumped against the wall, I instinctively reach for the back of my head. There's already a bump on it the size of a chestnut. I'm not sure how much more abuse my cranium can take. 'Dawn, this isn't about me.'

But none of that matters because when I glance up again, the space that contained Dawn is empty. She's heading for the door. It slams shut behind her, shaking the roots of the old building and fracturing the throbbing in my brain into a thousand painful splinters.

'Dawn!'

'Ma'am, are you alright?' The phone bleats pathetically from the floor beside me where it fell.

'This is all your fault.' Dawn screeches like a strangled owl through the locked wooden panel. 'You killed her. You killed Maggie.'

This can't be happening. Maggie's not dead. I didn't kill anyone. Maggie will be fine if she gets the right treatment, and I'm not sick. I jump to my feet, lunging at the door, just as I hear the key turning in its lock. Dawn is one seriously irritating piece of work. At this point in time, I'd like nothing better than to wring her neck; give the police two bodies. Even though I know the door is shut tight, I rattle the brass doorknob hard. So hard I hear Dawn shriek in terror from the hallway behind it. The satisfaction only lasts a moment; I cannot be shut in. Maggie needs help. And besides Maggie, I have my own problems to contend with—time is running out for me. With every click of the clock, I know Jayden will be closing the distance between us. Narrowing down all the options. Sniffing me out—fee fi fo.

'Dawn. I feel absolutely fine,' I spit through gritted teeth.

'How could you?' comes the reply. 'How could you...' and her broken words trail off, interspersed with footsteps as her flat feet thud into the distance accompanied by a smattering of high-pitched wailing.

'Ma'am?' The oh-so-small voice from the phone sounds forlorn, confused.

I bang hard on the door. 'Dawn. Maggie needs your help. For God's sake, get your phone. Do CPR.'

There's no reply. Just another pinched-nose bleat from my handset, which lies abandoned on the floor. 'Are you in danger, ma'am?'

I pick the phone up and sink down onto my lumpy bed. Am I in danger? Yes, probably. Probably I've always been in danger, but that's not the point.

'I...that was the receptionist. She's locked me in my room. She thinks I've got the virus.'

'Okay.' A brief pause. 'Is there anyone there who can do CPR, someone currently with the patient?'

I stare into the room, knowing the inn is empty; Dawn had told me I was the only guest. She'd seemed to think that was a good reason for her to scarper home. Locking me in my room has now apparently cleared her of all obligation.

Perhaps it doesn't matter. I'd seen how she applied herself to folding sheets and cooking breakfast; I couldn't imagine she'd be much use on the CPR front. Then again, maybe I was wrong. Maybe she wasn't scarpering from the building. Maybe she'd finally realised that in a situation like this, everyone has to pull their weight—save the day.

'I hope CPR is what the receptionist's gone to do.' My voice sounds flat.

'Okay, well that's...'

I hang up. I don't want any more questions. Glancing over at the unopened test, the full weight of the situation starts to settle. Say it is me? Say I am carrying this thing. We all know you can carry without showing symptoms. My God, what have I done? I part the curtains and stare out onto the street below, at the strip of marsh and mud sloping, oozing out into the distance. Clumps of tough-looking grass stand vertical between gulleys of endless brown swill. Put your foot on anything beyond that low concrete wall, and I'm willing to bet you'd be up to your knees within seconds. It's as though this whole place is built on quicksand. Below me in the street, I see Dawn break out of the building fast as a rat sliding out of a drainpipe. Once she's standing in the harsh cold air, she looks confused, stunned, staring side to side anxiously before setting her limp body to pace the tarmac. There's no way she's had time to go back to Maggie.

She must have run straight out of the inn without a thought for the poor woman upstairs. The best employer she'll most likely get in her entire life. The kindest friend. I'd only known Maggie for a few hours, but if, God forbid, that woman was dead, even I was going to miss her.

In the street below, Dawn's wimpy-wet arms beat around her blob of a body as if she's trying to ward off the cold, or the disaster, or both. Or maybe the flailing arms are a call for help? I'm not sure. The street's empty anyway. This place wakes up late, or maybe it's always like this—dead. Poor Maggie. It has to be a heart attack. If only bloody Dawn had more spine than gelatine running through her body, we might both be giving Maggie CPR. Things might be okay.

Although, a heart attack somehow doesn't seem quite right. Maggie wasn't that old. Maybe she had some kind of condition. Diabetes? Epilepsy? Maybe this was just a seizure, but if so, surely Dawn would know that? Then again, this latest virus—could it seriously be me? I stare in the mirror. Despite the battering, I look normal. I feel fine, but...I have got a headache. I'd had it since last night. Since Jayden whacked my head against the dashboard, to be precise. I'd thought it was the dashboard that did it, but maybe the headache had simply been waiting for an excuse to let rip. I run my fingers up to the bruise.

There are two bruises now, one on the front, courtesy of the blazing row with the psychopath I'm married to, the other on the back, courtesy of bloody Dawn. Just because I have bruises doesn't mean that the headache is related. Maybe I was feeling sick before the argument last night? Maybe that's why I pushed it, why everything blew up. Suddenly I can't help myself—I cough.

In the street below, Dawn continues to pace, steam pouring out of her mouth into the cold air as if she's a dying dragon. She must be waiting for the police, or maybe she's just confused, or waiting for some mysterious manager to check in and tell her she can go home. Hard to tell. If I am the carrier, does that mean he's got it too? My *ever-loving* husband. That would be an added bonus because that could mean that in some lay-by just off the A12, there's the hunched body of a man in his late thirties, his face stubbled as a scouring pad, his large angry fingers gripping the steering wheel rather than my throat, struggling for breath. I find myself enjoying the thought. Wanting to push just that little bit further with the embellishments; perhaps that homemade tattoo of a cross on his index finger, the one he's been carrying with him since his teens, well maybe that blue ink is even bluer now, now that his hands are luminous, bloated with the creep of death.

No, I think to myself. It's a nice thought, but no. Even if I managed to take out the whole of England with some new strain of disaster, there would be one person living through this. One person grinning that lopsided signature grin that he slides in and out of as effortlessly as the turn of a fish. Lopsided makes it sound attractive, but it's not. Everything about him is lopsided. I'd made sure to leave the USB, his flash drive, in the car. The man was neurotic about that thing, kept all his contacts on it and carried it everywhere. It was most likely in the glove with the map. He'd have found it. He'd know he didn't need to come after me.

Only, with him, that wouldn't really figure. He'd come anyway. It was a point of honour. That's what my mum said when he came to take me off her hands all those years ago. She'd "promised me". I wasn't old enough. I was fourteen. Even I knew it wasn't right. But she'd kept me off the radar, fattened me up like the witch in the gingerbread house till I was ripe. He kept me inside his house for two years. Two years of never feeling the wind on my face. Always inside till he could make it legal. I'd have signed on the dotted line for anything in order to get a little more freedom.

He might as well be here now, I realise with a wash of self-pity, because I'm still terrified of him. I let the curtains fall back into place. I bet he's enjoying this. He's a hunter, a poacher by heart. This little game will be right up his street. He might even be out there now, knowing exactly where I am but simply waiting, letting me stew. He's in no rush. Bastard. I pick up the test, rip the top off the foil package, punch a hole in the box so it can hold the plastic tube with its magic liquid swilling in the bottom, and get myself ready for the routine. I guess if they lock me up in some kind of facility, he won't be able to get in. If I have got it, cross my fingers it's so toxic I'm on for a long stay in something hermetically sealed with an armed guard.

IT TAKES a full fifteen minutes for the paramedics to arrive. More than enough time to inform me I haven't got the latest variant, and more than enough time to die if you haven't got anyone doing CPR. I watch from my window as an ambulance containing a man and a woman pulls up in front of The Wreckers. The couple are both wearing the caterpillar colours of the health service: green with yellow high vis. The woman has her long, dark hair tied tightly out of choking distance behind her head, and the man, mid-thirties, is all short-cut and buzzing energy. They look efficient. Up for the job.

In contrast, Dawn—pacing the street—looks a complete wreck of humanity, practically a different species. She's still outside, cold now. Her body concave as though blown inside out by the blustery East wind. Dawn keeps her distance even when they get out of the vehicle. But Dawn and her distress soon garner the full attention of the paramedics. She looks odd, haunted. I hope they're not going to start wasting time on her. I feel like tapping on the window and shouting at them.

Luckily, Dawn may look mad, but she's bent on keeping everyone two metres apart. She doesn't want anyone near. Fear of contamination has her edgy. This is good because Dawn is the kind to leach all sympathy out of a person before they'd even realised she wasn't the problem.

She starts gesticulating wildly towards the pub and then, as an afterthought, my window. They stare up. I pull back out of sight. I have no idea why, but there are only a few options here. Wave is all wrong. Smile is a pretty poor choice. Pulling back and out of sight seems like the most respectful option.

Within minutes, there's a thundering of feet on that old razzle dazzle carpet in the hallway. Then the heavy-footed thud-thudding growing quieter, receding into the distance. They must be heading straight for Maggie. I hope they're not too late. I think of her face last night. The only genuinely kind face I've seen for such a long time. The only person I've met who didn't seem to be working an angle. I think of her standing behind that bar downstairs with her concern and her food, and her warmth. That can't all be gone, surely. None of us can afford for that small but true spot of kindness in this big bad old world to have been wiped off the face of the planet.

A police car pulls up in the street outside. A young black police officer gets out. He looks a little apprehensive, as though he hasn't got a clue why he's here, although the second skin of the uniform he's shoehorned himself into is making him just that little bit braver. There's an older woman with him, her hair grey, giving her an air of gravitas, but he was driving. Cautiously.

From the way the woman talks to the young PC, it's clear she's in charge here. The young lad is all nods and fixed-eye-contact serious. When the policewoman finishes, the lad breaks away, pulling out his pad and walking towards the distraught Dawn, whose bendy blancmange body is still keeping itself away from everyone. Her mouth is soon going forty to the dozen, but she keeps stepping back, maintaining the distance as the young guy in uniform walks towards her, as though there's a magnetic field pushing their bodies apart. Maybe she is being safe, but she looks like a loony.

Meanwhile, the policewoman glances up at my window. She says something into the walkie-talkie she's got attached to her collar, then realising they've most likely extracted all the sense they're going to get out of Dawn, she nods her head towards the young guy, and they follow in the wake of the paramedics, trotting into the building.

Outside I notice a thin frill of water has started to creep back over the marsh. The tide must be on the turn. I wonder if Jayden's with us yet? I used to think I could sense him when he was near. It was as though he carried a little dark electric cloud above his head, and sometimes, I could feel that cloud when he was close, but the mud and the water must be throwing me out of step. If he is close, I'm not picking up on anything.

It's a good ten minutes before anyone bothers tapping on my door. When they do, it's the young guy's voice, not the older police officer, not the paramedics. I've become the newbie's responsibility. I suppose that's fair; I'm not dying, and I'm not going anywhere; the door is still locked tight.

'Hello?' says a clear voice accompanied by a light rap on the door.

'Hi.'

'I'm Special Leon Hutchins.'

A Special? I really am low on their list of worries. That's all okay. I'm happy with that because *Special* means I don't warrant serious police attention.

'Is Maggie alright?'

There's silence. Then SC Hutchins clears his throat. 'I'm afraid Maggie Reynolds is dead.'

I sink back onto the bed.

'Miss Adams?'

Maggie can't be dead. She just can't. She was fine last night. It was the crack of dawn, and she was looking the picture of health. This just cannot be happening.

'Miss Adams? Are you okay?'

It can't be.

'Miss Adams?'

Then I remember with a sinking feeling of drowning at my own over-flippant stupidity; that's me—Eve Adams. That was what I wrote in the bloody registration book last night. Eve Adams. I hadn't expected the name to come under scrutiny. I seriously hadn't expected anyone to repeat it ever again. It was a bit of a joke. I'd been tired last night, not thinking clearly, hadn't thought it mattered. I should have taken more care. Pulling a name out of thin air is just lazy arse and all wrong. I hadn't even had to bother with a car registration number. It should have been simple—just my mobile and a name, and I chose Eve Adams. What a berk. No. So much more. What an idiot. But when I reply to SC Hutchins, I manage to keep the ankle-kicking irritation out of my voice. That horse has bolted.

Eve Adams it is. 'Yes, sorry. I...'

'Miss Carpenter said that you hadn't done a lateral flow test? And that you came in from outside the town late last night?'

'I've done it. The lateral flow.' A sense of relief washes over me. At least I've got that nailed. 'It's negative. Absolutely. Not a doubt.'

A brief pause. 'Okay. Well, under the circumstances, we're going to have to keep you in isolation until you've done a PCR.'

This doesn't seem like a good idea to me. The Wreckers is far too easy to spot. Drive into town, and you'd come straight here. Those tests take at least forty-eight hours to process, which makes me a sitting duck.

'I'm sorry.' I hate the way my voice has risen an octave with the pinch of a liar. 'I can't stay here that long. I need to get back to my mother. She's sick.'

In fact, she's dead, but sick works so much better in this situation.

There's a brief pause. My guess is SC Hutchins is not good at emotion. He clears his throat before he wades back in. 'I'm so sorry, Miss Adams. But we are going to have to ask you to stay put.'

For a newbie, young Leon seems more than capable of holding his own. The *sick mother* doesn't put him one inch out of his stride.

'I tried to get Dawn to do CPR if she'd...'

Leon clears his throat. 'I'm not sure that would have helped.'

'How did Maggie die?'

Another brief pause. Now he's really out of his comfort zone. 'That's not clear at the moment. They're taking her to the coroners. But until we're one hundred per cent sure it's not the virus, we need to keep everyone who's had recent contact in isolation.'

This is all bad news. Maggie's death is heartbreaking, but unless they want more corpses on their hands, I really should be making a move. 'Like I said, I can't hang around, and I'm not infectious. I can show you the test.' It's unclear how far I can push this, and yet push is what I need to do. 'Seriously, I have to get to my sick mother. Cancer sick,' I add, just in case there's any confusion on the seriousness of the sickness stakes.

'Okay, can you just...' I hear Special Hutchins take a few steps away from the door, then the white static noise of the radio as he opens a line before he can be heard mumbling. 'Doesn't want to stay put.' A pause. 'Mother with cancer.' A pause. 'Not sure. Didn't ask.' A third pause. 'Okay. Okay.'

I hear him creak back over the floorboards.

'I'm sorry, Miss Adams, but you are going to have to stay in isolation until you've had a clear PCR. We'll post an officer on the door for you.' There's another pause which is just that fraction of a second too long. 'When one gets here.'

Well, at least the officer on watch will be a bit better than simply sitting behind a B&Q bog-standard locked door. Someone in uniform could help. 'And you're not allowed to let anyone in?' I ask.

'I'm sorry, but yes, that's right,' Leon says, misunderstanding my motives. 'You won't be able to see anyone until we're sure you're clear. In the meantime, I need to ask you some questions about your movements.' He clears his throat. 'Who have you come into contact with since you arrived in Attercoppe?'

Okay. Now it's time to play ball. I want whoever it is standing on the other side of the door working with me, not against me, and the easiest way to do that is to go full guns blazing with the old nice and helpful.

'Stan, he was the first.'

'Stan.' There's a pause as the Special scribbles it down. 'Do you have a surname?'

'No. He drove a Volvo. Too fast.' I can't help myself. I have to get the dig in somewhere.

'Maidstone? Stan Maidstone?'

'I don't know.'

'He drives a Volvo. Rust-coloured? Really old.'

Him and the car. But I don't say that. 'Yeah. Rust-coloured. I'd have said 1980s, kind of square-looking rectangle on wheels.'

'Okay. That's him. And how much contact would you say you had with Mr Maidstone?'

'Hmm, thirty minutes in the car. Forty downstairs in the bar.'

'Okay. And then there was Maggie?'

The name pierces me. Why do nice people have to die? What is all that about? It's a shame you can't trade souls. I know exactly who I'd be offering up instead of Maggie. Jayden, for one, and actually, the way I'm feeling, I'd even push the button on Dawn.

'Ms Adams?'

'Yeah, forty minutes in the bar.' The guilt hits. Did I really bring this in with me? I just can't see it. Wouldn't I be testing positive? Could the test have been faulty? Sure, I've got a headache, but now I have two good reasons for the head: my Hard Nut Hubby and bloody Virus Vigilante Dawn. I feel fine. 'I don't have the virus. Seriously.'

'And anyone else? Did you meet anyone else apart from Dawn Carpenter, the receptionist?'

'PC Green and Doctor Dancey...oh, and his wife.'

'Right.' SC Hutchins draws out the word, like this is anything but alright. 'That's a lot of people?'

He's not wrong. I bet I've got through most of the principal players in this small, muddy community in the space of one night.

'Yeah.'

'Why the doctor?'

'Sorry?'

'You weren't feeling well?'

Suddenly I see where this is going.

'No. I was fine. Bloody Stan ran me over.'

'Sorry?'

'We had a collision. Nothing serious. Maggie…' It still hurts to say the name. It feels raw as if my words are poking a dagger into an open wound. 'Maggie felt I should get checked out.'

'Okay. Hold on there just one minute.'

SC Leon Hutchins walks away from the door again, leaving me to stew. Poor Maggie. It must have been a heart attack. Nothing else acts that quick. Meanwhile, for me personally, none of this is looking good. Okay, so it's not as if Jayden, my fury-on-legs husband, would be stupid enough to come in through the front door if he saw the police cars. No, he'd bite down the anger and avoid the pub. But even if he didn't know I was in here, because how would he? The police activity would make him curious. Curious enough to wait. To watch. I might as well have flags stuck into the building—*she's here. Come pick her up.* If the autopsy comes back on Maggie quick, if they can tell it's not the virus, if I can do another lateral flow and it's negative, surely they can't keep me. I'll make certain I leave through the backdoor.

'Okay. You holding up okay in there?' Leon's returned with another jaunty knock.

'Fine. I was thinking, could I just do another lateral flow?'

'No, sorry...' I hear Leon take a deep breath in. 'They've located Mr Maidstone.'

'Mr Maidstone?'

'Stan. The guy who drives the Volvo.'

'Great, and he's okay. So...'

'No, I'm sorry.' SC Leon Hutchins coughs, but there's no power of virus behind it. I get the feeling that Leon's stalling for time. 'Actually, Stan's not okay. They found him on his doorstep. Dead. Early this morning. They thought it was hypothermia, but now...'

I can barely hear the words anymore. My brain is swimming. I must have this virus. It's me. I'm the carrier, patient zero, and the damn thing really does act like lightning. I stare at my pale face in the speckled mirror, but if that is true, then why aren't I dead?

8

ATTERCOPPE

I spend the afternoon watching TV. Gazing at the flickering blue lights until my brain feels as though it's turning to jelly. The box offers nothing but wall-to-wall virus coverage. Sadly, The Wreckers doesn't run to subscription channels. *Fancy* is a whole different world away. Here, you get what you're given. I'm feeling force-fed as a battery chicken with every channel trying, in what is quite literally the fever of the moment, to explain something they haven't actually got to grips with yet. We all know by now that it takes at least four weeks to fully understand the thing, to track it, to work out its MO. Only this fact is stopping absolutely nobody from voicing an opinion.

Everyone and their grandmother appears to be happily lobbing barely thought-out sentences at those soundbite-hungry media bods. In between an embarrassing and awkward vox-pox of interrupted pavement-stopped shoppers, there's a halfway useful sprinkling of experts. A scientist from the World Health Organisation tells viewers this latest variant originated in Asia, *probably*, but it's hit the UK hard. A virologist says it's too early to tell exactly what the rate of infection with Astrapi is, but the thing appears to be ripping through East Anglia quicker than any previous variant. A good case scenario would be an infection rate similar to SARS. A bad case scenario—the scientist doesn't even want to go there. Despite the greedy look of excitement on the blonde, bobbed presenter's face, the scientist leaves the nation hanging in uncertainty with an ironic upwards haul of his over-busy eyebrows.

The prime minister tells us East Anglia is now on shutdown. Is that different from lockdown? I'm not sure how and have no one to ask. Perhaps they simply wanted a different word for the same situation? The implication for the word change appears to be that there will be no piddling about for anti-vaxxers or masks worn at a jaunty angle—for *jaunty,* they mean they don't want your nose hanging out, not even if it's extra-large.

There's a whole news section about how to wear a mask properly, including an animation with a woman who has an enormous nose. I guess they want to ram the point home. We should know this simple procedure, have it muscled into the subconscious, but it would appear from the watch-with-mother antics the newscasters are employing that no one has been listening up. There's a little bit more, and this time I'm not sure if they're joking or serious, but apparently, if you're on the street, you better be carrying a fresh-that-day negative lateral flow test. They appear to be stopping just shy of pedestrians needing a time-stamped picture of themselves sticking a mandatory swab up their nose.

The point remains the same, though, as far as the East is concerned—everyone needs to stay put until the authorities can work out what they're dealing with. There's only one bit of sunshine on the horizon, sunshine for me, that is—there's no driving. You can walk in your area. You can drive if it's absolutely necessary, but only in your area. Cycling long distances is ruled out, even with the mask and the negative lateral flow test, and the no symptoms. Everyone in the East of England is going to have to stick within their patch, which has been handily designated as a five-mile radius. The upshot being—if Jayden's not in town by now, chances are he's not getting in until this latest panic has cycled through. That could be two weeks, but it could easily be more.

Keeping the TV on, I stare out of the window. I can still see it: the news reflected in the glass outside as if emblazoned on the dark estuary water that's crept steadily in over the mud. You can't even see the mud anymore, only cold, dark wrinkles on waves. It's ten o'clock, but it's been nighttime since five. I get the feeling that winter evenings here go on forever. In the reflection from the TV, a lady presenter, her head haloed by pictures of the army in action, tells us that food and supplies are going to be brought in by the army to any areas that have reported cases. There's no panic. The government is calling on us to keep calm and adhere to regional protocols.

Outside in the street, a little cluster of flowers has begun gathering by the lamppost opposite—tributes to Maggie. They started making an appearance at midday, only an hour after Maggie's body had been taken away. A few people were crying, actually blubbing. Nobody, not one person on the street below, looked as though they were there simply for curiosity's sake. By late afternoon we were on around five tributes an hour. The restrictions stopped no one. Though they were acting with caution, not standing too close, wearing masks, offering nods when people met rather than hugs. The latest global meltdown hasn't managed to put a stop to grief or people's need to say goodbye. I'd been surprised by the age range as I watched from my window. It wasn't only the middle-aged punters: Maggie's contemporaries, there were kids there, young mothers, teenage boys.

Even now, the handful of cars that still drive past the lamppost move slower when they reach the tribute. Unfortunately, it's rained again, and the puddles spray up anyway. Within hours of being placed, the bright flowers looked tarnished and sad. It kind of broke my heart to see them wilt so quickly. I'm glad that it's dark now. I can't see them wilting anymore, only the occasional glint of unmuddied cellophane.

I've done two lateral flows, both negative, and a PCR test. That's the one I'm waiting on. They've said forty-eight hours. This suddenly seems like a lifetime. If I'm positive, I don't have a clue what they'll do with me. There's been someone outside my door all day. I get a knock when there's a food delivery. It's basic stuff—a scotch egg for lunch and an early supper of a sausage roll at five. Processed pork products seem to be a speciality. There was nothing green on the plate. The sausage roll had been microwaved. Always a bad move. The sort of thing Dawn might do, though I doubt it was her handiwork; she'll be safely locked away, cowering at her parent's place. If she has parents. If they didn't abandon her at birth. The pastry was a soggy mess, with a taste less appetizing than sepia-tinted wet wallpaper. I ate it anyway. If it goes on like this for much longer, I'll be checking out for good with my own case of blocked arteries.

I've had to stay off social media. Jayden will be scanning all of that. I don't know if you can be traced by simply looking at social media accounts. I don't know, but he will. He can't trace me through the phone. I was ahead of him on that one, swapping it the day before yesterday when I got wind of our little trip out. The model was identical, but the phone was fresh. Sometimes it pays to be paranoid. The phone had eaten into my savings but had been worth it.

Besides, it wasn't a new one. I picked it up at CeX, trading the old one in. I'm not sure if that was a stupid move or not. The pimply girl behind the counter with the face piercings and the hair so dark I could almost see myself in it thought it was. She'd tried to explain to me three times that I was switching my old phone for the exact same model and being charged for the privilege. Then she'd wanted to know what was wrong with it.

Luckily, someone else was there to check it over. It was fine. She'd been about to relaunch into her argument when she'd glanced out of the window and had seen Jayden coming out of the off-licence looking for me, standing like a scowl in the doorway of the building opposite. She must have noticed me flinch because she dropped the argument and rang everything through extra quick, passing the phone over the counter sharpish. When he'd pushed open the door to the shop, she'd even managed to pull me up a copy of *The Evil Dead* from the shelf, as though that's what I'd been buying.

'I love this one. Good choice,' she'd blustered, giving me a look that said everything. We form our own little club—women who've been destroyed but are still standing. We stick together.

As I stare from the window of The Wreckers the lamp-light flickers on. A lone figure crosses the street, a woman. She's smartly dressed, her hair covered with a headscarf. Her coat, a cream woollen affair clinched neatly at the waist with a belt. Unlike the others, she's not carrying flowers. She stoops down beside the cluster of cellophane wrappers and petals. The road's quiet, which is lucky. No chance of getting splashed; that coat wouldn't take it. Not even dry cleaning would get the shadow out. It's just the woman in white out there now. The police have long gone, apart from the one on my door, and whoever my gaoler is, they can't see the road from the corridor where they're parked up.

The woman in white continues looking through the tributes, turning back the cards so she can see the names and what must be those small, sad scribbles of regret. I watch her, curious. Wondering why she's putting herself through this? Aren't the flowers enough. Wouldn't it be all too painful to read those well wishes that will never get heard? After a few minutes, the job must be done. Or as much of it's done as she has the energy for.

The woman stands back up. Straightening her spine, pulling the belt of her coat a little tighter. I wonder who she was to Maggie? A friend probably; that kind of outfit might be smart, but it reeks of middle age. Maybe they used to go out on a Friday, drive into Colchester for a curry and a movie. She'll miss that. She'll have to try to find someone else. Not always easy. The woman turns to go—to leave the weeping bouquets. To return to her small warm home, no doubt, and attempt to chase away the reek of death with a cup of tea and some mindless show on the box.

Then suddenly, she stops, tilting her head up towards my window, and my whole world vortexes out of control as the very blood seems to evaporate from every muscle in my body. Maggie! It's Maggie. She stares straight at me. Her eyes bore deep into my soul. I'm rigid. Unable to move, unable to pull back. A van shoots past outside, dragging an echo of black rain in its wake. When I focus again, Maggie's gone. The street is clear. The tributes are all as before, only perhaps a little muddier now from the wheels of the transit. I stand, petrified, gazing out onto the street. Stand stock still till I hear something odd: rattling. Something rigid like a bone china teacup jittering on a silver tray, and with a sick thud of realisation, understanding sinks through my gut— it's me. My teeth are chattering rigid and sharp in my skull. I glance at my face in the age-spored mirror. Now I really am whiter than lard. I don't just look like I've seen a ghost; I genuinely have seen one.

'Do you think I can have a book?' I ask when breakfast arrives. It's Leon again, the Special. He's so much better than Dawn at doing breakfast. I've got a bacon sandwich, still warm, and an egg sunny side over so it doesn't squirt. The door stands open between us. The tray is on the floor. He's standing a few good steps back from the opening. Mask on. He's even wearing those blue rubber glove things. It's enough to make anyone itch. I no longer feel like a human being. I feel like a bio-hazard petri dish. I, too, am wearing a mask.

'Book?'

'Yes.' The bacon sandwich looks tasty. I would love to tuck in, but room service here is not exactly Four-Star standard. Points of contact are few and far between. It's best to get all requests delivered in one hit. I seriously cannot listen to any more news flashes, and there's only so much "Place in the Sun" you can watch without actually packing your suitcase, and no one is going to let me do that. I don't even have a passport.

'The TV's driving me up the wall.' It had been my window into life for so long. My education, my friend. Everything I knew had come courtesy of the little rectangular box. Jayden never sat and absorbed, but I had consumed everything apart from reality trash. The art programs, the culture vultures, geography and a smattering of history, I had swallowed it all whole. Only now, now I could do with something to take my mind off things. 'I think there were some books in Maggie's room,' I offer helpfully.

'Not sure they've finished with it yet.' He sounds awkward, embarrassed. 'But I can find you something. If you can just...' Leon sweeps his hands forwards and backwards a little, and I realise he'll go, but he wants me locked in again.

The gesture means *step back*. I guess that's fair enough. He doesn't know me. If he did know me, he'd probably want to put me in handcuffs, chain me up, then lock the door. I pick the tray up and retreat into my room, not mentioning one word about seeing Maggie. Start talking about ghosts, and they'll be convinced I'm running a temperature, hallucinating. If I want to get out of here, I need to maintain absolute normality. Even if all of this is far from normal. I've put Maggie's visitation down to an overactive imagination. I'd seen her on the floor catatonic, then leaving the inn sarcophagused out on a stretcher. Seeing her outside beside the flowers, well, that must have been a case of me projecting my wants onto some random face in the street. Easily done. If the van hadn't driven between us, and I'd been allowed a little more time with the woman standing in the light, the mistake would have unravelled itself.

ONCE LEON IS GONE, I return to my gazing out from the window as I munch on the bacon sandwich. The tide's higher today, as is the watermark of tributes to Maggie. I'd like to say I don't believe in ghosts. Seriously, there's enough going on with the living as it is. Plus, my mother was deep into all that kind of stuff, crystals, spirits, cards. And anything she was into, I'd like to do without, but I guess superstition, it's like a religion, difficult to wash out even when you've stopped practising, but last night had to be just a trick of the light.

There's a knock on the door. Stupidly, I jump. My life is getting like some kind of spoof horror show.

'Left it outside,' comes Leon's voice.

When I pull the door open, he's standing there, a couple of steps back as usual, a pile of books on the floor between us.

'Wasn't sure what you liked, so I bought a few.'

'Thanks.' I scoop them up, injecting a little idle conversation into the hallway. 'The doctor and his wife? Are they alright?'

Leon nods. 'No bad news, yet.'

'And PC Green?'

'Doing fine. Climbing the wall so I hear.' He raises one knowing eyebrow. 'PC Green's what you might call a bit hands-on, so...'

'Doesn't like other people on his turf?'

'Something like that. Anyway, any news one way or the other...' Leon smiles, '...you'll be the first to hear.'

I take the books to my bed. There's a chair in the room, but it's more for decoration than sitting. I'm not convinced most people could fit their backside in it. Not exactly comfort central. The bed will have to do. I pull the pillows up towards the long fabric headboard. Luckily there are four. Feather, rather than foam, with innards that have sunk into the corners, but it's comfortable enough. I spread the books out over the coverlet and flick through the titles.

Great Expectations—Ironic, seeing as I am absolutely stuck in the marshes at the moment with no sign of getting out.

Brighton Rock—which feels a bit too close to the bone. People are after me, and sadly I don't have myself an interested party to pick up the pieces and follow the clues if I do get bumped off. Maggie was the only person who might have cared, but she was gone.

Then there's *Wuthering Heights.* That's exactly where ghosts should be kept, between the pages of a book. I open the covers. It smells of age-old paper, musty like the damp forgotten shavings from a sawmill. I used to dream of a time when I might be able to lie in my bed all day and read a book without Mum or Jayden dragging me out from under the blankets. They both hated reading. I need to just try to enjoy the moment. There's bugger all I can do to move my life forward, so it's time to take a rain check. I glance towards the door.

'You still there?' I call.

'Yeah,' comes SC Hutchins' weary voice. 'I grabbed one for myself while I was at it.'

'Oh. What did you grab?'

'*The Curious Incident of the Dog in the Night-time.*'

'What?'

He laughs. 'I know. Some title, right?'

'Practically a novel all on its own.'

'Yeah, well, I'm in training. Was never a big reader. Thought it might do me good. And you? What did you go for?'

'I thought I'd give *Wuthering Heights* a spin.'

'Oh, right. We saw that at school.' He coughs awkwardly. 'I mean a theatre version. Old Heathcliff's a bit of a bugger. A regular heartbreaker.'

'Yeah. Not my type. Bad boys are seriously overrated.'

'True…' there's a small pause, 'but he is kind of…'

Another brief pause from the Special, then a laugh. 'He's kind of my type.'

I smile. 'Oh.'

'Yeah, sorry, I'm crap at this. Probably shouldn't be telling you things like that.'

'I don't mind. I suppose there's no point in trying to seduce you then?'

'Not unless you've got Mr H in there with you.'

'You said yourself. He's a heartbreaker, nothing but trouble.'

'Maybe I could rehabilitate him?'

That, I'm pretty sure, is the oldest cliché ever fallen into.

It's the evening of the second day before there's any serious change.

'Miss?' A different voice. A woman's.

I've read *Wuthering Heights* cover to cover.

'Miss?'

'Yeah?' I don't bother getting up from the bed.

The key in the door rattles.

'PCR's come back. You're clear.'

For a moment, it doesn't register. I'm still up on the moors with the characters from my book, and then I realise. 'Great.' Only I'm not so sure it is *great*. What happens now? Staying still has suddenly become easy; moving forward, well, that's a different story. 'And everyone else? The doctor, PC Green?'

'Everyone's clear. We've actually lateral flowed the whole town. We're all clear. But there's no movement on or off the peninsula. Everyone's got to stay put.'

. . .

I HEAR the rattle of the downstairs door as it closes behind the PC. The old inn suddenly feels yawning and cavernous. I didn't ask about Dawn. Is Dawn coming back? When the PC had said *stay put*, does that mean it's okay to stay here? I have nowhere else. Can I help myself to whatever I want in the kitchen? What about the bar? Are there any rules? For a person who doesn't particularly like rules, I find myself wanting some. I've never carved my own path before. It was always Mum or Jayden beating out a track for me. Now, despite all the restrictions on movement, life seems impossibly open.

I step out into the hallway, the jazzy carpet greeting me like an old friend. The lights in this part of the building are on full. A little hard dining chair pulled up and abandoned where my police watch must have been sitting. But at the far end of the corridor, towards Maggie's room, dark shadows cluster. I can't help myself; I shiver. Okay, first things first. I need all the lights on. Maybe I'll get used to this place after a while, but for now, every corner needs to be lit. Every room that I'm not using needs to be shut off. I walk through the inn, flipping switches and shutting doors, relieved to find that the door to Maggie's room is already closed. There's no police tape over the frame. That feels like a blessing. It was natural causes: a heart attack, and Stan, well, silly old bugger, didn't get himself through his front door. What did he expect? Then again, maybe he didn't care. Maybe his mate's death was all too much.

When I get to the turning at the bottom of the stairs, catching myself briefly in the check-before-you-go mirror, I see the dark empty bar, silent as a black hole, and I can't help myself, my blood runs cold. I can almost see them, Stan hunched and hopeless on his stool, Maggie with her bright smile, doomed for eternity now in so many people's memories to wipe down that counter till the end of time. No. I hit the lights. The ghosts, if there ever were any, melt away.

The bar is empty; the table still sitting in the centre of the room, abandoned after my hasty cornflake breakfast. What a different world that had been with its plans of escape and worries about making my money last long enough to get some kind of roof over my head. The red wine bottle from the night of my arrival is still on the counter. I'd had one that night. Just one. It hadn't hurt. Drinking was an escape. I reach for the bottle, already anticipating that rich, fruity smell. I'm just about to lift it up and pour myself a glass when I get the sensation that I'm being watched. I turn, looking into the shadows of the room. The seats that are clustered around the walls, judge and jury, crowd in on me, empty.

Nothing.

Yet still, I have the odd, unnerving sensation that someone is watching. Suddenly, there's a tap on the glass. I jump, looking away from the benches of the room towards the dark windowpanes that dip into the world outside. A face looms out of the darkness. The features bleached and white from the wash of the pub lights. It's PC Green. Standing there, smiling. His arms clutching some kind of bundle that he's pointing to as he mouths words I don't understand. I take a deep breath. This place is enough to give anyone the jitters; company might help.

'THOUGHT WE DESERVED A CELEBRATION,' he says as I pull back the door, and he thrusts a warm bundle towards me.

It smells delicious. Oyster sauce, noodles, rice, bean sprouts. That kind of delicious—Chinese.

'Wow. Come in.' I stand back eagerly, letting him

through into the bar. A slap of wet air following him through. 'I'll get plates and cutlery.' I glance around the pub, suddenly remembering I have no idea where anything is.

'Over there.' He points to a service station standing tucked against the wall beside the door that leads to the main part of the inn. It's piled high with everything we are going to need and more.

'Thank you so much for this,' I say following him eagerly through the inn. I hadn't realised how hungry I was for something warm and fresh.

Green lays the cartons out across the bar, peeling back the paper lids from the foil-ringed clasps. 'Thought we deserved it. Besides, I was worried about you all on your own.'

I lay the cutlery out beside his place, beside mine. 'Is Dawn coming back?'

'She was pretty spooked.'

I feel the gall rising in my throat, remembering my frantic bangs on the door as Dawn had shut me in my room. 'If she'd acted a bit quicker. They were trying to take me through CPR. She locked me in my room.'

'Yeah. I heard.' He shoots me a concerned look. He knows how to deal with all this kind of shit. He pussyfoots through other people's recriminations and guilt every day. 'You couldn't have done anything anyway, Eve.' He drops his eyes to the bar. 'They're saying the time of death was around one in the morning.'

'Shit.' I sink down on my bar stool. 'So, she managed to fold my bloody clothes, put them outside with a test, messaged Dawn to tell her to cook me breakfast, then she...' I feel my eyes start to well.

PC Green reaches out his hand, placing it gently on my shoulder.

'Don't do that to yourself. Maggie was a good person, one of the best. She just ran out of time.'

I look at him. His body is slumped a little more than it was the last time we met. He can say all of that stuff about time and act like he's taking this in his stride, but Maggie's death is wearing heavy.

'Besides,' he heaps a large spoonful of egg fried rice onto my plate, 'it's good news that we've got no infections.'

'I guess. And they're seriously not letting anyone in or out?'

He smiles. 'It's a bit of a tradition here because of the island thing. They did it during the Black Death as well.'

'Yeah, Dawn told me.' I lift a sweet and sour crispy pork ball into my fingers and take one bite. The taste of batter and meat explodes across my tongue. 'This is amazing.'

Green nods between mouthfuls of prawn cracker. 'Thought we better jump in quick before the menu starts getting limited. I can't see monosodium glutamate as being a priority item.' He glances up at the optics. I've put the bottle of red on the back shelf, stuck a stopper in it. 'You have a glass of wine if you like. I'm sure the brewery won't worry if you write it all down.'

'No. Thanks. I'm fine.' I know how that story starts. Escapism is not where I need to be right now. 'Do you think I'm okay to just stay here?'

He shrugs. 'Can't see anyone objecting.'

I glance around me. The place is enormous. All this, just for one person. One person and, apparently, a shedload of history. 'So, what happened during the Black Death?' I reach for a spoon and dip it into some noodles.

'Oh, they just posted someone permanently on the road. No one went in, no one went out. You know the garage just before you come over the wash?'

I shake my head. I hadn't seen it when I'd come over with Stan. It had been pitch dark, wet and windy, and I'd been more interested in miles travelled than the place of arrival.

'It's called the Devil's Punch Bowl because they used to have this bowl of disinfectant-type stuff in the courtyard, so anyone who was paying for goods, coming in or out, had to put their money in the bowl first.'

'And the whole village, they all managed to survive?'

He chews through his mouthful before answering. 'The fourteenth-century plague, yeah. Only...it's a bit of an odd one really because, in the fifteenth century, the whole village got wiped out.'

I stop, my loaded fork heading towards my mouth. 'Unlucky. Black Death again?'

He shakes his head. 'No. They still have no idea what it was. There are a couple of theories. One is a suicide pact. They found twenty-five bodies in the mud. People would have had to walk out voluntarily through the tide, so it had to be suicide.'

I think of that vast expanse of brown slipping away from The Wreckers into the night. Despite the warmth of the food, my stomach starts to feel a kind of ice inside it. Yet PC Green is undeterred. He's told this story so many times it's lost its horror.

'Of course, they didn't have any kind of forensics back then, but the causes of death for all the bodies they found were all different. Legend has it that earlier, so in the four-teenth century, the locals had made this pact to avoid the Black Death.'

'Don't tell me, with the Devil?'

He nods, amused. 'Has to be. Though sometimes he's referred to as The Stranger. He has other names, too, there's lots of myths, but he's got the same kind of MO as Old Nick. Anyway, the pact was made, the village was saved from plague, but one hundred years later, the spirit, whatever it was, came to take payment.'

'Exactly one hundred years?' There's something about the circularity of the story which is beginning to spook me.

PC Green searches his brain. 'No, I don't think it's exact. It's just round about. I guess it would be three generations later. Thereabouts.'

'So, the original inhabitants sold out their grandkids?'

He looks at me shrewdly. 'Yeah. Hadn't thought of it like that. Not everything gets worse about society then.' He smiles to himself, a little ironically. 'And The Wreckers would have seen it all.'

I think of the mouldering flower tributes outside on the road and Maggie standing there in her white coat.

'You okay?' PC Green says anxiously.

'Do you believe in ghosts?'

He laughs, misunderstanding the trail of my conversation, setting us neatly back to the Black Death. 'There's a museum down on the front. You can read up about it all there.'

What purpose would it serve anyway to go telling him what I saw? Maggie is dead. I pull myself back to the living and my own needs. 'Can I go out? Walk about town?'

He shrugs. 'Sure. We're pretty safe here. Like I said, everyone's been tested. So, it's kind of business as usual till supplies run out. The military might be bringing stuff in, but I'm not sure how patchy that will be. There's even an author stranded here at the moment, Miley Clark. He's doing a book on *the pact*. That's what they call it—the reason Attercoppe managed to shrug off the plague. He can tell you more. Sorry to hear about your mum.'

'What?' My mum? Then I remember the lie I'd slipped to S C Hutchins. 'Oh yeah. Actually, she's a bit better now.'

I love it when you can just heal a person with a few words. I could even make her nice if I chose with just a short, gentle twist of my tongue, only I'm not sure I'm ready for the re-wash.

'Some good news.' PC Green smiles as if this is always welcome. 'And your husband?'

I'm not sure what to say here.

'I guess he must have been worried?'

'Oh yeah.' Though I wouldn't exactly describe Jayden as a worrier. He's more of a get-even kind of guy.

'Been married long?'

'Eight years,' I say, trying to keep the weary out of my voice. The beef looks good. I ladle a couple of large spoonfuls onto my plate, barely noticing the room's gone quiet. Turning to see PC Green, I realise he's staring at me curiously. It's that under-the-microscope look, the one I'd seen on my first night. The one I'm itching to avoid. Am I taking too much? My plate's piled high already; was that last spoonful of beef one too many? He must think I'm a glutton. I'm about to ask him—after the horse has bolted—if he minds me taking the last spoonful. But there's no need.

'You must have been a child bride.' His words are light enough in tone, but there's a shipwreck of other questions lurking under the surface.

Shit. I stare at myself in the optics. Eight years doesn't give me much time to have grown up enough for the altar. 'I look younger than I am,' I say, breezily, once again focusing on my food.

Out of the corner of my eye, I see him nod slowly. A little too slowly for comfort.

'And you? Wife doesn't mind you being out?' I throw the

discomfort back at him, but if there's a story there, putting a little scrutiny on it doesn't seem to bother Green.

'Married to the job.' He smiles.

'That old chestnut?'

'If it fits.' There's a brief pause, but only a brief one. 'So…' He draws the vowel out. 'How old were you then? When you tied the knot.'

The man is like a dog with a bone.

'Sixteen.' I've said too much already. He doesn't stop staring at me. 'Not feeling so young now.' I manage a large yawn. 'God, I'm tired.'

'Yeah,' he says, after a pause which feels way too long. 'Best get yourself a good night's sleep. You can explore a bit tomorrow.'

'You make it sound like a holiday destination.'

'When the sun shines, it's not too bad, and you can swim when the tide's in from a couple of spots along the bank. There are worse places.'

I carry on chewing through my Chinese. Only the beef doesn't taste quite as good as it did. Maybe there are worse places to be, but I'm not keen on PC Green's ever-hungry-for-facts eyes. Besides, there's something else bothering me. I can't help it; those twenty-five bodies—men, women, and children—walking through the mud to their deaths. If they found twenty-five, surely there had to be more? I wasn't so sure I'd be taking a dip out of choice in that cold estuary water.

9

———

WASHED UP

Morning arrived sharp and dry through the windows. I'd left a crack between the room's heavy-thread curtains when I'd fallen asleep. I'd gotten used to the sky outside being perpetually grey, but this morning the day surprised me, casting a lightsaber-sharp ray across my bed. Luckily, my head is starting to feel a bit more as though it is actually joined through the middle as opposed to suffering from some kind of painful tectonic drift; the light fails to make me wince.

For a brief moment, I wallow in the feeling of safety. With the peninsula closed off, for once, I am relatively safe. I have space to wallow; listening to the sounds of the building waking up; radiators from each and every corner of the old inn beginning to clank and groan. Hot pipes dragging them-selves reluctantly into action, solely for the purpose of my comfort. And that's not all; somewhere in this vast old build-ing, there is an entire tank of water heating up for me. Just for me, with no one to shout abuse if I use too much. I could drain the entire tank, and there would not be one *'stupid bitch'* or *'selfish cow'*. Not one slap across the head.

A full five minutes later, I emerge wet and steaming from the shower cubicle, my body glowing a delicious pink from the heat. This virus may be the best thing that's ever happened to me.

There had been no locks on the doors back home. Nothing bolting me in, so why didn't I walk out before? I guess I'd grown used to the cage. This is different. Outside my bedroom door, at least for the foreseeable, everything is mine. There will be no one to shuffle past in the kitchen. No one shooting disapproving looks if I don't put everything away in the exact right order or wipe everything down so not a trace of my living is left on the surfaces. The path I cut through this morning will be mine, absolutely, utterly mine and no one else's.

Drawing the curtains, I can see that the puddles from the last forty-eight-hour deluge have dried. Even the tributes of flowers to poor Maggie, clustered around the lamppost, aren't looking quite so shabby with the ditch water washed away. I throw my clothes on and head out.

Once downstairs, I grab the keys from the bar, locking the over-large rickety old door to The Wreckers behind me, and cross the narrow strip of tarmac to the waterfront in six large strides as clear, bright air pushes my lungs to full expansion, finding inches I hadn't realised were even there. Not a trace of virus to bugger the breathing process. Another good reason to be on this side of the causeway. It's not just my husband I need to be hiding away from. I don't particularly want to get sick either.

Yes, this is all working out well. I am back in my own boots, the ones Maggie so thoughtfully left padded with paper and drying out beside the radiators. The insides feel deliciously warm against my toes as if some small part of Maggie is still with me. Her thoughtfulness, at least, making the world just that bit better. Maybe that's the thing about thoughtfulness; maybe it goes a lot further than you'd expect. I'm not sure. Grant, Mum's ex-Traveller man-friend, was thoughtful. And yes, that did leave an impression. Perhaps thoughtfulness has as much resonance in the world as evil, or can at least help dilute all the bad stuff.

THERE'S a heady smell of salt and marsh weed breezing through the air, a morning freshness that expands my nostrils as I inhale. The tide is in this morning, bloated as a satisfied snake, although I get the feeling its high moment has passed. Every third or fourth wet-water grasp, the river sends out a swollen wave, but it's half-hearted, as though the large tea-dark body of estuary water is reluctant to slip back into some black hole on the other side of the horizon. Reluctant, even though it knows the pull is irresistible. I watch frills of foam flick against the grey concrete wall where, within seconds, they dwindle and die, losing the fight. The cycle is lost, but there will be others. One day the water may well win—reach up over the wall and spill across the road, head into The Wreckers for a quick "hello". Not today, though.

Staring out across the water's wide moving body, I can see the mainland, a far-off squint of low humps in dark green. There may be a cluster of houses spaced out along the opposite waterfront. It's difficult to tell. There's certainly some kind of man-made structures standing at the water's edge, broken as the sporadic underbite of crumbling teeth, but the buildings seem small for houses. It could be that the other side of the estuary is a nature reserve protected from property development. Or perhaps, the other side isn't even desirable—prone to flooding. There don't appear to be any access roads. But that doesn't mean they're not there. If they ran along the water's edge, I wouldn't be able to see them from where I'm standing.

The Attercoppe side of the estuary is more "developed". Though I'm not sure it's any more desirable. The Wreckers is detached. Its walls leaning outwards, randomly gathering energy and size as they pull further from the ground, top-heavy. It seems a counterintuitive way to build. Perhaps it has something to do with the possibility of flooding; the upper stories are a little bit wider, a little bit safer. A small gap between the houses on either side of the inn leaves it strutting in its own space. Although a good two stories taller than its neighbours, it would be difficult to say which came first—the houses or the inn. Perhaps they all arrived together. Although each structure is unique, they could be part of a medieval job lot. The rooves mark out a slight difference. The Wreckers, over the years, has acquired a deep, brown reptilian tile covering. The tumble of cottages flanking it, modest, squalid-looking lumps of wattle and daub, are all thatch. And yet, they're failing badly on the picturesque front; their barnets are so much more health-and-safety concern than quintessential chocolate box charm. Chicken wire fixes a mass of clustered brown material in place, as the thatch withers behind the metallic mesh-like old limbs or bloats into bulging blisters of thatch and moss. In short, these hand-woven rooves are the sort of thing that makes your skin itch.

The causeway linking Attercoppe to the mainland must be on the other side of the island, the side I can't see. From where I'm standing, you'd think you were on a regular island. Unless, of course, the road is under the water in front of me. Somehow, I doubt that. There would be a truncated strip of tarmac leading off into the waves, and that's not happening. Instead, the street curves around the waterfront before branching off a hundred yards or so to my right, where it splits into a tarmacked road, heading away from the water into the town and what looks like a vehicle-wide stone and dirt track hobbling along beside the estuary.

The town might be in the death grip of October, but I get the feeling that even in summer, this place will always have seen better days. The tidal habit is probably the thing keeping it safe from weekender exploitation—a fresh lick of paint and gainful employment for the local thatcher. The overly stressed and obscenely wealthy London hordes don't want the added imposition of nature cutting them off from their weekend hideaways. There's most definitely the feeling that this place has been left to quietly rot, a motorway away from living the dream. Yet for me, standing here in the warm October sunshine, Attercoppe seems like paradise.

I strike off down the street towards the unmade track. There's a sign just where the road splits, over-egging it slightly in claiming that the *Town Centre* is to the right, and the *Harbour* can be found along the stone and mud track. "Harbour" appears to be an over-inflated name for the row of blackened huts strung out and exhausted along the waterside path, a path so uneven the stones rumble awkwardly under my feet at every step.

Every few paces, I have to fling my arms out just to steady myself. The dark huts look on, unamused. Their window eyes darkened. Their waterlogged timbers a shadowy bitumen funeral-black. Crinkled patched rooves sit above the awkward frames. They're mostly corrugated iron, mostly rust red, but occasionally there's been some kind of makeshift job, a sheet of new corrugation thrown into the mix of rusted tan. The newly acquired metal squinting brightly in the sun, sending morse code to the seagulls. Louder, louder. It must be saying something because the damn things never shut up.

Almost all the sheds are locked; large cross-beams anchored, forbidding as thick folded arms, across the doors. Some of the doors are chained, some padlocked. I wonder if they're trying to keep people out rather than materials in? It seems unlikely anyone would store anything worth nicking in a structure that, with a bit of effort, you could probably just prise off a wall and fill your arms with "bounty". It's difficult to know what the huts are used for now. If they're used at all. Though some of the structures have lobster nets outside or stacked plastic crates as if something sometime gets carried in and out.

Glancing into the slivers of water to my left, lying just beyond the path, I note that the tide is racing out. Thick wedges of dirty brown liquid ooze eel-like through tributaries of mud beginning to peep through the high water as it slinks away. I find myself doubting the existence of lobsters. Doubting the existence of anything living in that water but eels and possibly the odd sea serpent.

Suddenly I remember stepping out of the car the night before Maggie died, stepping out onto the wet pavement and treading on…A shiver passes down my spine. I'd been in a state of high anxiety. Not surprising since I'd been clouted around the head earlier in the day. I had been twitchy as hell, held hostage by my imagination. The imagination will do that if you give it half a chance: keep you locked inside its own private horror fest. It's daft—for the first time in my life, I don't need to keep *anxious* on overdrive. I'm safe—no one's getting into Attercoppe. No one is getting out. I need to give my nerves a break. Once *normal* kicks in again, that'll be the time to dust off the old paranoia.

Small boats bob on the water, tethered to large iron hooks staked into the ground. There's no real harbour wall to speak of, just an end to the pothole and stone road, a little strip of tough-looking grass framing the edge, cluttered with the stakes, metal chains and bare strips of more mud: terrestrial as opposed to estuary gloop.

The boats are mainly for fishing—the no-frill type affair. Small basic structures, their paint cracked and peeling. There are a few pleasure boats, though my guess is that whatever pleasure the boats once gave has been long forgotten because no one is bothering to look after the things. Lay a picnic blanket out on one of those decks, and you'd most likely pick up something nasty. Most of the hulls are spotted with black mould, green mildew, or a mixture of both. Those that were, at one time, awarded the luxury of windows have their glassy offerings fogged, marked with condensation or split. You can barely even read the boat names anymore, letters are missing, or the fonts have simply worn away to a state where they're no longer legible. As I walk, I notice the tide pulling out from underneath the fibreglass bottoms. The hulls are starting to tilt in a lopsided manner as the vessels begin their inevitable sink into the mud beneath.

Flags tinkle and chime like splinters of glass floating into the bright autumn air, reminding me of a story I heard years ago. Not from my mother, of course. She did tell stories, only not the picture book type. No, this story must have been from one of my primary schools. One of the many. They weren't all bad. I liked school. I was one of those weird kids that actually wanted to go. This story had been *The Snow Queen*. It terrified me. Some kid got abducted by this beautiful woman. That was bad enough, but there was also a shattered magic mirror that let splinters of hopelessness fall into people's hearts and eyes. So that nothing you saw or touched gave you joy. My mum was like that—forever stealing the joy out of life.

I realise, as I pick my steps across the rotten, rumbling path, away from the cluster of sheds, that I've found my life in stories and fairy tales over the years. Nothing is ever original. Only my stories are always the dark ones, the grim Nordic affairs with killer dogs and women chopping off their toes to squeeze their feet into shoes. Disney princes don't get a look in.

I try to block the high-pitched boat tinkle and the Snow Queen out of my brain; try and find that sun; let it warm through my body as I walk down the wharf, avoiding the potholes and puddles. Despite the warm weather, there aren't many people out; just a couple walking a dog. Older. Retired. She's having problems with her back and is stooped slightly, his arm resting supportively under her elbow. Sometimes the potholes are too much for the couple; they step around rather than take the quickest route of going over. The man smiles at me pragmatically as I pass, as if to say—*slow progress. Thank God the sun is shining.* I smile back, but only the man catches it. The woman is too busy looking at her feet.

There's an avalanche of boxes outside one blackened hut and a door wedged open. I glance over to see an older guy, could be forty, could be a hundred, his face more beard than skin, although his movements are effortless, so I'm guessing he must be more on the forty side of the equation. Layers of shirt and jumper hang down over his oilskins where he's peeled himself free, hot from work. He has his large hands fixed roughly on a series of rusted buckets whilst he eyes me cautiously as I pass.

'Nice morning,' I say.

He doesn't reply, but I get the feeling as I leave him behind that he stops what he's doing and watches me. I guess they don't like outsiders here. Or maybe it's the pandemic thing. Maybe I should be wearing a mask? Mask-wearing might be difficult for an old hedgehog beard, though. You'd have to have extra-long straps at the back to get anything over the facial topiary he's sporting. A woman in her thirties jogs by. Headphones on, Lycra-clad, golden ponytail bobbing from side to side as if it's got some bright, sparky life all of its own. She's moving at a slow but upright speed, heading in the opposite direction, back towards the high street and The Wreckers.

'All good?' she shouts breathily as she passes the bearded guy.

'Not complaining. You?'

'So far.'

So, he does talk. Just not to me, it would seem. I feel a sense of relief when the huts dwindle away, and the pot-marked road fades into a footpath. I don't know where I'm heading, but quiet will suit me fine.

Initially, it's easy-going, easier on the grassy path than the harbour track at least. The footpath beside the water is well worn, a regular dog walker's route. They've even left their small pad footprints. In places, it's so muddy I have to skirt around on the verge of the track, but everything is relative—if I want to see real mud, I've only to glance to my left where the water is marching through its steady retreat, leaving a cranium of wet brown goo. I know I need to formulate some kind of plan. The lockdown will lift. Movement will start up again. So far, I've been lucky; all of my funds are intact. There's a chance the brewery, the owners of The Wreckers, might catch on that they've got an occupant and try to serve me up a bill, though this seems unlikely. Since

Dawn has abandoned her post, they probably haven't got a clue that I'm even there. Eve Adams. I grimace to myself. Seriously, couldn't I have thought up anything better?

In the bright sunshine, with the clear air filling my lungs, life seems like it might, for once, actually work out. Okay, so I'm in no way an optimist, but surely there are only so many times that a bread slice can fall butter down. Eventually, the tide of bad luck has to turn. One lucky break is all I'm asking for. Perhaps this separation might give Jayden time to cool down, just a little, just a degree, just cool enough for him to stop focusing his attention on me. He always did love a grudge, but I'd left his precious USB in the car. He has all his accounts, all his contacts. He doesn't need me.

Without evidence, it would be hard for me to go to the police. He might decide, after this little enforced separation, that I'm more trouble than I'm worth. He's had good use out of me. He could get something younger. I know he's thought about that. He told me that I was losing it. I wasn't certain I'd ever had *it*, but I did know one thing for sure: getting older was not going to help. Okay, so I had slammed his head under the bonnet when we'd stopped, but he'd practically shattered my face on the dashboard. In that instance we'd kind of come out quits on the abuse front. No. I stare out over the flat marshy landscape. The sun seems to be losing its brilliance by the second, allowing a cold blast of damp air to creep in over the tufts of coarse grass and mud channels. He would never see it as us being even.

THE PATH SPLITS. I can keep following the riverbed or strike out through the fields. The reeds are higher now. There must be water beside the bank. Straggling out through the rushes, I can just make out the tumbling structure of an abandoned pontoon. At some point in time, the river must have come up this far. I stare across the marshes. The edges of the grassland begin to blur. Glancing behind me, back towards the harbour, I realise that's gone now, shrouded in a layer of grey. A sea mist is rolling in. If this is an island, then following the river should just take me around. I turn right. It's the safest bet. I could go back the way I came, but there's even less of a path behind me now. It feels as if it's being eaten up. Chump. Chump. Chump. My mind starts to conjure up horrors, eels slithering unseen through the dark riverbed. I'll go forward. Provided I stick to the path, I'll be fine.

TWENTY MINUTES LATER, and the path peters out. I can barely see a metre in any direction. The air wraps itself around me, cold and wet. Filling my lungs with a damp salty taste. I must have missed a split in the track. The way forward appears to be heading straight for the riverbed. I turn around. I'll retrace my steps. I can't be far out. All I have to do is follow the path that brought me here. As I start to walk back, my pace becomes a little quicker. This is where optimism gets you. This is what happens when you turn your face into the sun and stop paying attention to the here and now.

There's another fork in the track. Perhaps I should cut in? The path going away from the river is better defined. I decide to follow it and after only a few minutes the thick foggy air starts to clear. Of course, walking beside the river was just attracting the mist. I turn up the speed again. I'll head back to the high street, find somewhere for breakfast, get some kind of update on the virus. I take out my phone, try to get a sense of where I am, but all it shows me is a single blue dot in the middle of a whole heap of nowhere. I need to keep walking. Stuffing my mobile back into my pocket, I continue on. Then, suddenly I catch something ahead of me, moving slowly away. It could be a cow? A solid block of white. Its edges blurred with the mist, but having a denser, solid core. Whatever it is, it appears to be going quickly, confidently. I increase my pace and realise to my absolute joy it's a person.

'Hey,' I call out. If they can just point me in the right direction. I speed up again. But the person in front also appears to go faster, always moving out of earshot.

'Hey. Excuse me.' The damp air wraps my words into thick lumps of muffled sound.

I increase the pace yet again. My feet sliding in the mud. I'm practically running. If I can just reach whoever it is. There's a sense of panic driving me forward. Nothing about this space is familiar. I know the dark water is out there, and the mud. Maybe even something worse; I can't help thinking of that thing, whatever it was, slipping and sliding under my shoe. Glancing out over the water, I can see the tide rippling oddly in a small whirl around what looks unnervingly like a hand poking out of the waves. That can't be right. I shake my head instinctively, trying to dislodge the thought. It's just a twig. I know that, but I can't help remembering PC Green's story—twenty-five people walking out into the marshes. Walking out to their deaths. A mass suicide? I tap my face sharply with my right hand. I seriously do need to snap out of it; that was a long time ago. I have to catch up with the other walker. I need...

'Hey!' I call. My voice rising sharply, cutting through the mist. The figure stops. Relief washes over me, but it's short-lived. The person ahead turns, and suddenly my heart stops. The figure is a woman, a woman I know—Maggie.

It feels as if my whole world has ground to a halt. As if time itself is turning backwards.

We stare at each other over a sea of mist before she raises one long thin arm, pointing in the direction that I've just come.

'Back,' she shouts, an air of panic in her voice. 'Back.'

Suddenly, my body jerks. I glance down. My right foot is starting to sink. My God! I've stumbled into the marshes. My left foot follows. There's mud crawling up my legs, past my knees, heading hungrily up my thighs. I gasp. Fear swelling through my brain, till there are no other thoughts. No other emotion. This is it.

'What the...' A strong arm grabs me from behind. I turn to see the bearded guy staring down at me. 'Idiot,' he says gruffly, a blast of tobacco breath clouding over my face. 'You need to stick to the bloody path.'

'BLACK COFFEE THEN, and one for your friend?' a gawky redhead asks from behind her counter. Her face full of questions.

There's a grill at her back, merrily pumping heat out into the small prefab café. We'd stumbled out of the marshes straight into the warmth of this place. I could have practically stubbed my toe on it. I seriously am feeling like a first-class idiot.

'Not my friend,' my bearded rescuer announces grudgingly. 'Found her about to step into the bloody mud.'

'Council should rope it off,' offers an old woman who smells as if she's been doused in Chanel No. 5. She tightens her bright silk headscarf around her tight curls and rattles some change down into the small tin mug beside the till as she settles her bill. 'Kev?' she calls over her shoulder.

'I heard you,' replies a mumbling bespectacled guy. His fine dark hair clinging to his large skull. He doesn't even bother to raise his eyes from the paper he's scanning.

'Well?'

Kev sighs. 'You can't rope the thing off; it's a river. People have to just use their brains.'

'Hmm,' my bearded mate grunts, as if this could be a problem around here.

'We're a parish council,' Kev states simply. 'Not a military state.'

'Not yet.' The redhead behind the counter pushes a coffee towards us. 'You seen the army on the other side of the causeway?'

'I want the coffee to go,' beard man grunts.

The redhead looks at him, irritated. 'You should have brought your reusable in then.'

His top lip curls in a snarl. 'I would have brought it in, but I heard shouting and had to go rescue this.' He glowers at me. I am the *this*.

'Well, I appreciate it,' I say.

'You wouldn't have to rescue anyone if the parish council did their job,' the older lady offers brightly as she packs an enormous gaudy purse back into her overly bling bag before heading for the door.

Lanky-haired Kev, who I'm guessing must be with the parish council, tuts, but refuses to rise to the bait.

'Well, I'll do it this once.' The redhead takes my bearded "friend's" coffee and empties it into a disposable. Fixing a plastic lid on the rim with efficient pale hands.

The bearded guy grabs it. 'Last time I do anyone a favour.' Grunting, he heads for the door.

The redhead bites the inside of her mouth as though to stop herself smiling. 'You will never live that one down.' She smiles. 'When Malik has a grudge, he'll take it to the grave. So, what can I get you?'

'Umm, a cappuccino?'

She looks at me as if I've just beamed down from the planet Tharg. 'You see any fancy coffee gubbins?'

I glance behind her. The answer is no. 'Okay, I'll go for a hot chocolate.'

'Right.' She pulls a mug out from the rack behind her. 'Leave your boots by the door, though.'

I glance down at my feet. I can see what she means; they're coated in mud.

I walk the few steps back towards the door, trying to go on the balls of my feet. 'If you give me a brush, I can...'

'No worries. I'm used to it,' she says, swishing her hands dismissively through the air in front of her. 'You take yourself a seat.'

As I pull off my boots, I steal a glance around the café. It's like something left over from the seventies: Formica tables and Americana-style booths. The parish council guy is sitting in one with what looks like accounts books spread out in front of him. There's another man in a window booth, head down, writing into his notebook and a third booth that looks like it's been recently vacated. A cup is sitting centre stage, crowded by a plate with a half-eaten sausage roll. What is it about this place and speciality meat products?

I choose a seat in a banquette pressed up against the wall. Out of the large rectangular windows, the mist is beginning to clear and I can just about see the creek where I almost came a cropper.

'There you go. Nice and strong.' The redhead puts a cup down in front of me.

'Thanks.'

'You got stuck here, then?'

'The mist came down.' I slip the mug into my hands to try and extract a little warmth from it. 'I missed my footing.'

'No, I meant in Attercoppe.' The redhead scrutinises me slowly. 'You came in with Stan.'

She doesn't ask but slides her backside into the bench seat opposite.

I nod.

'You know he's dead, right?'

I stick the spoon into my hot chocolate and glance awkwardly at the table, reluctant to meet her eyes. There's a sugar bowl sitting between the salt and pepper. I grab it. I'm going to need any kind of sweetness I can get hold of. 'Yeah, so I heard,' I mumble.

The girl gives me a long, hard stare. I say nothing, just pile three sugars into my cup.

'Stocking up?' The redhead looks on in absolute disgust.

I smile. 'Something like that.' Old habits.

'And Maggie's dead too.'

'Yeah. That's a shame. She seemed nice.'

'She was lovely. Not a bad word for anyone.'

I'm not sure if she's accusing me of something or simply likes to stick her nose into things so badly that she can't help but come off as abrupt.

'I had nothing to do with it.'

She pauses for an uncomfortable moment before nodding simply.

I gather I'm off the hook, yet she doesn't stop with the questions. 'They seem sick to you when you saw them?'

My mouth drops open, but my words seem reluctant to form. Luckily for me, someone comes to my rescue.

'Stan died of hypothermia, and Maggie had a heart attack.'

I glance up. There's a young black guy standing over our table. He must have been in the toilets when I came in because I didn't feel the door go, *feel* being the operative word; every time the door pulls open, it lets in a blast of ice-cold air.

The redhead stares up, irritated at the interruption. 'I was just asking.' She pulls herself from the booth.

'I'll have another coffee while you're at it, Rosa,' he says as he slides in opposite. This is getting to be tedious.

'Look, I really don't...'

'Remember me?' He looks at me, amused. 'Bad taste in men. Heathcliff.'

'Oh, sorry,' I bluster. 'I was just...SC Hutchins.'

'Leon, please. That's okay. You didn't recognise me with my clothes on.'

I hear a scoff from the redhead. 'Give me a man in uniform,' she mumbles. 'And I mean that—a man.'

Leon pulls the scarf from around his neck and hurls it at Rosa. He's smiling; somewhere underneath this banter, I reckon they must be friends, and I feel an ache somewhere near my heart. I've never had that— friends.

Leon turns his attention back to me. 'You doing okay?'

I take my spoon for another stir around my mug. 'Bit of an odd situation.'

He smiles. 'Odd, it's the new normal.'

Rosa arrives back with his coffee.

'And what about Hetty?' she asks as if they're mid-conversation.

'Hetty's okay,' Leon replies briskly.

'Only, my nan says she shouldn't be living on her own. Not with Davey gone.'

'Rosa, can you just mind your own.' Leon's shoulders start to rise.

'It is my *own*. It's my nan.'

I'm finding it difficult to keep up here. 'So...' I say, feeling the need to dig for a little more info, 'Hetty's, Davey's wife? Davey was Stan's best friend?'

Leon takes a swig of his coffee. 'That's about it. Hetty's fine. She's just grieving. Obviously.' He shoots Rosa a don't-be-such-a-dimbo look. 'She and Davey were together for like forever.'

'Hetty is so not fine.' Rosa shakes her head in an irritated fashion. 'She was leaving pans and gas on long before Davey copped it. Without him to look after her, she'll have that bloody house burnt down.'

Leon turns wearily towards her. 'I told you, Hetty's fine. We took her over to Green Acres this morning.'

Rosa gives a small, satisfied nod.

'Happy now?'

Rosa rocks her body forward and backwards on her heels. It seems like there's a whole tsunami of back-history lying beneath every word uttered in this place. 'About time. Everyone knows that should have happened long ago. It's my nan that lives next door. If that house burnt down, Nan's would be next.'

'Yeah, well, it's sorted. You want my job?'

Rosa laughs. 'Like hell.' She bends and whispers, 'You didn't want your job either,' then she flicks his ear before pulling away.

He looks irritated but not surprised. 'We went to school together. She thinks she owns me.'

'No one else would have you,' Rosa says, smiling as she

walks away to get a dustpan and brush for the mud I've tramped in.

'Actually,' he smirks at me, 'I do okay, but don't tell her that.'

I glance over and notice that the guy in the corner is writing ten to the dozen. His floppy blond hair falls across his face as his pen skims across the open page of his notebook. Is he writing down the conversation?

'SO WHY DIDN'T YOU LEAVE?' I ask Leon as we wander back down the *correct* path to the harbour. The mist has cleared, but the sun's failed to show its face again.

He pulls his tongue over his teeth as if reluctant to answer, but his eyes sparkle. He can't help himself. I've seen his type before—ask them a direct question and they cannot help but give you an answer.

'Failed my GCSEs.'

I don't tell him I failed mine too. I don't want to go into my educational background. People just assume you've got the requisite set of whatever if you say nothing. So, I just grin sympathetically.

'Just kind of fell into it. Phil, PC Green, he was a friend of my dad's.'

I note the *was*, but don't pick at it.

'I do other things. I mean, Special is just voluntary, so I work in a bar on the mainland most of the time, DJ.'

I'm impressed. 'Seriously.'

He smiles, trying to suppress his pride. 'Yeah. When we're not having this lockdown crap. I mean, there's no money in it. Not real money. It's not a real job. But I like sound mixing. Maybe I can get some work in that kind of general...' he throws out a hand, waving it in a wide circle, '...area.'

'So, you don't think you'd join the police?'

He sighs. 'I don't know. I mean, at first, it was just all a bit of a joke. Something to shut my dad up, but I'd have to go back, get my exams, and to be honest, the job can be a bit...depressing.'

'Oh?'

He slows till he's standing, takes in a deep breath and fixes me with his eyes. 'Dr Dancey died last night.'

'No.' I feel the news hit me like a punch to the gut.

He nods his head, shuffling awkwardly from foot to foot.

What the hell is happening here? Maggie, Stan and now Dancey? People I meet are dropping like flies. Leon, thankfully, hasn't cottoned on to my panic. He's moving forward, oblivious.

'I don't like being the first to know. Rosa'll be mad I didn't tell her. He was a nice guy. Delivered me.'

'I'm sorry,' I manage.

'Yeah. So he's kind of always been in my life.'

'The virus?' My words break a little as the word comes out of my mouth.

'Nah.' Leon lets out a snort. 'Appendix.'

So it's not me. It can't be me. Only the sense of relief doesn't last long. 'But...' This doesn't seem to work. 'He was old?'

'Exactly what I said. PC Green told me to stop being so naïve. First sharp thing PC Green's ever said to me. He was quite sarcastic, actually. He said the young didn't have a monopoly on peritonitis, that's...'

'Burst appendix?' There's a note of disbelief in my voice.

'Yeah. Apparently, it doesn't happen much when you're old, but if it happens, it's worse.'

'I'm so sorry.' I have no idea what else to say.

Luckily Leon continues forwards. We fall back into step.

'I hear your mum made a miraculous recovery?'

'Yeah,' I say as we walk off the path and onto the main tarmac of the street. Leon shoots me a curious look. One I'm willing to bet he borrowed from PC Green. Then I do the strangest thing. 'Actually, she died ages ago.' I find myself telling the truth. 'I just wanted to...'

'...get out.' He laughs. 'PC Green said he thought as much.'

'Seriously?' Now it's my turn to stop dead.

'Yeah. Full marks for trying, though.' He glances around him at the tumbleweed-empty street. 'Welcome to failure town.' Then he throws back his head and laughs. 'God, that was so depressing. I'm just on my way to a *good news* story. Fancy tagging along?'

'Good news?'

'Green Acres. Where they put Davey's wife to stop her burning down the town. It's a bingo thing. I put out the tables.'

'Um...' I hesitate, not sure how to get out of it, turning back towards the marshes framed over Leon's shoulder. My protest dries in my throat because standing there, out beyond the water, is the figure in white.

'Leon, do you believe in ghosts?' I don't take my eyes off the figure, the watcher, standing there on the flats beyond the water and mud, seeming to look straight at me.

Leon laughs. 'Living in this place? You got to be joking. Everyone believes in ghosts. My mum says they're just people with unfinished business, wanting to tell you something.'

He glances behind him; the figure appears to have gone. 'Yeah, sometimes this place can give you the creeps. Best to keep up with the living.' He glances back at me and shoots me a large, wide grin. 'Well, maybe the hanging-on-in-there. Come on. Green Acres. It's not like you've got anything else to do.'

I stare back down the length of the deserted high street. The Wreckers stands at the end of the tarmac, waiting like a bloated toad. Leon's right. I have nothing else to do. Besides, I'm not too keen on Maggie's ghost catching up with me. Whatever it has to tell me, I don't want to know.

'Okay. Count me in.'

10

GREEN ACRES

Leon is funny, bright, and generous with his time and enthusiasm. He tells me he lives out of town. His dad died a long time ago, and his mum's a bit of a recluse. He lives in one of her outbuildings on the marshes. Has all his sound equipment there. Once a week, he puts the tables out for the bingo at the old people's place. The oldies just love him. He hopes someday, when he's old, someone will do the same for him. I let his words wash over me as we walk, my head still buzzing with Maggie. Why do I keep seeing her? The second time she was warning me—stay back, marshland ahead—but she's still lingering, and she was there before, standing outside the inn with the flowers. I can't help but get the creeping feeling that even with its free rooms and "friends" with smiles, there's something odd about this place.

We don't have to walk past The Wreckers. The road we take heads into town, but we go straight across the narrow high street, with its one takeaway, two shops—convenience and chemist—and a Baptist-style chapel, before cutting through to the back of the main road where the land opens into fields. There's only one building out beyond the grass, a long low flat affair. It's sixties style, with those wide rectangular windows sitting above blocks of coloured metal. The centre section is slightly different. No blocks of metal. Instead, it's all window. The view out must be good.

A wide drive takes us leisurely towards the building with its car park at the front. But there are only a handful of cars filling the spaces.

'It's a shame. Normally this place is packed—rellies visiting,' Leon says. 'But what with the restrictions...'

I glance into the central room. There's a kind of tint to the glass, so I can't see clearly, but the place looks to be heaving. 'Bingo must be a big deal.'

'Too right.' Leon smiles, striding towards the door at the side and pulling it open.

I'M NOT sure I'm good with old people. The smell hits me first. Grant used to go hunting, and he'd string pheasants and things up in this makeshift larder in the camp. Green Acres smells the same.

'You okay?' Leon asks.

My hand's instinctively gone to my nose, dragging a piece of my T-shirt with it. 'Yeah.'

'Best put the belly away...' he says, glancing at my naked stomach. 'They can have too much excitement.'

'Leon.' It's the headscarf woman I'd seen in the café.

I shuffle downwind of her, hoping to acclimatise. She's still wearing a perfume factory of Chanel, but now I realise there's something not right underneath all that high-end scent. Something rotting.

'Hi, Mrs T. You're looking lovely.'

'Aw.' She blushes. 'No getting around me with flattery, young man. When's this situation going to be over?'

Poor Leon, he just can't shake that uniform off, even if they're not paying him.

'You know they don't tell me anything.'

'Well, you're in good company. Can you make sure there's only three seats to each table?' She leans in towards him. 'Alice Hardcaste always cheats. Best if she's out on her own.'

'I can sort the chairs, but I'm sadly powerless to stop them shuffling.'

'Hmm.' Mrs T looks serious. 'Well, just do your best. We so desperately need something to brighten the mood.'

I glance around into the sitting room, the room with the wide windows, and something else appears to be somehow not right. The room is empty apart from an old guy sitting hunched and worried in a bright red V-neck by the door. It doesn't stack up; I could have sworn that I'd seen people in there.

'Where is everyone?'

Mrs T fails to pick up on my confusion. 'They'll all be here in half an hour or so.' She glances at her watch.

I must have been mistaken. The bingo hasn't started yet. Despite the shaking, the old guy in the V-neck squashed into an overly tight, tartan armchair has the kindest, sweetest face I've ever seen. Bright blue eyes and, despite his age, a cloud of curly hair, but something is clearly bothering him. Perhaps he knew Davey and Stan?

'You alright there, Terry?' Leon calls out amiably.

Terry nods and flaps his arms.

'Good. I'm good,' Leon says, moving his fingers awkwardly in reply. Then it hits me. They're signing.

I turn to Terry, it's been a long time since I've done it, but my hands find *Hello* and *Pleased to meet you* easy enough.

'You sign?' Leon's face shows he's impressed.

'Yeah, a...friend taught me when I was a kid. But you do too.' I'd just seen him.

'Nah.'

Terry's now standing. Looking at me with an intensity that I can't quite place.

Leon laughs. 'I can manage *Hello*, and *I'm good*, but that's about the size of it.'

'Great, well,' Mrs T is saying, in her all bluster, no-nonsense tone, 'shall we get those tables sorted?'

She ushers us forward, leaving poor Terry slumped and desperate for conversation out in the hallway.

THE ROOM I saw from outside, the one with the floor-to-ceiling tinted windows, is completely empty. Perhaps it was a trick of the light? Maybe the tint casts some kind of odd shadow. As we start to set up, a few old folks begin to cluster into the high-backed chairs, smiling at us as they come through the door, keen to banter with Leon to ask him about his mum. To find out more about Maggie and Stan. I notice that Leon doesn't mention the doctor; just because you have bad news, it doesn't mean you have to deliver it. Two deaths are enough.

'Everything's stacked in the utility cupboard.' Mrs T's voice sounds curt. She's clearly irritated by the banter, which is slowing us down.

'That one's a bit of a dragon,' I say as Leon unlocks the door to the cupboard.

The rectangular tables are folded and propped against

each other; the plastic chairs are stacked in a tower to the other side.

'You get used to her. I mean the bingo's a good idea. Mostly, they enjoy it.' Leon's voice might be saying positive things, yet I can tell he's not happy; there's something awkward underlying the tone.

'All okay?'

He sighs as we stand in the darkness of the cupboard. The small tight space smelling of wet plastic and trapped air, but curiously it's preferable to what's on offer outside.

'It's Terry.' Leon rubs his fingers into his forehead as if trying to ease away the concern. 'He's deteriorating so fast.'

'The guy in the red V-neck?'

'Yeah.'

'He's pretty old,' I say.

'Does that make it okay?'

I'm not sure.

Leon tilts an edge of the folded table towards me, and I grab it. 'Can you carry it on your own?'

I nod.

'Great. We'll get this done in half the time. I guess Terry's one of my...' he drops his voice, 'favourites.'

Once outside the cupboard, Leon has to show me the "trick" of unfolding the damn things. I'm not so sure we'll do this in half the time. Effortlessly, he swings the legs into place and fastens them with a clasp before twisting the table the right way about.

'Terry used to help do this. Before he got...'

We glance back towards the hallway where Terry sits, looking agitated. He's still shaking. I wonder if it's Parkinson's.

'He may be old, but he was a regular handyman. Ex-military.'

I look at the shrunken man twitching in the tartan armchair.

'Admin on account of the...' Leon waves his right hand towards his ear.

'Hearing?' I offer.

'Yeah.'

'So, was he from London?'

Leon strides back to the cupboard for more tables. 'Nah...born and bred here. Even managed to stay on the island when the military kicked everyone off.'

'Seriously?'

He hands me another table. 'Yeah. About the only one.'

'No.' I stop, the unfolded table propped against my body. 'Everyone got told to leave?'

Leon smirks. 'Yup. All the locals got moved off the island in the fifties.'

'Flooding?' I ask as I wait for him to grab his own table.

'No, the island was used by the military in the war. Then they started up something else in the fifties.'

'The military? They took over the island?'

Leon shrugs. 'I think they own it. They own a lot of them. Foulness. Osea. There's one in Suffolk, too, a radar base. Foulness, you still have to get permission to go on.'

'Wow.'

He laughs. 'There's about forty islands in Essex.'

'I didn't know that.'

'No.'

This time I manage to clip the legs of my table into place and get it turned around and upstanding extra quick. I'm curious as hell. Why would the military clear everyone off the island in peacetime? It doesn't stack up. Luckily, Leon has no qualms about spilling everything he knows.

'When the military cleared Attercoppe off completely, in the fifties, Terry was already signed up, so they let him stay.'

'What were they doing here?' I follow Leon back to the cupboard, and he hands me another table.

'I have no idea.' Through the crack in the cupboard door, he glances over at Terry.

A cluster of women are gathered around the old guy. They're yapping ten to the dozen, but the poor bugger can't understand a word.

'He used to be a bit of a live wire, but now he's got cataracts, so lip-reading is a problem.'

'Not Parkinson's?'

Terry's right hand taps intermittently on his left leg. Trapped in his own world. He looks far from content. He reminds me of a polar bear pacing its too-small enclosure in a zoo. Those cataracts must have provided that added, final kick in the balls from life.

'Parkinson's? Not so I've heard. Four more tables, and we should be done.'

'That's Davey's wife over there,' Leon says, carrying a large stack of chairs out into the room and indicating with his head towards a shrivelled woman slumped like a small "c" in a chair with a ridiculously high back. She's dressed all in blue, an A-line skirt sitting above her belly, a once pretty blouse tucked into the skirt's over-large waistband. She's wearing odd socks and dribbling. I've had enough. I don't need the chit-chat. This place is giving me the creeps. Old age is scary. Suddenly, my mission is to get the chairs out asap, then go.

. . .

'You are a darling,' Mrs T says as we move back out into the hallway. 'Darlings,' she corrects herself in order to take me in.

'No trouble, Mrs T. Couple of hours?'

'That should do it.'

I shoot Leon a grimace—we have to put the damn things away!

'Sure.'

If Leon is aware that I am shooting him a *seriously* look, he doesn't pick up on it. He might be bound to this, but I'm certainly not. I turn my attention back to Mrs T. Behind her, I can see an old woman, moving surprisingly fast, taking her chair towards the front line: a table which is already sporting three chairs. Okay, so Mrs T may be a bit of a dragon, but she clearly has her work cut out for her. These old folks are sneakier than toddlers.

'Lost?' Mrs T says, looking curiously over my shoulder.

I turn to see Terry. He's standing in the doorway, blocking our way out.

'He's not been the same since his eyesight failed,' Mrs T offers, her voice more statement of fact than sympathy and too loud to be tactful.

Oblivious, Terry grabs my arm.

'Oh, right, well...' I mumble awkwardly, keen to pull myself away. Only when I look up into his eyes do I see a note of panic, or is it relief? I'm not entirely sure.

'Well, I'll leave you. Till next time.' Mrs T wanders back into the lounge, keen to keep control over the shifting chairs.

'You alright, Terry?' Leon places a gentle hand on the old guy's shoulders.

Terry begins to sign.

Leon drops the hand, looking embarrassed. 'Sorry mate, I don't really...'

'No, I do, though.' Suddenly it all becomes clear. This man is desperate to communicate. I'm rusty, but surely I can remember enough. I sign for Terry to continue.

Relieved, he nods. Instantly his hands are moving; he's telling me he has a message for Leon.

'Okay.' I nod. 'He wants to tell you something.'

Quick as lightning, Terry's hands begin to move again.

'He says...you're in danger. No, I correct myself,' as Terry gesticulates all around, taking in the whole building. 'We're all in danger.' I sign for Terry to go slower.

Terry nods before, much slower, reassured perhaps that he's getting through, he begins again.

'He says we're all in danger. If you can, you should get off the island with your mother, and...' Terry indicates towards me. 'And me...And...' The movement gets wider. 'Anyone else you can take. Anyone who's...' I stumble over the words, unclear of the meaning. 'Everyone who's alright?' What does he mean? —*alright.* But he's not stopping. 'The island is shutting down.'

'We know that,' Leon says simply. 'Eve, tell him we know that. Not to worry. It's the virus, but it's not here.'

Terry shakes his head. He must have lip-read that part. His fingers move wildly again.

'He says it's not the virus.'

'Think I got that bit,' Leon smirks.

'Can everyone please take their seats?' Mrs T's voice comes through loud and clear from the other room.

Terry looks frustrated. He starts again.

'He's asking about Davey.' I give Leon a puzzled look, unsure where this is going.

Leon sighs. 'It is really sad. He was a regular old boy.'

I may not be looking at Terry, but I can feel he's been signing the whole time. I turn back towards the old guy in the red jumper, standing there pitiful and small, trying so desperately to communicate.

'No, I don't think it's about Davey. It's more about...'

Terry is hitting his ear.

'What Davey heard. Heard?' I say. Struggling to keep up despite the fact that Terry is going slow. Whatever he's trying to say doesn't fit with any kind of normal, standard communication I went through with Grant.

'No,' I correct myself. 'Davey overheard?'

Terry nods emphatically. He's standing so close to me now he could practically touch my lips.

'Davey...' I start again. A little more confidently now. 'Davey overheard his parents in the fifties talking about something. Something he'd...forgotten?' I ask.

Terry nods.

'He heard them talking the night before they died. His parents. His parents died.'

Terry nods again. I'm getting it. He's signing once more.

'But what they were saying didn't make sense, so Davey...'

Terry taps his head with his right hand before flapping it away.

'He put it out of his mind.' I glance at Terry. He nods. 'Because...' I continue, '...shortly after...in the fifties, the same thing happened.' I stop. 'Same thing?' I ask, exaggerating my lip movements.

Terry readies his hands again.

'People started dying,' I read.

Leon puts his own hand once again on the old guy's shoulder. 'Tell him not to worry, Eve. It's not connected. This is all natural causes.'

But Terry shakes off Leon's hand. His eyes look desperate, a touch of insanity hidden behind the washed-out cataract blue. He starts to sign once again. Frantically this time, as if his life depended on it.

'He's saying, what about your phone?' I'm a little surprised. This seems totally off track, but I've most definitely nailed the interpretation. That one was easy.

Leon looks uncertain, taking his mobile from his pocket and pressing it into action. 'What about my phone? It's fine.'

Again, Terry's hands start to move.

'No. He says it's not fine.'

'Look.' Leon slides the phone under Terry's eyes. Close enough so that even with those milky blue pupils, the old guy can see the handset has all bells and whistles working on go. 'Look messages, from Mum; from PC Green...'

Terry's hands slice through the air again.

'But...' I translate, 'nothing from outside of the island.'

Leon takes a closer look at his handset. 'Well, not since yesterday.'

I turn to face him. 'Would you normally get something?'

He shakes his head non-committally. 'Difficult to tell, but yeah. Yeah, normally, I guess...something.' Leon stares at the phone. 'Not even junk mail,' he mumbles.

Terry's eyes are wild. He's looking close to dropping with exhaustion.

'Terry, we're starting,' Mrs T shouts from the other room.

One of the other old men, a tall man with a thin white comb-over and a stoop that suggests he's permanently looking after others, moves out of the community room towards us. Slipping his palm neatly under Terry's elbow. 'Come on, Terry, old mate. I've saved you a card. I can do your numbers. Let's give the old girls a run for their money.' He laughs.

As the tall white-haired man leads him away, Terry turns back one last time towards us. One more frantic attempt at communication. His hands insistent, over and over. Before the tall guy places his own gnarled fingers over Terry's.

'Not too excited, hey? We have to win yet.' He sets a long arm around Terry, turning him effortlessly back into the room.

'What did he just say?' Leon asks.

'Get out.'

'No.' Leon shakes his head. 'Even I could see he said a lot more than that.'

Feeling unnerved, I stare into Leon's dark open eyes. 'Get out.' That was it. The words seem curiously haunting when aired. 'He just repeated it, again and again and again.'

11

———

THE TWENTY-FIVE

'You don't mind if I skip the put-away?' We're back at Leon's. Sitting in his kitchen. His mum, Bea, a sweet woman with greying afro hair and a round, homely face, has just made us a couple of hearty doorstop sandwiches. Roast beef, thick sliced from the Sunday roast. Horseradish, homemade and a handful of rocket. The kitchen is small, eclectic. The kind of place you'd expect someone who is not so keen on company to have. Everything she could ever need for her and her much-loved son is here at her fingertips. There are pictures Leon did as a kid covering the walls. One is of a long stringy PC Green standing next to a police car, a black guy and a small curly-haired kid.

'Is that PC Green and your dad?'

Leon laughs. A splutter of horseradish slipping back out of his mouth. 'Yeah. Sorry. I mean about the horseradish laugh. Table manners were never my strong point.'

His mum is nowhere in sight. She had been pleasant, asked a few questions to show interest, just a quick rundown as to who was still rocking and rolling at Green Acres. Leon didn't tell her about the doctor. I wondered who Leon was keeping Doctor Dancey alive for, himself or the rest of the community? Then again, I guess Bea hadn't given us much time. As soon as the sandwiches were on the four-person, life-worn pine table, Leon's mum disappeared.

Leon nods towards the painting. 'An artist at a young age.' His voice is mock-pretentious as he sinks his teeth into another bite.

'What do you think Terry meant about the no mobile thing?'

Leon looks puzzled. 'To be honest, I'm not sure. But he's right. It is odd. Have you been getting anything?' He eyes me curiously, before a smile seeps across his features. 'Ha!' He laughs. 'You don't have a phone, do you?'

'I...'

'That's why you're not constantly fidgeting with it. You don't have one.'

I pull my device from my pocket as though clearing my name. The battery's dead, though. 'I'm not expecting any calls.'

'None?'

I shake my head in a wide arc.

'Your husband?'

'Hopefully not.'

Leon eyes me cautiously. 'You do know, you are a bit young to be married.'

'Yeah.' I glance awkwardly at my hands, suddenly self-conscious. 'That's another story.'

'I'm listening.'

Toying with my sandwich, I pull out the strings of rocket so that when I take a bite, it doesn't sprawl down my chin. I could lie at this point. I could find something neat and fitting that would shut Leon's questions down. I'd use my sincere phone voice, and Leon would be none the wiser. 'Another time, maybe.'

He laughs. 'Well, well, well. You...' he points his sandwich at me, 'are a dark horse.'

Thankfully, he doesn't press the question. Instead, he turns his bread doorstop around again, readying it for the bite. 'I seriously get it about the old folks' home, you not wanting to go back. Arthur can help. He was the big guy who offered to read Terry's bingo card. Helpful is Arthur's middle name. But sure, you dip out. I mean, they've kind of got me by the goolies for the rest of my natural, but you... you are footloose and fancy-free.'

I can't help but smile. For the first time in my life, that might describe me. Although there's that haunting feeling, the feeling that something isn't quite right about this place, and the ghost, Maggie, what's she trying to tell me? 'I thought I might go to the museum.'

From his face, I get the feeling museums are not Leon's kind of thing. 'We had to go there as kids. School trips. Cheap day out.'

'Does it have stuff on the military?' I just can't get my head around the place being cleared out. Maybe all these deaths are connected. Could it be something in the soil, an old leak that's suddenly taking its toll?

Leon takes a moment to chew the last chunk of sandwich he's taken before replying. 'Military, what like you mean all the top-secret stuff?' There's a hint of irony in his tone.

Ask a stupid question.

'To be honest,' he wipes his mouth using the back of his hand, 'I'm not sure there's that much to tell. It was after the war. Threat of the cold war, maybe? The islands were just coastal defences. The stuff on the twenty-five is way more interesting. You know about that, right?'

'The pact, isn't that what they call it?'

He nods.

'Why pact?'

Leon has to wait again, chewing hard before continuing. 'I mean, this is like way back when. Long time ago, but the people who found them…'

'The twenty-five?'

'The twenty-five. Well, the people who found them…I don't know, it's written in some account somewhere, some old parish records or something.'

'Yes?' I say, wishing he'd stop stalling.

'Well, the twenty-five were chained together.'

'Uggh.' I put the sandwich down on my plate. 'But…?'

Leon shakes his head. 'No one knows why. They've got some of the links, links of the chain, in the museum. At least that's what the description says.' He stares at my plate. 'You not eating that?'

The thought of twenty-five people chained together and drowning over five hundred years ago turns my stomach, it seriously does. Apparently, not so for Leon, though.

'No.'

He eyes my abandoned sandwich. There's only a quarter left, but he's clearly after it. I guess he's so used to the myth it's stopped haunting him.

'I'm writing an opera about it—the twenty-five.'

I laugh.

He gives me an over-the-top hurt, WTF look.

'Sorry. It's just…opera?'

'Yeah, the lyrics. So a friend's doing that. But I want to get the seascape, capture the marsh sounds. You want to see it before you dive off?'

'See it?'

ONLY THAT'S EXACTLY what he means. We soon find
ourselves in Leon's shed at the bottom of his mum's garden.
You have to admire him for his strike out at independence.
There's a double bed with a series of rough dark blankets
strewn over it. An old-as-the-hills couch, kettle, fridge and
two rings of some kind of primitive electrical hob are set in a
corner. There's only one window, but that's curtained out
with a thick felt blackout blind. Homemade, I think, but
neatly sewn—his mother. There's no heating, but there are
plenty of electrical sockets, so Leon has access to a few electric radiators and a wood burner. The walls are painted
black. I think it may be some kind of artistic statement. If so,
it goes about my head. However, the most impressive thing
in the room are the screens which are truly enormous. A
series of blank-faced monitors plugged into a sound deck.

Leon flicks on a switch. The screens fire into action. I've
never seen anything like it. Horizontal lines of green patch-
work appear across the top half of the largest display. Each
line is filled with a waveform, an intricate mountain range of
sound. Below the audio lines are multiple dials and sliders.

'That is so impressive.'

He laughs. 'You have no idea what that is; it could be
shit.'

'Is it?'

He leans forward, rolling the curser along one audio line
as if gently stroking it. 'No. It's good. I think it's seriously
good. You want to hear?'

'Okay.'

He manoeuvres himself into the seat, wiggling a little to
embed himself into its leather, and before the altar of this

sound wall, Leon's fingers hover about the keyboard, sincere as a musician sitting in the pit of the Royal Albert Hall. He raises the fingers of his right hand, about to release the first bars of sound. Then stops, turning towards me.

'Eve, I want you to be honest, okay? If you don't like it, I need to know.'

I clear my throat. 'My name's not Eve,' I say, unsure if this is the right time or the right place, only knowing I need to get it off my chest; start owning up to being who, what, I am. 'It's Ella. My name's Ella Tanner.'

Leon stares at me for a moment. In a strange way, it feels as if we're both standing in front of each other naked; Leon with his never-before-heard opera, me with just my name. It feels good, being honest. After what seems like the longest, deepest moment in eternity, Leon simply nods, turns back to his deck and hits play.

The music is amazing. I've seriously never heard anything like it in my life. It seems to be mainly strings, but he's captured the haunting nature of the landscape. He'd said there were no lyrics, but I could swear I heard a woman's voice underneath it, not singing, but hugging the notes with her haunting song moving just above the chords, just below. It feels as if fingers are actually reaching out from the speakers and washing gently over my entire body. I don't want it to end. Ever. When, after thirty minutes, Leon hits the off button and pushes his chair away from the console, I feel bereft.

'Got to get back.' He glances at his watch. His voice oddly quiet; to speak after what we'd both just heard seems almost blasphemous. I simply nod, stand, grab my coat, and push out of the door. Glad, in a way, for the break. The music stirred up so many emotions I felt a burning need to be out in a wider landscape. A place where no one can scrutinise my features.

AFTER POINTING me in the right direction for the museum, Leon strikes off towards Green Acres. He didn't need to go back down to the road. Apparently, there's a footpath winding through the marshes, popping up bang-smack outside the old people's home.

It feels odd being alone again, standing in the street with the day at my disposal. Back home, Jayden had me fitted into a rigorous time frame. Mostly that would be on the phone. My voice reassuring people that despite the fact their card had been stolen, we—The Met—were on to the perps. I didn't dream up the scams. Jayden had a mate who did that. I just delivered the voice of trust.

The museum was easy to find, opposite the café. It might only be three o'clock, but the afternoon is so dull, an all-encompassing battleship grey, that you could be forgiven for thinking night is about to come crashing down. The lights in the café are on. Inside, the figures look like creatures in an aquarium. Rosa's frenetic pale arms cleaning tables. A detergent spray in one hand, a cloth in the other. Each table getting two squirts and a circular rub. Her red hair, so obedient this morning, has hatched a wilful escape from the tie holding it back. It's been a long day for her. The guy who was writing in the book, the one with the floppy blond eighties pop star hair, the one who I had felt certain was scribbling down our every word, is still writing. Though a little more thoughtfully now, not the manic scrawl of earlier. He occasionally pauses, letting his eyes run back over what he's written. Never smiling. Occasionally taking his pen and drawing a line through whatever he thought had been so important to get down.

Ahead of me, on the path, I can just about make out the black shed where grumpy-beard Malik had been earlier in the day. My reluctant saviour. Maybe I should ferry him down a coffee tomorrow, a thank you. But he's gone now, or maybe he's inside. The door's shut anyway. The buckets abandoned, left piled up in a Pisa-style tower outside.

Glancing over the swelling estuary, I can kind of make out the spot where I got stuck. It's underwater now. Deep underwater. My footprints are long gone. A black wrinkled wet blanket hiding the mud and the treachery. I wonder what would have happened if I hadn't been pulled out; how far above my head would that water reach now? The thought makes me feel cold to the bone. Vulnerable against all this elemental, raw tooth and claw nature; the river, the mud, the sky that stretches on forever. I pick up my pace. Keen to turn my back on the expanse, replace it all with something vaguely human.

When I arrive at the museum door, the place is closed; a sign stuck against one glass panel of window. It reads *Back in five*. I have no idea if it's a real sign—an active one—and someone seriously intends to be back in five. Or, for that matter, where the "five" minutes started. Chances are, the sign is telling the truth. I decide to amble along the harbour a little, towards the fishing huts. There will be no wandering off track this time. It's just a short five-minute stroll. Should be perfect timing. Walking along the same path I trundled this morning. I seem to have gained a better sense of balance, no longer having to put my hands out on either side to keep myself from toppling. The boats are all in almost exactly the same places, give or take a few feet due to the push-pull of the tide.

All the huts are empty. Large padlocks on the doors, apart, that is, from Malik's hut. There is a lock on the door, only there's a light spilling out from the crack. Which is kind of odd. Why would you lock yourself in with the lights on? And I doubt there's any electricity running this far down the harbour. Certainly, not anything hooked up to the main grid. So it's not as if a light has accidentally been left on, which is curious. Moving a little closer, I stare hard at the thin blade of orange between the lock and the door. Suddenly it breaks. A shadow. There is someone in there. Someone moving. What can he be up to?

Old Malik had struck me as shifty as hell, and it kind of takes one to know one on that front. There was something caged and trapped in his eyes, and that beard was much more *disguise* than *on trend*. I would have preferred for my "saviour" to be someone neutral, living their own best life badly like most of us. The guy writing in his book; the parish councillor, head down in his accounts. Even pearl-clutcher, bingo fascist Mrs T. Although the possibility of her getting herself muddy would have most likely had her neatly turning her back on me as I slipped under. Maybe bearded guy had saved me, but I might just skip that peace-offering coffee. He's up to something, and I've been involved with too many up-to-something type guys to want to reopen that can of worms.

When I get back to the museum, the sign is down. I turn the handle and push. Nothing. I lean my shoulder into the door—a large rectangular slice of the thickest wood I've ever seen in my life. I'm not sure they make trees that solid. But the result, when I do get in, is worth the effort. The place is an old Victorian customs house. The rooms are small, neat, and lined with gleaming glass cabinets. The building still retains the last vestiges of a society which feels the need to impress. I can see into three rooms from where I'm standing. All have intricate cornicing. Beautifully plastered high ceilings painted a slick brilliant white. There must be underfloor heating because the place is toasty. The lottery logo, those hopefully crossed cartoon fingers, is emblazoned on a glass panel which separates the desk from the rest of the museum.

'Well, well. I wondered when you would get around to us.'

I turn to see a small, neat woman, her raven dark hair swept up in a chignon, a pair of fashionable ink-black spectacles sitting on an aquiline nose, sheltering a mouth so intricately lined and filled with blood-red lipstick, she could have just stepped away from a beauty counter. Everything about this woman is petite and perfect and centred.

'I'm Charley.' Her voice is precise. Confident. University educated without a hint of anything or anywhere regional. 'Or Charlotte, if the gender-neutral thing bothers you. I can do either.'

'Eve,' I say. It's okay to blow my cover with Leon, but imploding it wholesale would involve way too much explanation.

She smiles cheekily. 'I know who you are.' Her face creases in concern. 'I hope everyone's being nice?'

'Yeah, I...'

'There was a lot of talk when you arrived. They're a superstitious lot here. *Nice* doesn't always come automatically, and the deaths were a shock. Suspicion is part of the whole island mentality. Even though we are not...of course... an island most of the time.'

'Yeah. I got that.'

She nods as if to say, *of course you did.* 'A couple of our hardcore drinkers were spouting down the pub, saying, loudly, that you'd dragged a curse in.' She eyes me curiously as if she's not wholeheartedly dismissing this position but too rational to jump in on the proposal without hardcore evidence.

'No,' I say, hoping to lighten the tone. 'No curses. Just me, stuck in the wrong place, wrong time.'

'Irritating, huh? The whole lock-in thing. Hopefully, it won't be for too long, and in the meantime, well, we are very pleased to have you, Eve?'

'Adams,' I say, and see something in her eyes flicker through as if she's got the joke.

'Eve Adams. No serpent?'

'No,' I say. Beginning to feel irritated. 'Just new beginnings.'

'Everyone needs those,' Charley offers lightly. 'So, this is us.' She turns in towards the museum, waving her slim, gel-nailed fingers around the room. 'Lottery funded.' She points to the glass panel with its logo. 'As you see. But we've been here for years. Originally in one of the sheds along the harbour wall, then gravitating to this building around a hundred years ago, when the river had finally silted up. No more boats, nothing needing a customs house at least,' she says lightly.

'It's a long time to have a museum.'

'Aha, that would be because we are an area of historic importance. You know about the pact?'

'A little.'

The light in her face dims just a notch, and I get the feeling she was itching to relate the story.

'Well, all the gruesome relics are here.'

'And the military occupation?'

She stops for a moment, her smile freezing as she takes a brief pause in order to step behind the reception desk and regain her authority. 'Well, you have been doing your homework. Although it was not strictly an occupation. No. That would be totally the wrong word. Gives the wrong idea. Words are very important.' She holds me fixed in place a little too earnestly with her burning green, over-sincere eyes. 'Get the word wrong, and, well, nothing works.' Sitting down on her seat, she pulls her thin black-cashmere-clad arms across the desk, clasping her hands together in an authoritative gesture. 'It cannot be an occupation if they own the land.'

'The whole island?'

'Peninsula, now. With the causeway,' she corrects, pointing one red lacquered nail at me as though punctuating my mistake. 'But yes, the military owns the entire peninsula. All houses are leasehold, not mortgaged or privately owned. The area was useful strategically in the war.'

'But they moved everyone out in the fifties?'

She shrugs, sending her chair on a short, controlled sideways swivel. 'As I said, the military owns it. If that's your interest...' There's a distinct air of disappointment to her voice. 'We do have some photos in room three.' She waves a hand behind her into one of the rooms leading off from the main trunk. 'You're the second person today. Don't tell me you have theories that the land's contaminated somehow. All these recent deaths, people who have lived here all their lives, maybe they've ingested something. Maybe their bodies are ticking time bombs waiting to go off.'

'I...'

'Maggie been haunting you?'

My mouth falls open. Does Charley know something? Is she being "haunted" too?

She nods sadly. 'She was a wonderful woman. Meet her for ten minutes, and you'd fall head over heels for that warmth.' She fixes me with those green eyes, a little warmth flickering through them this time. 'Truth is, people just die. It's kind of what we're meant to do.'

She hadn't meant *haunting* in the literal sense. She hasn't been seeing Maggie too, but just because Charley's not having visitations, it doesn't mean I'm not or that Maggie isn't trying to tell me something.

The door rattles open behind me. I don't see who it is but catch the brief look of disappointment on Charley's face. It's only brief. She props that lipsticked smile back up in a nanosecond.

'Ah, Mr Clark. I wondered where you'd got to. I took the sign off a full...' she glances at the watch sitting neatly on her wrist, 'three minutes ago.'

I turn to see the guy from the café, the one who was writing. He's taller and thinner than he looked spread out in the booth. He brushes his long fringe back from his eyes. An affectation, I think. A tic which shows he's a little rattled; he's intelligent enough to get the sarcasm. Or perhaps it's simply that he's self-conscious enough to pick up on the sting. Underneath his arm, he carries a notebook, a classic racing green, leather-bound. I'd seen them before in shops. They're expensive. In his right hand, he's actually carrying a pen, as if no moment can be wasted. Everything must be recorded. The pen looks expensive too. His fingers are inky where he's failing to master it. Yet the pen is at the ready, as though no moment must be lost.

'You had to go out?' he says. Throwing the interrogation back to where it should rightfully belong.

'Nothing serious.' She flicks her wrist dismissively towards me. 'You've met Eve...' She draws out the name, a little too keen to indulge in the full piss-take for my liking. 'Eve, Miley. Miley, Eve. Miley is a writer.' Charley yawns. 'Sorry, so terribly stuffy in here.' With her right hand, she lifts her cashmere cardi, giving it a quick shake at the neckline. 'Eve's interested in the military, Miley.' She smiles neatly, pleased with the alliteration, even though she's clearly disappointed with the content.

'Seriously?' Miley, for his part, looks genuinely disappointed.

'Just curious,' I say, feeling painfully self-conscious. It's as if I'm being cross-examined on a quiz show, humiliated for offering up all the wrong answers.

'Do you know about the curse?' Miley asks with relish.

'Yeah.'

For a moment, there's silence as Charley and Miley look me over. Charley is actually leaning her body over the table and propping her heart-shaped chin into her palms as if cupping a goblet. 'I mean if you know about the...'

'The pact,' Miley says eagerly.

'Or the twenty-five,' Charley adds, tilting her head.

'Exactly. The pact or the twenty-five. It's the same difference, really.' Miley shrugs.

Charley raises one eyebrow as if she wouldn't, exactly, describe it as this.

I clear my throat awkwardly. 'I just thought it might be interesting to start with the military.'

They both look at me with attitudes of bewilderment on the part of Miley and bemused curiosity for Charley.

'But I guess. If you're here and...free. I'd...yeah, I'd love to hear about the twenty-five pact thing.'

Charley looks impressed, clearly liking what I'd done with the name conjunction. Miley doesn't really notice.

'I can do it, Charlotte,' he says over-enthusiastically.

She gives him a be-my-guest shrug before opening her perfectly formed lips wide and yawning once again.

WE'RE SOON STANDING in front of a large book, protected by a glass cube, illuminated by a dim violet light.

'These are the parish records,' Miley whispers, even though we are clearly the only people in the museum.

The pages on view are yellowed. The leather of the binding, at least the part that I can just about make out behind the leaves of paper inside, is so old that it almost looks chewed.

'Earlier on in the book, before this open page, are details of the plague years.'

'An account?' I ask.

'Not really an account; a little more info about the inhabitants. There were fifty people living here then.'

'Not many.'

'Actually, that's pretty healthy for a rural community. The entire UK population was about five million.'

I'm not sure what I'm supposed to say to this.

Miley notices my blank expression and nods in a slightly smug way. 'Today, it's around sixty-seven million.'

'Wow.'

'Indeed.' He sweeps his right hand through his thin blond hair, causing it to cow-slick a little at the front. Glancing at himself in the reflection of the glass case in front of us, he eases his hand through the other side of his head, matching the height. 'And this here...' he continues, as if oblivious to the brief vanity stop. Pointing with his little finger, though not touching the glass, at the other side of the book. 'Just at the bottom there, that's 1425.'

'This is when the pact was made?'

'No, no, no.' He emits the negatives a little too abruptly. Softening them with an indulgent smile. 'The pact was made in 1350.' He points again to the first page on the left-hand side.

'And the pact was?'

'Hmm.' He smiles. 'Good question. Okay. So, 1350 and the plague is rampant in these parts. At its height. You happen to go to the local villages, and a lot of them were wiped out.'

'But not Attercoppe?'

'Exactly. There was a monastery in Leiston, Suffolk. No longer there. Just ruins now, but some of the books from the library were preserved. There was one written by a travelling monk, Oswold of Dunwich. He'd travelled what we would now call the East Anglian Coast, collecting stories, making a census after the Black Death had done its worst.'

'Can I see the book?'

Miley shakes his head. His hair lolling forward. 'Sadly, it's in the British Library. Yes, you can see it. But you need an appointment and an academic introduction. It's a point of contention, really. It should be here.'

I think this might be taking us off topic. I need to bring him back unless I'm happy to stand here all night. 'So what did the book say? I mean about Attercoppe.' I'm not interested in a whole census of villages in the Middle Ages.

'Right. Well, Oswold said that the village of Attercoppe... Wait.' He stops. Pausing to dive into the canvas messenger bag at his side and draw out a phone. 'Here.'

He thrusts the mobile towards me. It takes a moment for my eyes to refocus. This part of the museum, beside the book, is dark. When my eyes do settle, I can't help but feel disappointed. There's a photo filling the screen; a mass of curvy squiggles on a tea-brown strip of textured paper. I can't even read it.

'I can't really make that out. It's...difficult to read.'

'Yes...?' He looks at me curiously. 'I supposed you get used to it.' He pulls the phone back towards his own eyes. 'In short, Oswold says that despite all the villages around this area being devastated, many being empty, the peninsula of Attercoppe had a thriving community. At first, he thought they must have blocked themselves off completely. Apparently, although they took precautions...'

'The bowl of disinfectant at the Devil's Punch Bowl?'

He smiles. 'Exactly so. Though probably, it would have been a mix of vinegar, urine, or possibly salt. Sometimes ashes were also used.'

'That's probably more detail than I need.' I'm aware it's getting late. We seriously could be here all day.

'Course. Sorry.' He lowers his head, his hair flopping forward in a bashful, more endearing way. 'It's my passion.' His voice sounds a little apologetic.

'That's good—to have a passion.'

'I think so. Only, yes, so...' Whatever he was about to say is lost. He's back on the plague. 'They took precautions, but it didn't really explain why no one had died. Then he, Oswold, overheard some of them talking. Even though they'd survived, not everyone was happy. They talked of a pact with a demon, their safety for two generations. After that, the people of Attercoppe would have to pay.'

'Pay what?'

Miley takes in a deep breath before shaking his head. 'That's unclear. If Oswold knew, he didn't go into details. It's only a short extract on the village. His book covers the whole of the Eastern region, so...'

I glance back towards the book. The 13,000 entries—the names of the people who struck their bargain.

'And so this...' I point to the right portion of the page, the collection of names. 'These are the people that paid?'

He nods. 'Yes. You see, after 1425, no entries.'

'Not even on the other pages?' I dip down as if I'm seriously able to see through the glass, through the paper, to what's written beneath.

'No.'

'So these are the people who committed suicide?' There are around seventy-five names.

'Some of them died. You can see here.' He points to the left-hand side of the paper. In a column next to the names are black crosses, in another column, the date. The names with the crosses run down the page until all crosses stop beside a Madeline Beaumont. 'These people with the crosses, they died before the pact?'

I glance down the list. 'A lot of them dying in August 1425.' I look again. 'A hell of a lot.'

'Fifty,' Miley says confidently. 'And with fifty gone, that left the island of Attercoppe with only twenty-five people. A mix of men, women and children. The twenty-five who walked into the sea between August the twenty-sixth, when the last of the fifty died, and September the third, when a group of migrant workers arrived to help with the harvest. They discovered twenty-five bodies, chained together, dead in the estuary.'

Everything is so not right about this. Is the place truly cursed? Is that what Maggie's trying to tell me, just like Terry with his frantic signing back at Green Acres? Are they all trying to tell me to get out?

. . .

THE LAST GORY detail in the whole gorefest that is the Attercoppe museum is a thick length of rusted chain.

We stand in front of it.

'This is the original?'

Miley nods. 'One of the twenty-five was the blacksmith. It's well made.'

BY THE TIME I stumble back past Charley's desk, I'm feeling suitably traumatised.

She gives me a wave as I walk by. 'Found everything you needed?' she says brightly.

'Yeah.' I stumble out of the heavy door, feeling a sense of total relief as the hard slap of salty marsh air hits my senses. I don't know these people, there are centuries between us, but somehow their strange sacrifice is the kind of thing that can turn a person's stomach inside out.

12

TARGET

Walking quickly back across the front, I zip my puffa to the top and pull my hood over my head. For once, I'll be relieved to get back to The Wreckers. I'm growing weary of people. Everyone seems to want something, even if it's only a reaction. There's food to eat in the fridges, so no need to drop off at the shops. I should have taken Leon's number. I could do with a chat with someone normal, but no doubt he's busy. He had the chairs to put away, PC Green on his back and an opera to write. It's only me that has nothing to do with my life, and that kind of nothing is dangerous because if you're not careful, someone will helpfully fill it up with crap for you.

The street is deserted. We must still be cut off; I've only seen a handful of cars on the road, and always the same ones. The streetlight opposite The Wreckers flickers on into the gloom. Its base wrapped with the tributes to poor Maggie. I'll pick some flowers myself in the morning if I can find anything growing wild. If it hadn't been for Stan finding me, for Maggie taking me in, I don't know where in the hell I would be now. Most likely, Jayden would have found me. A small pool of water underneath the streetlight shines a shimmering dab of orange.

Over the other side of the wide band of black tide are the crumbling white teeth of what had to be military buildings. I can see no lights. Yet even as the thought flickers through my head, there's a spark of illumination. Someone is over there, watching us, I wonder. I'm not sure, but the idea of a human presence, sitting on the other side of the dark swirling water, gives me a little comfort. The world is still there, getting along with its everyday, virus or no.

The Wreckers may be empty, but it's far from silent. When I come through the door, the electric light buzzes into action. The fridges behind the bar are already singing their tune. I go through to the front bar, slip behind the wide tongue of wood separating the optics from the lounge, and grab myself an orange and lemonade, not bothering with a glass. There's no one here, and I can't be bothered to wash anything up, so the bottle will do me just fine.

In the kitchen, I pull open the wide walk-in fridge. Propping the door with the mop. If the thing slammed shut with me inside, I'm not convinced anyone would come looking. Maybe, after a couple of days, Leon would pull off his headphones and wonder where I'd got to, but that would be about the size of it. There's a stack of industrial Tupperware in the fridge, neatly labelled in what must be Maggie's curved cursive hand: a beef stew, a chicken chasseur, two stroganoffs, one mushroom, one beef. I fix on the chicken, taking it out of the freezer, knocking the mop out of the way on my exit. It's large, so going to take forever to defrost. The tea-brown contents are so cold I can't even get them out of the Tupperware, so run a Belfast sink with a good five inches of hot water and put the plastic container in it to melt.

Grabbing a French stick from the bread bin, I'm disappointed that the golden baton is hard as a pickaxe. Reluctantly, I stuff it in the bin. There's probably bread in the freezer. I'll defrost some for tomorrow. There are some catering bags of tortilla chips piled on a shelf, waiting for someone to fix a chilli. Grabbing one, I pop open the mouth and start to munch. There's a remote up there too.

Scanning the room, I notice the blank screen of a TV nestled in the corner above a worktop. It might be good to catch the news, find out what the virus is up to. I hit play, and the dead dark screen wows to life. To my utter amazement, the scenes on the box are not all doom and destruction. Instead, a bright-faced group of young women are telling the behind-the-camera news presenter about their joy at being able to present the UK at The Film Innovation Awards in Milan 2026. There is a circulating strip banded at the bottom informing me that a few areas of the UK are still in lockdown. No death tolls being touted.

During a brief recap on the headlines, I'm told by a plastic-looking newsreader in a bright red trouser suit and impossibly shiny hair that although the Astrapi variant appears to have burnt itself out, a few areas are still locked down. A few? Then why is the military on the other side of the causeway when we've got no cases here? If they're not trying to stop anything from getting in, then what are they trying to stop getting out?

As though on cue, I suddenly feel an ebb of cold air. There must be a window open somewhere. Switching off the TV and placing the remote back on the tortilla shelf, I wander out of the kitchen to the back of the building, the glass entrance porch where Maggie had propped my boots that first night. It's not the stateliest of structures, a lean-to greenhouse-type affair. Used for utility rather than glamour, and cold, despite the radiator where my boots had rested. There's another freezer down the length of the annexe. A coffin-shaped one. It's clear I'm in no danger of starving.

Suddenly the door bangs, the glass rattles. Someone has left the door to the annexe open. It could be anyone. The pub is practically community property, but I can't help feeling a little unnerved. Had it been open this entire time? Open while I slept upstairs in my bed. I pull it closed, turning the key in the lock. That should hold anyone out who fancies helping themselves to a quick pint from the bar. The Wreckers is spooky enough as it is, without the possibility of others wandering around. Passing back through the glass palace, I pull the connecting door closed behind me as well. This is solid wood. No one's getting through it without an axe. I turn the key and slide across both sets of bolts: top and bottom.

In the kitchen, the lid to the chicken stew comes off with the slightest of tugs, revealing a gooey line between the solid stew and the edges of the container. Slamming a knife down through the centre, I put half of the iced casserole into a microwavable dish and the other half back into the fridge. It's going to take a while to defrost. Maybe twenty minutes. I put the dish into the microwave and set the timer. I've got enough time to run a bath.

It's only a shower in my room, so I stop off on the way up the stairs and choose another. If the new room was better than the one I'd ended up in, I'd have swapped, but it's pretty much the same story; dark beams in unpredictable places; heavy wooden furniture with drawers that don't open and handles that rattle. The bed in the room with the bath is lumpy, the eiderdown pink rather than brown. Perhaps I'll take that one back to my room when I go. I give it a sniff. No feet, instead a faint trace of perfume. I'll definitely take that one back with me when I go.

Setting the taps on full in the en suite, I pass back out through the door and down the corridor towards my room. The corridor seems darker than before, emptier, its beams appearing to narrow around me with every step that I take, but I refuse to let the place spook me. It's just a building, just four walls, a crapped-out lean-to and a reptilian roof. Pushing open the door to my room, I stop dead.

Every stick of furniture, every inch of upholstery, has been trashed. The drawers from the side unit have finally come unstuck and lie abandoned at odd rectangular angles. The foot-smelling brown quilt is scrunched on the floor. The chair is on its side, and the mattress is curiously half on, half off the bed, revealing a nest of rusty brown springs. On top of this, over every inch of the room, strewn carelessly as if blown by a hurricane, is my hard-earned cash. In the bathroom, my towels are on the floor. My toothbrush ground into the tiles. Dawn? Surely not. She wouldn't say boo to a ladybird. Somebody here doesn't like me. Someone still blames me for the lockdown, for the deaths of Stan, Maggie and the doctor. I'd felt I had begun to fit in, the helping out, the banter, the visits to all the local hot spots, but I'm still the outsider, the easiest one to blame.

I could just lock the room. Set myself up in the one with the bath, but I'd got used to this one. This was mine. After switching off the bath, I return to my room and pick up my money, setting it back in the felt purse. Then I haul the mattress onto the bed again. It probably needed an airing anyway. I hope the intruder gave it a good punch. I remake it. Plumping my pillows. Setting the pink bedspread from the other room across it. Re-erecting the chest of drawers is more of a problem. They seriously don't appear to want to go back in.

Eventually, after a little trial and error, I get them back on their runners, then fold up my clothes, pick up all the tissues scattered from the wastebasket and my toothbrush, and head back down towards the kitchen. The waste needed emptying anyway. It wasn't done in the way I would normally do it, but now was as good a time as any to get it all sorted. I'll just have to be more careful in the future. Somebody doesn't like me. So I need to make sure all the doors are locked when I'm inside and when I'm out.

Hopefully, this little show of hate has helped its perp get all the angst and bitterness out of their body. I lift the large lid of the bin in the kitchen, am about to pour the contents of the wastebasket inside when something catches my eye. Underneath the rock-hard French stick, there's a plastic bag. A Co-op bag. The bag I'd stuffed my felt purse in. I pull it out, and my heart sinks because in the corner of the bag, slunk right down and hiding, I can feel the outline of something small, rectangular and hard—Jayden's USB.

BANG. My heart jumps. Someone is in the building. My room was turned over by some xenophobic Attercoppe resident. BANG. Or, so much more likely, my room's been turned over because someone is looking for this flash drive. Not someone, nothing so neutral. Jayden is looking for his USB. I should have left it out for him to find. BANG. I duck down behind the units. No, that wouldn't have worked. If he's here, he'll want to finish the job. The banging is coming from the front of the pub. I could slip out of the back. If I go out through the lean-to, I could cut down through the high street. Make my way to Leon's. BANG.

'Eve?'

I've never been so glad to hear another human voice in my life.

'Leon,' I mumble, not that he can hear me. I get to my feet. Sprinting out of the kitchen, through the bar-room and towards the front door. I can't seem to turn the key quick enough; my breath is coming fast in excited, relieved bursts.

'Leon,' I say, throwing open the door wide and grabbing him into a hug.

'What!' He staggers back a little.

'Someone's been in. My husband. I think it's my...' Then I stop. His face is ghostly, flaccid and in shock, but not from my news.

'Leon?'

'There's a problem,' he stutters. 'Green Acres.'

'I don't follow.'

He shakes his head, unsure how to go on. Words failing him before he manages a barely audible. 'They've shut it off, the army.'

'That doesn't make sense.'

He's leaning heavily in the doorway, his face ashen.

'Leon? The virus, is that what all this is about?'

He shakes his head nervously, looking scared and confused. 'They were fine earlier. Weren't they fine?'

'Sure. Fine.'

But he shoots me a scared look.

'Okay, show me.'

13

THE FIRST CLUSTER

We hurry down the empty street sticking to the shadows. Leon's voice barely grazing up and over a whisper. My shitshow of a burglary and the possible arrival of my husband is lost, trumped by whatever this is. Leon's eyes are wild, but he doesn't stop his continual quick pace forward down the street through the darkness.

'We need to keep to the shadows,' he says, his voice low as he pushes forward.

That suits me just fine. I keep checking behind me just in case Jayden is on the prowl, but so far, so good; no one is following. Maybe he paid someone to ransack my room. The man has contacts everywhere. It wouldn't be so difficult, even with the phone lines down. Jayden has ways of issuing orders to a grubby ever-ready team, just waiting to carry things out.

We turn off the street that runs along the front, cut down the narrow link road and come out on the high street. It's dead. Not a soul. Then again, we haven't seen anyone since we left The Wreckers. I'm expecting us to go across the road and towards the main drag, the road that would take us straight to the old folks' home, but Leon grabs my hand.

'Footpath,' he hisses, taking my arm and pulling me gently off the road and onto a narrow, now darkened byway. It smells of dank undergrowth, and gnats flick through the darkness. Once we're out of the line of houses, Leon loosens up.

'I came over to help put the tables away.'

'Yeah, you said you were going to.' Our feet trudge across the cold, damp grass.

'Only, when I got here, there was...' A beam of light sweeps the grass. Without stopping to think, Leon places a hand on the top of my head and pushes me down. I cringe under his palm. What the hell is going on? The light sweeps slowly across the empty grassland as we cower below its reach. Finally, it clicks off again, leaving us in darkness.

'When I got to the home, there were two military vehicles parked in front of the building.'

His tone is tense, scared, but I can't work out why. 'Maybe they were bringing in supplies?'

Leon shakes his head. 'There were four guys out the front with guns.'

Guns? None of this sounds right. 'Did you call PC Green?'

Frustrated, Leon shakes his head. 'I've been trying to get hold of him all morning. He sent me this message.'

He grabs his phone out of his pocket and starts to read the time stamps. 'Ten twenty.'

– Need to talk. Out by boat shed around three.

I can see the little blue bubble of reply from Leon.

– Sure.

But there's nothing else.

'I went over to the boat shed after I left you.'

'And?'

'Nothing.' He looks frustrated. 'So, then I came around here, and...' Leon gestures towards Green Acres.

The building has a few lights on, but not enough to illuminate the front parking area. It's only when I look harder that I realise the armoured vehicles are still there. 'He could be inside?'

Leon nods. 'That's what I thought. Something came up, and he had to come over.'

We both stare back towards the low-slung building.

'Only what?'

'You think the old folks have got the virus?' Why do I suddenly feel guilty? I haven't got it. I'm not doing this.

Leon shrugs. 'I don't know. I mean, that would be a bloody quick reaction.'

'It's called Astrapi,' I say, trying to keep the *guilty* out of my voice. 'Lightning.'

'Hmm.' Leon doesn't sound convinced. 'So why haven't we got it? Besides, I couldn't see anyone moving in there. I zoomed in on my phone, but nothing.'

'Surely, if PC Green needs you, he'll text.' My words might sound rational, but they don't appear to be doing anything for Leon's peace of mind. 'And there was that lady police officer as well. The one that came around when I was locked in at The Wreckers.'

'Sandy,' he says before shaking his head. 'She's on annual leave. I tried to get hold of her anyway, but she's not picking up.'

'Right,' I say, still not entirely certain what we're doing here.

'I thought maybe we should go in.'

'What!' I can't help myself. My exclamation is on the loud side. Leon clamps his hand over my mouth.

'I've got this really bad feeling.'

I stare at Leon through the darkness. This is not the young guy who jollied me along when I was stuck locked in my room, not the guy I met in the café with his banter and easy smile, not the guy who showed me his opera with such pride and excitement. This Leon has aged, worry lines etched across his forehead.

'PC Green's on his own, against...' Leon indicates towards the armoured vehicles. 'I just want to check he's alright. He might find it difficult getting a message out. If I just turn up, well, then maybe we can help. Besides, what about Terry and the others?'

My instinct is to run, to tell Leon that none of this is my problem. I don't really know these people. Yet, despite the instinct to get out of here fast, there's something about Leon Hutchins and his love for this small washed-up community that makes me want to be a part of it.

'Why did you come to me and not Rosa?'

'You haven't exactly got a lot on.'

I think of my turned-over room and my panic at having narrowly missed an intruder, about to tell him the whole story, but Leon's not waiting.

'Besides, Rosa's mouthy as hell. You seriously think she'd keep the volume down if she was out here with me now?'

He's got a point. Rosa would be taking the military on. She'd be out on the road, up in their face, asking for answers. Whereas stealth is kind of my middle name.

'Okay.' I nod. 'We're not going to get in through the front, though.' The guys with guns are way more gatekeeper than anything Tolkien could have come up with.

'Around the back.' Leon flexes his head towards the building. 'There's a door in the kitchen that faces out over the marshes. We can get in that way.'

Luckily, the ground is firm. The undergrowth cut short, with a band of longer grass standing between the Green Acres "lawn" and the watery mud. From the creek, the tall, silhouetted reeds rustle like a ballgown as we pass louder than village gossips, their sound covering our footsteps. Leon knows exactly where we're going, where to tread and where to avoid. Born and bred on the marshes, there's no building in Attercoppe, entry point or exit that's a mystery to him. Keeping low, we reach the building.

First stop is the backdoor, but it's shut tight. We shuffle along the building, our knees bent, our backs scraping against the wall for support, Leon running his fingers across the windows as we pass: testing. The lights are off, but I can just make out shapes inside, dark rectangular units. A stainless steel mixer, an industrial extractor fan: the kitchen.

His fingers fall away, disappointed; the window is shut tight. He moves on to the next, shuffling forward, me following, the scrape of brick against my coat making a hissing sound. There's a small gap at the bottom of the second window frame. Leon shoots me a look. We could be in luck. Although, I'm not so sure I want to get in. If I'm found breaking and entering, that's going to bring up one hell of a lot of questions. There'll be no handing out false names for them to swallow, then. Perhaps I should stay on the outside. No one is going to worry about Leon. Everyone knows his face, and he's even got a uniform back home. But me? Leon pulls gently at the UPVC frame. It folds out towards us. He turns towards me; the full-on beam of his smile irresistible. I know in an instant, wherever he's going, I'm following.

He snakes his way through the window headfirst. The top half of his body reaching down inside, trying to get something hard so he can lever the rest over and through the window. He can't find anything. There's a break in the kitchen units at just the place we need it. Kneeling on the floor, I bend my knee and point to it. Leon glances at it critically, then nods. The extra foot or so should give him leverage. He places his heavy boot on my thigh. Luckily, he doesn't leave it there long; just a quick, short push, then he's through. There's no knee for me, though. Leon uses his arms to instruct me, indicating that I should lean through the window. I do as I'm told. It's too late for cold feet now. We are in this together. He pushes up my puffa, grabs the belt at the back of my jeans, and yanks me through.

I crumple onto the hard tiles on the other side of the window.

'Okay?' he hisses.

I nod, pulling my trousers back into place. 'A door would be nice on the way out.'

'Wedgy?' His features crinkle as he tries to suppress a snort.

I really don't want to go there. 'Can we just get on with this?'

Now it's his turn to nod, but he places one finger over his lips. 'Listen.'

I listen hard. I can hear the reed beds from outside and the usual hum of the kitchen, but apart from that, not a sound.

'There should be noise.' His voice is laced with concern.

'If they've got the virus, aren't we...?'

'We won't touch anyone.' He pulls two white paper masks from his pocket. 'Came prepared.'

I'm so not convinced that this slip of soft folded paper with ear strings attached is going to cut much of a deal, but I put it on anyway.

Masks on, Leon pulls me to my feet, and quiet as cats avoiding a Rottweiler, we set off across the kitchen.

The place stinks of bleach. Okay, so people use bleach in kitchens, but this is on a different level, industrial. A kind of municipal toilet or hospital disinfectant. The kind of cleaning that's been going on here is just that bit too deep.

'That smell?' I gag slightly.

'Not a good sign,' Leon says anxiously. 'Normally, this place smells of custard creams or stew.'

There's a glass panel in the door from the kitchen to the rest of the home, one of those small panels laced with meshed wire: in case of a fire. Leon walks towards the door, his toes barely hitting the floor, and peers through the panel into the hallway outside. I'm not far behind.

'Well?'

'No one. Not even any lights.' He sounds confused. His eyes dart around the framed corridor as though trying to work out the best way forward. 'I think we should split up.'

'Seriously?' I hiss.

'If those jokers with guns come in, it's more difficult to explain what the two of us are up to. One of us, and we can just bluff.'

I'm good at bluffing. It's something I've spent my adult life doing, but even for me, this is going to be a stretch.

'Tell them...' He hesitates.

'Don't worry,' I say wearily. 'If push comes to shove, I can find the right story.' I don't need a script anymore. Lying is part and parcel of my every day.

'Great, and my story's simple—I'm just after PC Green.'

Whatever ruse I come up with, his is so much better because it's got that hint of truth.

'Ready?'

I puff out my cheeks in an exaggerated fashion. It's clear that I am not actually ready for this, but I'm along for the ride. So, what the hell?

'You take the community room.'

Great, I think. Then again, at least I know where it is.

'I'll do the bedrooms.' And with that, he pulls open the door.

The hallway beyond the kitchen is warm. Too warm, but there's that smell of bleach again, and on the carpet, there's a mark. Someone's been trying to get it out, there's a scum of foam in the mix, but despite the cleaning, the imprint is still too visible for comfort. It has the unnerving size and shape of a body. Leon's noticed it too.

I shake my head, a look of fear shooting through my eyes. We shouldn't be doing this, but Leon just rests a hand gently on my shoulder. With Jayden, the hand would be a push and a squeeze, accompanied by a bitter hiss in my ear. It was always clear who the boss was. With Leon, it's different. He might be the uniform-wearing type, but we are so in this together.

Not looking back, he walks away from me down the corridor. I just have to do one room. One room, and I'm done, easy-peasy. If there's no one in there, which stands to reason since the lights are off, my job will be done and dusted in less than five. Moving cautiously past the stain on the carpet, I hover by the door. The room is cut through with dark shadows. Through the windows, I can see the driveway outside, three large military vehicles parked up on the tarmac. The sort of vehicles that can do without roads if necessary. I can spot only two men with guns. The others must be inside the cars. I can't afford to switch on the lights. Even the smallest flicker of light from my phone could bring unwanted attention. Luckily, the soldiers have their backs to me; at least the two I can see have.

The room is empty. The tables all put away in the cupboard. Somebody must have tidied up. Maybe PC

Green? Maybe the tall, white-haired guy who helped with Terry? The room still smells odd, though. Bleach, yes, but something else. Something underlying, something not so preferable. Something that's old and most definitely off.

Apart from the smell, which is almost physical, there's nothing here. Not even a bingo ball or counter. I might as well find Leon. Going back out into the corridor, I'm not entirely sure where to start. The place feels dead. There are two corridors leading off from the main atrium. Leon won't be in the kitchen. So I take the opposite corridor. It's lined with rooms. The white doors pulled closed. Each door has a small brass plate: *Mrs Thompson*. She's the closest to the action. This must be the Mrs T I had kept bumping into. I try a light rap, then the door. It's open.

The room is small but contains everything you would need if you were over seventy and slow of movement: a chair, a sofa, a false, electric fireplace which, undaunted, is still flickering a strange orange glow into the room. There's also a neat row of kitchen units, just enough to stand behind and warm yourself up something in the microwave or grab yourself a slice of toast. The surfaces are all wiped down. The room is immaculate. Mrs T's garish purse lies abandoned on the coffee table. Her handbag is next to the armchair. There's something a little creepy about the room. A touch of the old *Marie Celeste*. I step inside, letting the door close behind me, and the silence of my entry die away. The purse is just sitting there. These are desperate times.

Once this lockdown, lock-in, lock-up, or whatever you care to call it ends, I'm going to be out on my own, running again. I take two steps towards the leather purse. No one would know. Mrs T must be busy somewhere. No doubt organising Christmas. There's a long way to go till the festive season, but Mrs T strikes me as the kind of woman who would like to have everything sorted, entered in a spread-sheet, and posted on a wall. There will be rotas, secret Santas, and trips. My right hand reaches forward, the purse within my grasp.

The door pushes open. 'Shit!' It's Leon. 'You scared me.'

'Goes both ways.'

The moment is lost. The purse too far out of reach.

'You have got to see this.'

I'm not so sure I do. There's something odd going on here. Me thinking I'd filch Mrs T's purse is most likely the least of our worries. This old folks' home is modern. The walls are concrete, the angles square, yet it feels as if they are closing in on me, as though the shadows have more depth than they should, as if someone is watching.

As we walk down the corridor, Leon holds my hand. I'm not sure why, but it's very sweet, and I'm glad of the way everything about him feels different from this place—alive. At the end of the passage, we stop. There's a double door in front of us. It's different from the others—the ones like Mrs T's that are the doors to someone's living space. This door has a set of those rectangular meshed windows. I look at the plaque on the wall. *Chapel.* I shoot Leon a curious look. He comes behind me, places both hands on my shoulders and manoeuvres my body, so I'm standing in front of the glass panel in the door. Inside, there's someone in a hazmat suit walking slowly around what looks like a shrouded, hori-zontal body. The hazmat guy inside moves to the side, and my heart bangs inside my ribs. Beyond the hazmat, resting on the long rectangular bingo tables, there are rows and rows of long low lumps draped in white shrouds. The person in the white suit knocks against one of the tables. An arm falls out from the shroud. An arm with a red sleeve. I gasp, moving back—Terry.

Leon, eyes wild, fixes a hand over my mouth. But it's too late; the person in the white suit turns slowly towards us. I can't see the eyes, but I know they've clocked me. I get the desire to run, to sprint, to grab hold of Leon and just get the hell out of there. The person inside the room remains perfectly still. Then with one hand, lifts off the mask: Erin!

We cluster in the kitchen. It feels like the safest place. Erin's pretty sure the military is staying out front. She'd warned them that the grass behind the building went off into the mud, so they should be careful if walking back that way. They'd been stationary ever since.

'I trained as a nurse,' she tells me as, exhausted, she leans against the units. 'That's how Stuart and I met.'

So she wasn't just about arnica and hocus pocus.

'Surely they brought a doctor in from the mainland?' Leon asks, sounding bewildered.

Erin shakes her head. 'No. They're moving the bodies out tonight. We're just waiting for the...' she hesitates. 'They wanted a refrigeration vehicle so they can do accurate autopsies.'

I feel a dull thud of sickness at the base of my stomach. What the hell is going on here? 'Is it the virus?' My voice sounds small and frightened, even in my own ears.

Erin shakes her head. 'I don't think so. I mean, they'll have to do autopsies, but every one of the deaths seems...different.'

'Oh?' Leon wants more. Vagueness is no longer enough.

'It's difficult to say.' Erin sighs.

'Try.'

'Okay.' She draws her hand through her grey hair. 'Well, it looks like a few heart attacks. At least one, and thrombosis, and Mrs T...You know how proud she was of her hair?'

'Oh my God, yeah.' Leon rolls his eyes. 'All natural.' He

delivers a quick impersonation before they fall in together. 'No HRT.' They both smile at the ingrained knowledge.

'Well, her hair's all fallen out.'

'Can it do that?' I ask, instinctively touching my own.

'Never seen it before. Not that kind of speed. She was fine this morning.' Erin glances down at her hands. 'She came into the surgery for her prescription.'

'But the heart attacks.' Leon's voice is level. He's attempting to sound neutral, playing devil's advocate. 'They are all old.'

Erin shakes her head. 'The ones who had heart attacks weren't the ones who had any problems. You forget I know these people inside out. I've got the lowdown on who has high blood pressure, low blood pressure, their family histories.'

Leon's looking worried. This is so above his pay grade. 'Have you told PC Green?'

Erin takes out her phone, her expression one of absolute frustration. 'I've been trying to get hold of him. Nothing, and I can't get a signal to the mainland.'

I remember what poor Terry had said. 'That's been going on for a while,' I say. 'It seems like you can phone anyone on the island, but the signals have been blocked from going further.'

'By who?' There's a touch of indignation in her voice.

There's a brief pause before, as if choreographed, we all stare back towards the front of the building. We can't see the military from our huddled position in the kitchen with the lights off, but we all know they're there.

'There's going to be a meeting at six.' Erin glances at her watch. 'Kev's called it.'

'Kev?' I ask.

Helpfully, Leon fills me in. 'Chair for the parish council.'

Kev must be the guy I saw in the café, the one with the accounts' books spread out over the table.

Erin sighs again. 'Probably PC Green will be there. Some big-bod military guy is also going to speak.'

Leon instinctively straightens up. 'Coming to the island?'

'No.' Erin shakes her head. 'That'll be online. Did you not get the message?' She glances at us both.

We look sheepish—obviously not.

From outside, we hear the rumble of a vehicle approaching. Erin grabs her mask.

'You two should go.' She pulls the fabric of the face cover over her head, and I stare into those sad green eyes. She's barely had time to bury her husband, and now to have to deal with all of this.

14

USB

Leon and I cut back across the small strip of grass outside, taking care to stay as close to the long grass as we dare. The damp air wells around us in cold eddies, accompanied by the gentle slosh of salt water against mud. We only look back once, just in time to see a large van pull up by the front entrance. The arc lights adjust till they're aimed at the van and the door to the home. The military is busy as a mound of ants that's been kicked, moving with motives we don't understand but seem to make sense to them. A gurney goes into Green Acres. It's followed by a second. We don't wait to see the bodies come out.

'What do you think?' Leon asks. The sound of our feet hitting the tarmac as we spill out of the footpath seems oddly comforting.

'I don't know, Leon. To be honest, I'd say it's got to be the virus.'

Instinctively, he takes a step away from me.

'I seriously think it's too late for that.'

'Yeah.' We cross the road and head down the high street. 'Probably right.'

The shop is closed. The Chinese is closed. There are lights on in a few of the houses, but everyone appears to be lying low until the meeting tonight. Leon checks his phone.

'Still no word from PC Green?'

Leon rubs his forehead with his free hand, concerned. 'It's just not like him. He always keeps in touch. Too much in touch. It's not just the *Special* thing. It's because of my dad. They were friends and...You know, Green's always looking out for me.'

'He's probably with the military. He'll be at the meeting tonight.'

'Yeah.' Only there's an edge to Leon's voice, an underlay of worry.

PC Green's like a father figure to him. Why would the man go AWOL? Nothing is stacking up.

'You know, before you came to The Wreckers, something odd happened,' I say.

'That place is always odd.'

'Yeah, but...' I lower my voice. 'My room got turned over.'

He stops. 'Seriously?'

I nod. 'Seriously.'

His eyes narrow. 'That's weird. There's no crime here. You can leave your door open. Worst that ever happens is someone scrumps an apple off a neighbour's tree when it's hanging over their garden. That's the level of trouble we get.'

No wonder he wants to be a Special here. 'Well, this was serious wreckage. Even for The Wreckers.'

I don't laugh. The thought of going back to my room is unsettling. It can't be Jayden, not with all this military activity. They're clearly not letting anyone on the island, but that doesn't stop me from feeling uneasy. Leon must be able to tell because his eyes switch from curiosity to concern.

'Look, you come back with me. Come home with me

until the meeting. Then I'll walk you back to the pub, check the place myself if PC Green hasn't materialised and make sure everything's locked up.'

I feel something welling in my throat—a hard lump—and realise, to my absolute shame, I want to cry. I barely know Leon, yet here he is, putting himself on the line to be my conquering hero.

'Great,' I say.

'And you can listen to the rest of my opera.'

'Always a catch.' I laugh.

We cut back in the opposite direction, skirting the shops and heading towards the far end of the peninsula and Leon's home. As we walk past the causeway, the tide is out. We could just walk across, be back on the mainland within twenty minutes. Only at the far end we can see the barricade. The military vehicles. The camouflaged figures stamping their limbs to keep out the cold and dampness. I guess I should feel relieved. Jayden's not getting across that causeway, but the situation is too odd. It's like they're waiting for something to explode. Something beyond one foulmouthed man with flying fists.

THE SWELL of notes fills my ears, making me feel as though my body is drifting away on the tide, that I'm held firmly in the grip of a gentle but firm wave carrying me out towards something bigger, better.

'So that's the opening.' Leon's fingers fly across the keyboard as he tweaks the sound levels just that one step more, in constant search for perfection.

'It is seriously beautiful.'

He smiles proudly. 'Thank you kindly.'

There are bowls on the makeshift coffee table. Bea's beef hash is something else. That woman can cook. My bowl is cleaner than it would be if it had just come out of the dishwasher. Not one bit of deep, warm liquid went to waste.

Leon pushes his chair away from the deck and glances at his watch. 'Thirty minutes. We don't want to be early.' His body shakes in mock revulsion. 'I can't do all the *Haven't you grown? What are you up to?*' He flicks the side of the console. '*Don't you look just like your dad.*' There's a brief pause. 'I hate that one. Those people must see me around most days but stick them in the village hall, and they're way too keen to dish out the clichés.'

'I can imagine.' I stack the bowls and, without standing, lean over and put them beside the door. 'What happened to your dad?'

'Oh, stupid. Car accident.'

'I'm sorry.'

'Yeah. What about you?'

I drag my hands through my hair, bundling it in a tie at the back of my neck even though I have no clip or elastic to fix it with. 'Nothing to tell.'

'Your father?'

'Actually, I never knew him.'

'Seriously?'

'Oh yeah. Not even a name. There was this guy once, Grant, friend of my mum's. That's where I learnt to sign. I guess Grant was the closest thing I had to having a real dad.'

'PC Green, stand-in type affair?'

'Kind of, yeah. He looked out for me. Till Mum took me away.' I can't help it; when I say *Mum*, my tone always turns bitter.

'She was a character?' Leon's trying to keep his tone

neutral, but since I discovered the attraction of honesty with Leon, I don't want to put myself back into a box of lies.

'There was something wrong with her. She's dead now, two years ago.'

'Sorry.'

I shrug. 'No need. She walked out when I was fourteen.'

'Oh. Can I be sorry now?'

'Please.' I allow a small smile to crease my lips.

'So you went into care?'

How easy that would have been. 'No, she kind of...' This is so difficult to explain. I'm not even sure I understand it myself. 'She kind of sold me.'

There's a brief pause. 'Sold you?'

'Yeah, to this guy. Jayden. My husband.'

'Ew.'

'Definitely, ew.'

'So how old was he?'

'Jayden? He's late thirties now.'

Leon eyes me curiously. 'And you're early twenties?'

'Twenty-three.'

He leans forward, taking my hands between his. 'You know none of that's legal, don't you?'

How can I explain to Leon, law-abiding, community-spirited, Special Leon, that most of my life has been lived on the wrong side of legal?

'Yeah, I know.'

'Thank God you got out.'

I glance at the floor, the sense of tension welling up across my back as if it's laced with strings and someone is pulling them taught.

'You didn't get out, did you?' He eyes me curiously. 'That's why you were on the road running.'

Hooking my bottom lip under my teeth, I look up into

those kind, deep brown eyes. 'Initially, I thought Jayden may have turned over my room.'

'No.' Leon relaxes back into his chair. 'Can't be. I swear, no one is getting on this island, not at the moment.'

'Is there any way he could have come in with the military?'

Leon mulls it over. 'So he looks like he's in the army?'

I think of Jayden's dark, shoulder-length Jesus hair. A stomach that hangs a little too enthusiastically over the front of his trousers. That homemade cross on his index finger and his manic, angry blue eyes.

'No. But he could get away with being delivery driver come hired thug.'

'Nice,' Leon says, his words laced with sarcasm.

'He could also have paid someone to do it.'

'Phones are down.'

'The man always finds a way.'

Leon nods. 'That sounds more likely. Okay.' He sighs. 'Leave it with me, Ell. I'll figure out a plan. If he is paying someone, it'll be one of the "usual suspects". I'll find out what I can.'

15

BREAK-IN

Leon leaves me in the shed while he goes back into the house carrying the bowls. We haven't got long till the meeting. My clothes are a mess from where we trudged through the footpath. I try and sponge my trousers off, but they just look worse. I should go back to The Wreckers and change. I've got the spare set of clothes Maggie left me.

Besides, Leon needs a bit of time with his mum, and I can't keep living scared of my own shadow. Leon's right—it's a chance in a million that my husband will have got onto the island. Whoever it was that turned my room over left the money, but did they leave anything else? Anything personal that might give me or Leon a hint as to who they are. I know The Wreckers well enough by now. If I go back, grab my clothes, check for clues as to who broke in, I could switch the tables. Currently, I'm waiting for Jayden to catch up with me. How about I catch up with him? Take him by surprise. I find a spare bit of paper on Leon's desk and scribble down a note, leaving it on the coffee table for Leon to find before heading back out into the night.

I strut through the darkened streets, my hood up against the wind. The town is busier now, with an odd collection of people milling around, putting out bins, chatting over the news on doorsteps. Nobody gives me a second glance, but I should change my coat when I get in. Maggie must have something I can borrow, something left over and hanging forgotten on a hook. I need to err on the cautious side. There might be photographers at the meeting—newspapers. Jayden knows what my puffa looks like. For most people, it's slipping under the radar black, but for him, the coat is an invitation to come get me.

I push open the rattling door to the inn, holding it with my left hand to stop its brittle bone chattering and easing it gently back into the doorjamb in my wake. I turn the key in the lock and stand for a moment beyond the door, soaking up the smell of hops, beer, and slop trays. A smell that will go on for years, even if nobody ever pulls a pint in the old place ever again.

The tables and chairs are in the exact same positions. The breakfast table that Dawn had set in the centre of the room is still standing there as if waiting for its guest to arrive. Yet there's something different about the room, the place, a kind of live energy. The hair on the back of my neck begins to creep—someone has been moving through this very space only moments before me.

Glancing down, I see a curve of a wet footprint on the carpet. Cautiously, I take one step forward, painfully aware that my coat rustles louder than a crisp packet when I move. Holding my breath, I peel the coat, inch by inch, arm by arm. Walking cautiously on my toes across the empty room, I stash the coat behind the bar in the large blue bucket where the bottles get thrown. The coat is a giveaway. Hanging the thing on the hook by the door would scream that I was back. Without the coat flagging my presence, I at least still have the element of surprise on my side. I glance down at my shoes. They're squelchy from the marshes. They'll have to come off too.

Whoever is in the building must be here because of my husband. I need to know who they are and how much Jayden knows. Then it hits me with a sickening lurch. Who am I kidding? My scheme is too elaborate. The simple story always works best; it has to be my hubby. Somehow he's got himself on the island, and he'll be mad as hell. There'll be no holding back. No fear of being found. No fear of the police. We are all alone. In a full-on fight, Jayden will always win. He's got the weight to lay me low and an angry power behind every punch. I should have known as soon as I saw that USB stick that nothing would stop him. The army, the lockdown, none of that would make a blind bit of difference.

Half of me, most of me, wants to run back to Leon, but Leon, with his wide innocent smile, stick thin arms and single mum, doesn't deserve to be pulled into this. This is my mess. Deep in my heart, I know that the only way Jayden will ever stop hunting me is if he's dead. It's me or him.

Shoes off, I inch through the dust-smelling downstairs on the balls of my toes towards the kitchen and the knives. There's a clutch of blades standing, handles ready, in a block on the counter by the hob. I pull one out. It's too long. Too flashy. I need something small. A little something that I can keep in my pocket. Something that, allowing for the right placement and pressure, will do the trick. It will be easy enough to get rid of the body. Perfect timing. People are dropping around me like fruit flies. What's one more to the pile? Nobody apart from Erin's even asking questions. Which might be seriously odd but could work in my favour.

Can I do this, though? Can I seriously kill a person? Take

someone else's life? My fingers hesitate over the knife block. The answer is, I'm not sure. Despite the fact Jayden's held me captive for so long, actually killing a person is a whole different ball game. Me or him, I think to myself. That's what I've got to keep hold of. I can't wimp out now. It's not that I'm killing him. That doesn't come first. The right way to think of this is that I have to stop him from killing me, whatever the cost.

I find two small, sharp knives, their stainless steel blades so hungry they cut my skin when I draw them across my thumb. Putting the smaller one in my right pocket, I clutch the other blade in my hand, its sharp edge extending out in front of me as I creep out of the kitchen. Cautiously I head back through the bar, placing one hand on the newel of the stairs. A large part of me wishes I was back at Leon's, waiting in his shed, allowing the stew his mum made me to stick to my bones and warm my heart. And yet there's this other bit of me, a really big bit, which is saying, this is your chance. Your chance of freedom.

There's a bang from upstairs which sets my heart thumping against my ribcage. The bang wasn't loud, not angry. Somewhere a drawer is being shut closed, and there's the sound of rustling. He's hunting for that bloody USB stick. He won't kill me until I tell him where it is. Why the hell hadn't I checked the bag before I'd run? If I didn't have the USB, maybe he wouldn't be here. Getting to the island must have been difficult.

Probably, with the army's presence, more than teaching me a lesson was worth it. Jayden would have fumed for a while, strutted the other side of the marshes, and then given it all up as a bad idea. Gone home to find himself that "something younger" he was permanently hankering after. The USB is the thing that's brought him here, not me. It's important that you don't always put yourself centre story. The world is perfectly capable of ticking along without any one of us. Everyone has their own unfathomable motivations. Having said that, there's one thing I know for sure: Jayden will make sure I'm in pain, try to squeeze the info out of me, but he won't kill me until he knows where I've stashed his flash drive, and while he's not killing me, that's when I need to strike.

I creep slowly up the stairs, one step at a time. I can still hear him rummaging. Heavy footsteps marching across a room, more drawers being opened. Cupboards being slammed. At the top of the staircase, I realise the sound isn't coming from my room. It's coming from the other side of the building. The side where Maggie had her apartment. I could run, and it was tempting standing there at the top of the steps, the small knife clutched in my hand.

If I turn back now and hightail it down the stairs, I could sprint all the way to Leon, find PC Green, confess everything. There would be a court case. I was bound to get into trouble as well. There were all the phone cons I'd been part of. The door to the house I'd shared with Jaden hadn't been locked. Technically, I wasn't a prisoner. There would be questions. Would anyone believe that it had always been Jayden masterminding the scams and pulling the strings? He was the puppet master who had brainwashed me since I was a kid. Fourteen. When I'd told Leon the whole sordid truth, it hadn't sounded as though I was relating some Bonnie and Clyde high jinks caper like I'd always thought it was. Even though I'd never loved my *Clyde*. Repeating the story out loud, it sounded as though I was spilling the beans on a sordid story of abuse and manipulation—my abuse. Surely the courts would protect me? Yet still, I keep climbing those stairs.

When I reach the landing, that jazzy Wes Anderson carpet discoing its way lazily on either side of me, I know I have to do this. I can't bank on anyone having my back. I have to get this thing over and done with now. Taking a life is wrong. There are no two ways about it. In a normal world, normal people shouldn't have to kill other people. My right hand begins to shake. Supporting it with my left, I continue to move helplessly forward because my world is not a *normal* world.

The banging is getting louder. Jayden can't be aware that I'm in the building because he's making one hell of a racket. I plant each footstep carefully on the long strip of red ahead of me. I need to do this, do it fast and give myself not one minute of time for regrets or hesitation.

I swing around the door-frame, raise the knife above my head, fix a snarl on my face, then stop dead. Maggie is standing in front of me, wrapped in a long white coat, her soft, kind features startled into a grimace of shock at the sight of me. A wave of terror passes through my body. A wave so strong, my knees give and my hands, suddenly hot and sticky, melt. The knife clatters to the floor. My chest collapses, and I grab the door-frame to steady myself as the apparition floats towards me.

SITTING IN THE BAR, Julia—Maggie's sister—hands me a whisky. I hesitate for one moment, but only a moment, before knocking the amply filled tumbler back, enjoying the burn of it as it eases down my throat and fills every muscle in my body with a sudden burst of ease.

'I didn't mean to startle you,' Julia says. 'I just wanted to get a photo of the two of us, me and my sister, with Dad.

Maggie had a shoebox with all the old photos. She...' Julia smiles sadly. 'Maggie was a bit of a hoarder.'

I pull the cashmere jumper tighter around my shoulders, one of Maggie's cast-offs. Julia had wrapped me in it because my teeth kept chattering uncontrollably. It wasn't just the shock of thinking I'd seen a ghost. I could have gotten over that easily enough. It was the fact that I'd been hyping myself up to kill someone. Julia doesn't know that, of course, and I'm not about to enlighten her.

'How are you managing here?' Julia glances around the bar-room. Moving closer to me, bringing with her the strong smell of Coco Mademoiselle. There must be some expensive perfume concession on this island because so many of the women here seem to be wearing high-end scent by the gallon. Maybe they smuggle it in over the marshes. The Wreckers certainly has the name of a venue with that kind of history.

'The place, it's...' I don't want to wake any ghosts or invite trouble. In truth, I'm grateful for the roof over my head and the bottomless fridge of food. 'It's okay.'

'You don't find it a bit...' She sighs, flicking her eyes across the gloom of the bar.

'Yeah,' I say. Julia doesn't need to fill the *creepy* bit in. It is creepy, but with creepy, it's always best not to go into too much detail. I don't need to spook myself any more than I already am.

'Never bothered Maggie,' Julia says lightly as she pulls up a stool next to me, pouring herself a hefty slug of alcohol from the bottle. 'Got to go slow on this. The grief's still there in the morning even if I try my damnedest to drown it out.'

'I'm so sorry.'

'Yeah. Me too. You know she rang me the night before.'

Of course, I remember when we came in, Maggie was just putting down the phone.

'She was on edge, well you know what with everything —Davey's funeral, Stan practically knocking you down, and then the whole pandemic thing, icing on the cake.'

'She seemed like a lovely woman.'

Julia shoots me a wry look. 'She was, and the best sister.'

I don't bother to ask for details. None of it matters. I need to be living in the here and now. 'Do you know what happened at Green Acres?'

Julia shakes her head. 'No. I think it's quiz night tonight?'

I don't bother to inform her that there are going to be no answers to the quiz this evening. She'll find out soon enough. I feel a curious sense of belonging; Julia hasn't heard about the latest tragedy, but I'm in the know. 'Apparently, there's a meeting tonight in the village hall. I was wondering where it is. The hall, I mean?'

She waves one arm out over the bar. 'Other end of the high street. Tucked around by the causeway. It's a new building, well, new-old. Forties, I guess?' She helps herself to another slug of whisky as she glances around, a hint of distaste wrinkling her nose. 'This used to be the village hall.'

'So it wasn't always a pub?'

Julia shakes her head. 'No, The Wreckers was always a pub, but they also used it as the courthouse, village hall. Market place if it was raining.'

I feel the shadows closing in as if the ghosts of the past are peering over our shoulders.

'It's where the twenty-five met before they…So legend has it.'

'Oh.'

'Exactly. *Oh.* Yet, Maggie, never had any problems. Never

heard anything or got spooked. Until...' Julia's voice dries out at the edges, allowing a weighty silence to descend.

'Until that last night?'

She nods her head slowly. 'Yeah.' She downs the rest of her drink. 'But, odd times, hey?'

'Too right.' I glance at my watch. It's coming up for six. 'Will you go to the meeting?'

She smiles, a cheeky smile animating her lips. 'Try stopping me. Kev Butcher's the best-known sedative on the planet. One hour in that man's company, and I'm snoring. So yes, absolutely, count me in. Save me from popping a few Temazepam.'

16

COMMUNITY

When we leave The Wreckers, I'm wearing a different coat. I was right. There had been a number to choose from hanging abandoned by the backdoor. Nothing exactly high fashion. A wax Barbour, smelling as if it had just stepped out of a tannery. A plastic rain mac, luminous white, with fabric that squealed at every rustle. Or a long, 1950s button-to-strangulation wool coat in dark blue. The kind of thing you'd wear to the solicitors or for an appearance in court. I went for the long navy coat. I had my hoodie underneath, so I could sink into that if needed: hide my face. If Jayden did have a friend on the island, there was a strong chance they could be at the meeting. Hopefully, the long coat would put them off the scent.

Although walking next to Julia, who is wearing her otherworldly blazing white robe, might not be too sensible. She clearly likes an attention-grabbing outfit. Sadly, it's difficult to say to someone, *can you walk on the other side of the road, please?* Without causing offence. Besides, I'm glad for the company. If Jayden's mate is around, I probably won't have a clue. But if Jayden's managed to get himself by some nefarious means to the island, I'll feel him. I know I will. Those heavy, menacing eyes will be boring into my skull. When people are operating on neutral, they give off very little presence. Jayden doesn't do neutral very often, and currently, he's going to be operating on hate. Hate is an emotion which practically glows in the dark. I'm going to have to trust my senses and stick to crowds as far as possible.

We leave by the front door, its rattle echoing into the lamp-lit evening. All along the street, I can see other people stepping out into the cold, dark night. Feet shuffling by the doorstep as they lock doors behind them, calling out various *How you doings* Fred, Ted, or Mary. Or offering simple, silent nods of recognition.

'Julia,' a man in a dark grey windcheater calls as we pass. 'Sorry about your sister.' His voice trails away.

'I know, Dale. Me too. You know what this meeting is about?'

He shrugs. 'Kev just pushed a note through my door. Said meeting, and...' He raises his shoulders idly as he turns the key in its lock.

Behind us, the tributes to Maggie rustle in the breeze. I wonder how long they'll be left there. How long is decent? Is there etiquette for these kinds of situations?

We walk around the corner. The one that The Wreckers stands on, heading left, away from the harbour wall and the cut through to the high street. Other people ease out of their houses, silently or with a nod to Julia. Footsteps of flat shoes, trainers, heeled boots, and rubber-soled wellies fill the air, forming a persistent soft beat as we move slowly forward in this strange parade.

When we've bent around the corner, leaving its curve behind us, I get a better sense of my bearings. Over this side of the island, you can see the causeway. The one I must have driven over with Stan in what seems like an age ago. Or at least a different life. The low-slung, slightly raised outline of the causeway slithers lazily across what is currently a low belly of water on either side. The thin, straight road looks like a tentacle, reaching back towards the real world. Lights are dotted down its length every fifty feet or so, so that the illuminated sections well with a brief splurge of a glow and then dip into darkness. Reminding me of those pictures taken of the Loch Ness, a series of humps protruding from the waves. But more than the humps, the suggestion of something slithering and moving just out of sight beneath the dark, wrinkled water. The thought makes me shiver. It smells around this side of the peninsula as well. A heavy stink of rotting fish constantly buffeted by the wind towards me. Although, the scent is always there, an underlying decay of unpleasantness. Perhaps fish get washed up, caught on the road to the mainland and can't help but rot. The air feels so heavy you could cut yourself out a chunk.

Ahead of us, standing on our side of the causeway, there's a brightly lit building, a handful of people already pouring from the street through the open door. Their bodies illuminated briefly by the bright exterior light hanging over the entrance. I catch a brief undertone of curiosity. *Know what this is about?* style questions. No one has any answers. Their faces look blank, confused, worn. This lockdown is taking it out of people. I wonder how many of them have heard about Green Acres. That's going to be a blow when it hits. I scan the faces again. People are looking tired but not distraught, not scared. Not yet. Over this side of the peninsula, they must have seen the military trucks arriving. So they'll have picked up that all is not right. If they don't know about Green Acres, there's going to be panic. An outpouring of grief and fear. I'll slip away if that happens. I'm not good with emotion.

As we draw closer to the doorway, a man with a child in his arms, too young to be out this late, jostles my shoulder. I can't help wondering, under the circumstances, is this level of close contact a good idea? Doesn't the virus spread through contact? They must have thought of that, surely.

'Sorry,' the man says as he rights his path, whispering into the ear of the child. 'S'alright, Jamie. We'll get you back to bed soon.'

Jamie has his PJs on under a bright red coat, and his curly, mop-blond hair is still mussed from sleep. He rubs one weary eye, glancing at me as he does. I smile. He doesn't bother to reciprocate.

'So, if you can all take your seats.' Kev is standing on the podium, a notepad in one hand, his thin straggly dark hair still clinging to that shell-white skull. 'You'll notice they're spaced out,' he says, as though trying to reassure us. As though this kind of spacing is seriously going to make a difference. Behind Kev, there's a large screen displaying a real-time feed of a high-backed office chair. A chair that's set somewhere else. In a safe place, presumably. An office, all heavy teak furniture and man-cave.

We shuffle through the door to the hall, sheep-like, confused. The lights seemingly over-bright. The smell of dead fish is even worse in this trapped space. Maybe it once had some kind of commercial use. Other people are also touching their noses, trying to block it out as they search for a place to sit. The orange plastic chairs have been laid in rows, a slip of paper on each alternate seat. LEAVE printed in large handwritten magic-marker strokes. The crowd shuffles obediently into the lines, some of them pulling off the paper. Some of them are wearing masks. One person has even got those blue throwaway gloves on. Despite the formal wool coat, I feel underdressed.

'Mask?' a voice I recognise grabs my attention. It's Charley. Her eyes immaculate beyond a heavy lid of blue makeup. She's wearing a mask herself.

'No thanks,' Julia answers for both of us.

Even though Charley has most of her face covered, I spot the *please yourself* glint of irony that flashes through her eyes. The mask-taking doesn't bother her either way. As long as she's sorted, all is right with the world.

There's a heavy clatter at the entrance. Malik's arrived. He shoots me a *still here* snarl. Only my interest in my bearded "friend" wanes the moment I turn around because suddenly I feel a rising sense of panic. Behind us, stationed on the inside of the door, still as stone pillars, are two large military guys dressed in khaki. Guns slung across their chests. Guns?

'As I mentioned,' Kev's voice calls me back, 'gap between each person.' He points helpfully to the front row, which is already neatly seated in the prescribed manner. Dawn, I notice, is in the centre of the row. She has things on the seats on either side of her just to ensure no one messes with her space. She's also wearing a mask and a set of gloves. I see Leon one row back. He's next to his mother—no space between them. He glances around at me, holding one hand up in a wave.

'Apologies for the call out,' Kev continues.

'You still on for tonight?' a bright voice I recognise whispers from behind us.

We turn to see Rosa. A puzzled look crosses my face briefly before I realise; she's not talking to me.

'I've read it,' Julia says. 'You think it'll still be on?'

'What else are we supposed to do? Die of boredom.' She glances around the room quickly, checking no one's listening. 'Is Miley seriously going to come in and talk about it?'

Julia suppresses a half smile before lowering her voice. 'Is there any way of stopping him?'

Miley has set himself up in a wide space along the wall. A notebook clutched in his hand. He's already writing furiously, even though the meeting hasn't begun.

'Back?' Julia asks, nodding towards the closest row of seats.

I slip into the row, Julia and Rosa following suit.

'Means we can make a hasty exit if needed. Besides...' she whispers, barely audible, taking a pew as a ripple of people turn to offer her sympathetic looks. She meets each one with a small, sad smile. 'All the sympathy is doing my head in.'

Rosa slips a hand into Julia's lap and squeezes her knee.

'How are you holding up for supplies at the café?'

'Fine.' Rosa draws the hand gently back; the support has been noted. 'An army vehicle brings stuff every other day. I write a list. Whatever I want arrives. To be honest, it works better than before. Can you smell something?'

Julia sniffs the air. 'No.'

'Yeah,' I say. 'Rotting fish?'

Rosa nods and is just about to say something else when the high whine of feedback screeches through the air.

'Okay, everyone...'

When I glance back at the podium, the high-backed seat on the screen has been filled by an unsmiling, heavy-jowled man. His military torso blown up to a giant size. His barrel chest sporting a variety of badges and even the odd, glittery medal.

'So, thank you for coming,' Kev barks into the hall as quiet descends. 'We've got a feed directly to Brigadier Morston.'

The man on the screen nods but doesn't smile. I'm not sure what it would take to get a man like that to smile. Even though the image is transported through the ether in millions of digital blocks and reassembled for our "entertainment" miraculously, the impassioned stance of the man appears to have been ferried along with the cold, hard digital information.

I get the sensation of movement from the back of the hall, a door opening, a clatter of heeled feet. I turn briefly to see Erin slipping in. She looks exhausted. The white/grey hair that I know for a fact she spends her evenings winding tightly in rollers, falls in flat unkempt strips across her head. She's lost the hazmat from Green Acres, pulling on a pair of smart jeans, topping the look with a fluffy, mohair jumper. Hand knitted. Although nothing about her looks comfortable and homely now.

The standard issue Covid mask may be doing something to interrupt the impression, but there's more; she looks run ragged and worried. Her fingers flick in over-animated circles against her thighs as she moves quickly towards the front. No doubt, under the impression that she's going to be speaking, but Kev holds up one hand. Erin stops in her tracks before leaning her back against the wall as though waiting in turn. Brigadier Morston clears his throat with an efficient un-virus-like cough.

'As you may realise,' he begins, an air of absolute hush filling the room, 'you are still being held in quarantine while much of the UK has had restrictions lifted.'

'Too bloody right,' a gruff-looking large man shouts.

The father and Jamie combination twitch. The father

placing his hands protectively over poor Jamie's sensitive young ears.

'So come on then, Kev, Brigadier bloody Morston. What's that all about then?' the man from the floor continues.

'Certainly, as Greg...' Kev throws his hand out towards the gruff man, as if introducing him to the brigadier, '...implies, we have questions. It's an odd situation, but...I'm afraid this has become serious.' He lowers his head, the lank hair falling forwards over his eyes. Whatever he's going to say, Kev clearly doesn't want to say it. 'We had a severe outbreak of the new virus today at Green Acres.'

A hushed whisper of panic rounds the room. Although my eyes remain on Erin. She's looking confused.

'Yes,' Kev continues. Glancing towards the brigadier, who nods effortlessly, taking over the conversation.

'That's right. Thank you, Mr Butcher, and thank you, everyone, for coming out tonight.'

'Should we even be doing this—if there's an outbreak?' Bea asks, clutching Leon's hand as if to anchor herself.

'Well...' The brigadier draws in a deep breath. 'Luckily, the outbreak has been contained.'

Erin frowns.

'What about my dad?' A tall thin guy is standing now. 'Greg Tyler. My father's Neil. Neil Tyler. He's at Green Acres. I haven't had any texts from him since this afternoon. He said he needed to talk to me.'

'And I can't get a message out to the mainland.' The man with Jamie fishes in his pocket, holding out his phone to the brigadier as if offering proof.

An air of panic circulates the room.

'Yeah, me too.'

Phones are pulled out, their shiny glass faces examined. I don't bother fishing out mine.

'There's a problem with the radio mast,' the brigadier tells us.

Gruff man is straight back in there, standing now. 'We're not all on the same service.'

'That's right.' Julia draws in her lips, concerned. 'I mean, I can't get a message to work.'

Brigadier Morston holds up his hands. 'Please. The situation is temporary. Be assured your places of work have all been informed.'

The muttering dies down a little.

'For the moment, Green Acres is the concern,' the brigadier continues.

The tall thin guy has sat back down, but he's leaning forward in his seat, his angled body hanging over the empty chair in front, eager to hear all and not convinced he's going to be satisfied.

'So far, the residents are doing well.'

There's a brief murmur, but I don't get caught up in that. I continue looking towards Erin. She's still leaning against the wall, but her face has blanched. Her eyes are cast down, her mouth hanging open in disbelief. When I glance back at the podium, Leon is turning towards me; our eyes lock. What the hell is going on? Back by the wall, Erin's pulling herself together, standing a little taller, about to open her mouth in speech now. Just in time, Leon locks her gaze, shooting his glance back towards the door—the men with guns.

'What about...' Leon gets to his feet, turning back to the screen as if in an interview and about to introduce himself. 'Special Constable Leon Hutchins, sir,' he says.

The brigadier nods, a quick one-beat pulse of acknowledgement.

'Is PC Green working with you?' Leon asks.

'Yes. Of course.'

'So, he's no longer on the peninsula?'

There's a brief pause.

'I'm sure he'll check back in with you when he's ready, Special Hutchins.'

The brigadier hits the *Special* just that little bit too hard.

'Then why are the lights out?' Gruff Gregg comes in sharply. Another rustle of discontent rounds the room. 'All the lights are out at Green Acres.'

'Power cut,' the brigadier says, without missing a beat. 'That's...' he draws out the "s" as if stalling for thinking time, '...been sorted. We're asking you to remain on the island until further notice.'

'But...'

'We appreciate your cooperation with this.'

'Can anyone visit us?' The child with Jamie is looking concerned. 'My wife, she hasn't been back on the island since this thing began.'

The child looks miserable. The man pulls him to his chest, shushing him a little, even though the child is not actually making any noise.

'Visits have not been possible,' the brigadier announces.

'But she lives here.'

'Mummy?' Jamie mumbles.

The father turns to the child, taking his face in his hands. 'Shh,' he says gently. 'She'll be back soon.'

'There is a full lockdown in place. No one has been on the island since the outbreak began, and for the foreseeable no one will be able to get back onto the island, apart from the military. This situation will continue until we are sure the virus has been contained.'

My heart begins racing with excitement. No one, I think, as the brigadier continues, stating that the postal system is still working. Letters can be collected from the café. Rosa rolls her eyes theatrically, her shoulders sloping in a more-work-for-me attitude. But I don't care about any of that. If no one has got on the island since the outbreak, Jayden can't be here. I glance around the room. Malik shoots me an odd look. He's standing beside an old upright piano. One arm leant across it. His large, calloused fingers hanging down over the shiny dark wood. He looks totally out of place and so shifty. Jayden had "friends" everywhere. A network of people. If he couldn't get onto the island, would he have been able to get a message through, instruct a "friend" to check up on me?

'Please be assured we are doing all that we can to secure this situation,' the brigadier drones on, but I'm not interested. My heart, bizarrely, is beginning to feel a whole lot lighter. Jayden's not here. Not a physical presence. Malik pulls his body away from the piano and slinks towards the door.

A couple of people shout out questions to do with loved ones, supplies, phone signals.

The last one strikes me hard. Sure, Jayden has "friend" colleagues, but if there's no signal, how did he get a message in? It must have been that first night. The night that I ran. He'd got straight on the phone and asked people to keep a lookout. He'd have known the USB was missing. So the message would have been something like, locate the girl, find the flash drive.

I watch as Malik, the man who saved my life once, slinks away, guilty as sin. He knows I'm on to him. Then again, what can he do about it? Jayden's text messages will have gone dead. The pressure is off. The promise of money, or drugs, or favours, or whatever it is that Jayden had been offering, that's all been frozen. For the moment, I'm safe.

'If you can make lists of emergency supplies or medicines which are needed and give these to Mr Butcher,' the brigadier continues.

I'm safe!

'Please be assured we will have things back to normal as soon as possible. Thank you.'

The line goes dead. The discontented murmur swells.

Things back to normal. No, I don't want that. This, whatever this is, suits me just fine. Then I remember the bodies at Green Acres. The dead bodies that are now supposed to be alive, simply sick. I may have gotten away from Jayden, but I'm not entirely sure what I've gotten myself tied up in.

'Okay, so...that's it for the moment,' Kev says.

'It,' the tall man interjects sharply. 'What about my dad?'

'Well, the army is handling it, Simon. They know best,' Kev says, attempting to smooth things over.

'So, we just carry on as normal,' Rosa asks. 'Opening the café, going to the book club?'

Kev nods.

'I'm not staying here,' someone mumbles from behind me. 'If it's on the bloody island, this is stupid.'

There's a unanimous scrape back of chairs.

'Please, don't panic,' Kev calls into the air, his voice rising a little shrilly at the end. 'The virus has been contained.'

No one is listening. I get the feeling no one listens to Kev much around here. His suggestions most likely get nowhere. His pleas to the council on planning, or positive peninsular implementations, most likely all sit in a drawer, never read.

Dawn is already up and hurrying towards the door, a look of sheer panic on her face.

'You are free to go about your lives as normal,' Kev insists above the clatter.

'It's not normal if we can't get off the bleeding island,' a woman says, wrapping her coat tighter around her in readiness for the cold air outside.

'Or see our parents,' the tall guy interjects. He doesn't look like he's going anywhere. He's still got questions.

'We should go,' Julia sighs.

Rosa gets to her feet, pushing her orange plastic chair back with her calves. 'Looks like everyone's off work but me.'

'Well, defo for the book club then.' Julia squeezes her hand.

'What are you reading?' I try to put an air of normal into my voice, but I'm scanning the crowd. Leon's headed over to Erin. She's keeping her eyes down, shaking her head.

'Miley's last book,' Julia says as if it's a chore.

'He made us,' Rosa interjects.

I stare over at Miley. He's stopped writing. Instead, he's taken out a slim black object. It looks a little like a TV remote. He's surreptitiously aiming it around the room. Is he recording us?

'Excuse me.' Bea is standing beside us. She gives me a nod of recognition and a brief smile before reaching out for Julia's wrist. 'I'm so sorry about...'

Julia nods, lowering her eyes.

'Lovely woman.'

'She was.'

'I wanted to apologise for not going to the book club tonight.'

'No problem. A lot of people are taking the night off,' Julia says kindly.

'I'll be there for sewing circle,' Bea says gently before removing her hand and walking towards Leon and Erin.

'Is there a club every night?'

Julia unclips her bag, drawing out a tissue. The *sorrys* are getting too much for her. There are no real tears, but her eyes are wet, in danger of spilling over. 'Monday is sewing circle.'

'Tonight's book club,' Rosa says as we squeeze our way out of our line.

'Thursday, quiz night. You get the picture?'

I nod.

'People have to make their own fun around here.' The word *fun*, sounding a little bitter in her mouth.

'Here's the key.' Rosa hands Julia a thick wadge of key rings. They rattle as she passes them over. 'Remember to lock up after, and if there's any…'

'Mud?' Julia fills in the blank. 'Yeah, sure. I'll sweep it up.'

Rosa gives a shrug of her shoulders, easing her large puffed jacket down over her body and pulling up the zip. 'Just drop the keys back through mine on your way back.'

Chatting, they walk to the door, but I hang back. A lot of people left quick. The lowdown on the virus is making people cautious. Only something stinks here, not just the rotting fish. Something is going on. Something weird that the powers that be don't want the islanders to know about. I glance over at Erin and Leon, their heads still locked in conversation. Erin had said she didn't think it was a virus that had whipped through Green Acres. She'd felt it was "natural" causes. When Leon and I broke in, none of the old folks was still standing. The army had removed all the bodies in a refrigerated truck. So it wasn't exactly business as usual up at Green Acres.

'Leon?' Kev calls from the platform. 'Could you...' He waves one arm around the hall taking in the abandoned lines of chairs.

'Sure.' Leon glances over at me. I nod. Maybe Kev has a little more info. Although, looking at his wide open, slightly flaccid features, I doubt it. Whatever lie you told Kev, he'd swallow it whole, tail and all, without even burping up one question.

I start to stack, moving quickly around the hall. Miley's about the only person left. He's got the recording device close to his mouth. I only catch the end of what he's whispering into it...

'An ancient and disturbing dream.'

I move closer to him, pretending to stack, but he's clearly finished whatever it was he was up to. The Dictaphone goes back into his pocket.

'THANK YOU, LEON,' Kev says, offering a kind of salute. 'And, Eve?'

'Yes,' I say.

Leon shoots me a look which I know is a reprimand, but it's easier to live with the lie now.

We tumble out into the street, leaving Kev musing over parish records. This is probably the most action he's had since landing himself in office. He's enjoying the status.

'What was that all about?' Leon hisses to me as we regroup outside of the building. 'They're not just sick at Green Acres.'

He draws one hand over his face, rubbing it back into life.

None of this is good.

'And PC Green?' He sighs.

'Well, maybe old Morston had a point. Green'll be in contact when he can.'

'You don't understand, Ella. He texts me all the time. Not just police business. In fact…' Leon glances around us at the quiet street, the gentle wash of the waves the only sound. 'Hardly ever police business. He asks me if I got home alright? Does Mum need anything? Are we okay for chopped wood? Most of it's not about police business.'

'When did you hear from him last?'

'This morning.' Leon's features seem to hang a little longer on his face. They've lost that boyish playfulness he had when I met him.

I reach out gently and touch his arm. 'He must be tied up with something.'

With his free hand, Leon pulls his phone once again from his pocket.

'He'll call soon. I guess the good news is, my husband can't be on the island.'

Leon eyes me curiously.

'I know this is odd, Leon, but I feel the safest I've ever felt for ten years.'

He looks uncomfortable, and I wish I hadn't said it. People are dying, and all I care about is avoiding Jayden. Instead of being judgemental, Leon being Leon, rubs my shoulder supportively. 'He must be one hell of a bastard.'

I nod, unable to express exactly the full shitshow of how Jayden is exactly that.

17

THE MARSHES

Saying goodnight to Leon, giving him a hug, feels so nice, so warm and caring. Despite the odd lockdown on the island, and the tragedy unfolding at the old people's home, for the first time in my adult life, I feel like a real person, a proper person, not a shadow of someone else. Leon cares about me, and oddly enough, I care about these other people. Whatever is happening here, we have to get to the bottom of it. My bet is still on the military. This whole thing seems way too elaborate for a virus, but for the moment, I'll keep that one close to my chest. At least until I get some more evidence.

After the hug, we go our separate ways; Leon heads home to his mum and his opera. I don't really have a home, and The Wreckers can wait. Besides, the night air feels good. Whatever that awful smell was at the community hall, it seriously got up my nose. It feels good to be out, to be alive, to finally put some distance between myself and the monster I'm married to.

On the other side of the island, the front road, with its low, narrow wall keeping back the tide, seems quieter than dead. The Wreckers is still crouching in the shadows, and the only lights blazing are the ones I left on. Jayden's "friend" on the island has to be Malik. At the meeting in the hall, he'd looked at me as if I'd been marked. I could confront him. Offer him a truce. Some money? Though I'm not sure that would work; he'd left the money scattered across my room. No doubt scared of reprisals from Jayden. Malik's mission would have been to get in, intimidate—foreshadow a taste of what was to come—and then grab that USB stick. It might be worth trying to turn Jayden in. But to who?

The tributes to Maggie rustle as I move past, and I stop for a moment, stooping to pause over the cards stuck beneath the cellophane.

To Maggie, miss you.

My eye catches on a bunch of white Harissi lilies, brown stamens crushed and crumbling in a mucky smudge against their wrapper. A battered, weather-beaten card nestling against the white trumpets.

A joy to all who knew her.

I read the words again. Letting them seep beneath my skin. She seriously was exactly that—a joy to everyone she came into contact with. Loosening the card from its spray of flowers, their scent wafts up, engulfing me, bathing me momentarily in something sweet and cloying. I flick the damp card through my fingers, wondering how people would describe me. The words fail to come. Not a *nice person*, or a *good laugh*, or a *sorely missed.*

No one would ink a card, tuck it into a bunch of flowers and leave it beside a lamppost or even a grave for me. I'm invisible. I'm not even convinced I have enough about me to like or dislike. Leon may have noticed me briefly but walk away from this place, and everyone will forget. I'll be gone as easily as the tide pulling away from the mud twice a day. I glance out over the dark waves, rustling, hurrying downstream. Racing quickly towards the sea. I need to get more presence in my life. Help these people. Stop being the stranger that no one cares about. I tuck the cellophane back around the flowers, a little protection against the wind, but I keep the card. This is something to aim for—*A joy to all who knew her.* It might take me years to get there, but I know one thing for certain: standing alone in the cold night as the damp air seeps into my skin, I want people to speak those words about me.

Walking along the front, I stare in through the houses. Most of the windows are in darkness. A few spilling bright orange cameos into the night for my entertainment; Jamie and his dad huddled on a generous peacock-blue sofa. No doubt, the sofa is a testament to the *lost* wife's style. Its bright shouting colours are too much of a statement choice for Jamie's father—the kind of man who looks as if he would like to be invisible. The book lies open across Dad's arms. Its pages are comfortingly over-large and welcoming. The process of reading, therefore, exaggerated. Dad's face nestles into Jamie's halo of blond curls as he draws the words from the page. Suddenly, the father looks up, aware someone is on the outside. My instinct is to lower my eyes, scuttle on past them crab-like into the dark street, but instead, I raise one hand, nod my head. Dad looks back at me, an air of sadness in his eyes; his wife is still so far away. The world is being turned upside down. Will a letter be enough? He offers me a half-smile in return.

I stop looking into windows after this. I have made a connection, seen a slice of island life. The kind of life I'm on the outside of in so many more ways than just the literal. Increasing my step, I move towards the end of the long link of thatched houses. The harbour wall lies ahead of me. The café to the left. Its lights on. I can see Julia inside, her white coat slung over the back of a banquette. She's setting up for the evening, but the chairs are not formed into the regimented lines of the village hall meeting; these chairs are drawn into a circle. Book club. Although I think it's unlikely they'll be talking about books under the circumstances. It can't just be me that feels we're not being told the whole story. What the hell is going on here? My guess is they avoided telling everyone about Green Acres.

The military is not keen on panic, and they don't know what happened. When the autopsies come back, when they have more information, they'll tell us then. But what about PC Green? Where the hell is he? Suddenly I feel very alone. Perhaps I should make an appearance at the book club. A little village chatter might provide a little slice of normal. I hadn't read Miley's book, but then again, Miley would no doubt bring us all up to speed. Staring out towards the open water, I can see the empty boats tugging anxiously at their anchors. The tide is receding fast now, slithering away like a snake down the estuary channel. I move closer to the harbour wall, careful not to step over the path onto the soft marshes. The lights from the café spill out across the dark water, creating curious rectangles of blinding white light.

Only...

I narrow my eyes, taking a step forward. There's something out there. Lying just outside one of the illuminated rectangles, something is straying up through the water. A tree? I take another step into the soft ground, peering at the corrugated waves of dark water. The air is clearer here; the rotting fish smell gone. Standing on the harbour wall, there is nothing but raw, salty oxygen, carrying with it that undeniable bladderwrack mud taint. The tide ripples fast as I squint into the cold, dark water. There is definitely something poking up above the waves. Something…in the café, a light goes on, another patch of water is thrown into illumination. Instantly, I step back in horror, my heart racing.

'No!' The word escapes my mouth, an involuntary gasp because poking above the rippling tide, waving just about the water's surface, is a hand.

'Help!' I splutter the word so confused it barely leaves my body. The water is fast, unforgiving. I need a life ring, a rope. My mind whirls. I need…I stumble back. My torso thumping into something warm, something large. Turning, I see Miley's inquisitive hazel eyes boring into me.

'There's…' I throw one arm back out into the darkness in a wide ungainly arc. 'We need…'

'It's okay.' He places one hand firmly on my shoulder.

But it is so not okay. Why is he smiling? Why isn't he reacting? This is all wrong.

'There's someone in the water.' I hit each word hard; there's no room for misunderstanding here; we need to act quickly.

Everything about his reaction is wrong. He's smiling, his eyes flickering in an amused fashion towards the wide, watery estuary mouth. 'It's the twenty-five.'

I glance erratically towards the slithering estuary. Is he mad? That was hundreds of years ago. Their bodies can't still be out there.

'A statue,' Miley says calmly, still not dropping the amused tone.

'Statue!' I find it hard to keep the disgust out of my voice. Glancing back out at the receding waves, I can see it now; the hand is fixed, not moving, certainly not waving. It protrudes rigid and still above the water.

'Gormley style,' Miley offers.

I must look confused because he continues.

'You know those statues Antony Gormley does on Crosby beach. Sometimes they're in the sea, sometimes they're on the sand.'

Gormley. It rings a bell. I'd heard something about his work. How they spooked people. Life-sized statues of people standing on buildings or haunting the coast. Well, he'd certainly got me. Was that the whole intention? Some big joke. I stare at the grotesque hand peeking above the deep water.

'So, those are ours.' Miley sweeps his left arm towards what must be the protruding limb. 'Only not Gormley. Obviously. Council couldn't afford him.'

Speechless, I continue staring out at the dark metal hand as the water drops a little more, revealing a slender arm.

'There's not twenty-five either. That was quite expensive. There are seven figures and a series of flat rectangular posts representing the others. That there...' Miley holds up one arm, aiming it at the hand in the water, and narrowing his eyes as if taking a shot, '...that is Madeline Beaumont.'

'The entry in the parish records. The first person who didn't have a date of death next to their name?'

He nods. 'Well done. Yes, that's Madeline. The rest are whoever. Artistic licence. She's the tallest. So we get to see her first.'

The wind appears to have picked up. I'm not feeling confident and at ease with the world anymore. Although I'm not sure that this is entirely my problem; this world is not an easy place to feel at ease with.

'Do you think Madeline led them into the water?' I ask. My voice sounding a little too monotone and lost. 'I mean because she was the eldest?'

Miley draws in a long breath. 'Could be. Impossible to know. Fascinating, though.'

A door bangs somewhere behind us. We both turn together to see the aquarium windows of the café filling up.

'Book club,' Miley offers, and a sense of normality washes over us. To-do lists have the habit of scaffolding even the weirdest situations into place. The twenty-five have been relegated once again to the past.

'You're speaking?'

He draws up a large serious-looking tome which I hadn't noticed he was carrying.

'My last book. Sold over a million copies.'

'Wow.'

Miley allows himself a small, smug smile.

'Exactly. But this next one...'

'It's about the marshes?'

'About Attercoppe, the twenty-five, the pact. This next novel, it's going to be a *Times* Best Seller.'

I don't really know what that is, but it must be impressive and already in the bag because Miley's beaming from ear to ear.

'That's fantastic,' I say because I feel like I should say something. He's looking at me all expectation and hope.

'Once it's written,' he says, coyly.

I'm not sure there's any answer to that. Luckily, he's not looking for one.

'It's just this one bit that I can't get right.'

'Oh?'

He glances down dismissively at his last project as if drawing comfort from it. The book's pages rustling briefly in a gust of wind. 'Writing is a complex activity. The transition of the four-dimensional onto a page. And...' He hesitates, his eyes narrowing as though perusing through a subject he's given a lot of attention to as he runs his tongue briefly across his bottom lip. 'How can you convey something orally toxic?'

'I'm not sure I...'

But he cuts me off, waving his hand as if he's absolutely certain that, actually, I wouldn't have a clue and that his question was rhetorical rather than serious.

'Right,' I say.

'Come along if you like?' He gestures a quick over-the-shoulder thumb back towards the café as he pulls away from me, heading towards the large bright windows and Julia.

'Thanks. I'm good, though.' Whatever Miley is talking about, I'm not convinced I'm interested. 'Fancied a walk.'

He smiles a quick goodbye as he takes another step away. 'Make the most of it while the rain's stopped.'

'Exactly.' I turn to go, but Miley's not finished.

'Mind you don't stray off the path.'

I glance back at him.

His face glints with curious excitement. 'Those twenty-five, they're always waiting.'

I smirk, a kind of got-ya acknowledgement, then turn my back on him, gazing out towards the statue. It's still only Madeline's arm that I can see. Curiously, by what must be a trick of the light, it seems to me as though she's no longer waving, no longer offering a call for help, no. Now I get the distinct feeling that Madeline Beaumont's arm is offering more of an eerie invitation: *join us if you dare.*

Who, in their right mind, would commission a statue so blatantly horrific? I kick on down the road, the stones rumbling under my boots, and I see my answer as I pass the museum. Charley, with her cross-finger lottery money and her forensic way of looking at the past: under the microscope; a dead, inert thing; academically interesting but has little or no room for emotional engagement. For Charley, the past has mutated Madeline and the other twenty-four poor tortured souls into anecdotes for a dwindling tourist trade, as opposed to real people. The lights in the museum are off. The door closed. The sign inviting admittance turned around on its cord, announcing to the world that the museum is closed.

Up ahead of me, the track is empty, all the fishing huts dark, apart from Malik's. Do I have the nerve to knock on the door and try to strike a deal? I could give him the USB—explain the contents. The information is worth a lot: a vibrant underworld trade directory. He could use it to start up a business or blackmail my husband's list of contacts.

Before long, I reach the start of the huts, their weather slats chipped. The bitumen black slapped on so thick that it drools and dribbles down their sides. Malik's hut might be a little better on the presentation front, but that could be because it's where he works; the paint and bitumen did their job, holding it together. He probably didn't have the brains for blackmail. And if he was lacking the blackmail brains, there was no way he would be setting up a start-up. No, the USB wouldn't be my ticket. Unless...I could offer it to him. Malik might be many shades of unpleasant, but he didn't strike me as a murderer. He'd already saved me once.

Okay, so that was an accidental *save*. Most likely, he had no idea who I was when he wrapped his arms around me and hoisted me out of the bog. But if Malik's remit had been to take me out, I'd be dead by now. So I'm pretty certain Malik's deal is petty theft. Criminals who murder are a whole different breed. If Malik knew Jayden was after my blood, would that evoke some kind of sympathy? Or, at the very least, prompt him to realise he should steer clear of this whole little prank. It could get nasty, like fifteen years in a maximum-security prison as an accessory, nasty. I would give Malik the USB. Offer it up freely.

As far as Jayden was concerned, Malik's job would be done. Easy. Only I needed something too. Malik had a boat tied up on the pontoon beside his hut. In that shed of his that he so lovingly tended, he most likely kept an outboard. In return for me handing over the USB, no more hunting around at The Wreckers, no threats, no looking in places that would only ever prove fruitless. Malik would get me off the island. Get me out and away just before this quarantine lifts.

I'm almost at the shed now. A rim of orange light squealing out from the closed door. I'll just knock, present him with my deal, see what he says. He could get nasty, try to force me to hand over the USB, but why? All he has to do is agree to get me out on the next high tide, and I'll hand him the bloody flash drive. There's no point in staying here. These people are lovely, but they're not my responsibility. No doubt the military will have gotten to the root of the problem by tomorrow. PC Green will be back in town, and the quarantine will be lifted. I need to get out.

The large buckets are still stacked on either side of Malik's hut, and there's a makeshift path angled obliquely towards the door. I take a deep breath. Giving my shoulders a shake as though I'm about to go in for a keynote presentation, I tread quickly down the path and knock. There's a moment of absolute silence.

At first, I wonder if there is anyone in there. Maybe he always leaves the light on at night, a ruse to keep burglars' hands off his outboard. Then I hear a shuffle. Heavy feet scraping across the wooden floor inside. I take a step back so I won't be standing nose to nose with him when the door opens. I need to give him his space. I'm striking a deal here, a business transaction. There's nothing emotional that needs to be opened up. We can simply lay all the facts out on the table and find the best-case scenario for both of us. The door flies open, and I feel my stomach knot in sheer terror. Standing in the doorway, framed in the orange light, is the heavy-set frame of my husband. The world stops as we stare at each other in shock. Stare till his lip curls upward into a snarl, and his heavy fat arms swing out of the wooden structure like a jack-in-the-box. I duck, step back, and run.

18

LOST AND FOUND

The gravel on the track scatters under my feet as I run for my life, no longer worried about where the path stops and the marshes start. No long thinking of the mud or the water or the twenty-five. I have to get away. Jayden's growl echoes into the damp air behind me, shocking a raft of sleeping marsh birds, causing them to swoon in a shadowy wave into the dark air, their flapping wings filling the night with panic. I sprint along the path, mud soon replacing the slithering loose, packed stones. The switch is no better, the mud may not be deep, but it slides from underneath me. I need to be careful, I can't afford to slip, and it's hard to see. There's barely any moon, the torch on my phone, even if I had the battery, would only help Jayden pinpoint me. From close behind, I hear the heavy thunder of his boots, hard and unforgiving as the Devil's hounds. He's not shouting, though. There was only that one single holler. Now he's saving his breath and his energy, putting every effort he can muster into closing the gap between us.

My heart fills my ears. The mud grabs at my feet. I have

to push forward, but it feels like I'm running through time itself. I shouldn't have run into the marshes. The café would have been safe. He wouldn't have tried anything if I'd been inside with the others. And yet, deep in my heart, I know that wouldn't have worked. He would have just waited outside in the shadows. He's waited this long. What difference would a couple of hours make.

The path splits. My feet are peddling against the ground so frantically, my mind racing along with them, that I've lost all sense of direction. If I go on, turn right, will I come to the water? Or is this the same path that doubles back around and ends up close to the café, the path I'd stepped away from when I'd ended up in the mud? I'm not sure. The only thing I'm certain of is that I've been here before. I'm convinced this junction had a path heading off into fields, a path that could now be an escape.

But if I end up taking the wrong track, ending up in the mud...There's no time to hesitate. I glance back over my shoulder. I can't see him. The reeds are high here, but I can hear him. Closer and closer he comes. I need to get off the path. Stepping into the cold, dark water, I pray to God the mud will hold me. My foot squelches a little but doesn't sink. I squat down in the reeds, the cold squeezing the air from my lungs as I ease my body nervously away from the track, groping into the watery edges of the marsh.

Suddenly a thin hiss of pain slices into my finger as I grope into the long grass. It could be teeth. It could be that thing I had felt slithering under my boot outside the inn. The pain is sharp, clean. Replacing the need to scream with another action, I bite down hard on my bottom lip. Not a noise, though. I cannot afford any noise.

Only my mind won't rest.

As I wade further into the water, my imagination has set

itself on conjuring nightmare images as fast as if they're on special offer, a two-for-one, bulk order deal. Images of eels with razor-sharp teeth, rats or worse. Pulling my finger back, I peer at the pain centre. The light is poor, all definition is lost, but when I rub my other hand across it, the pain bites again. Wood? It's a splinter. The pontoon! There had been an old pontoon here. I slide my muddy body quietly across the weeds, every squelch, every rustle sounding impossibly loud. He'll hear me. I swear he'll hear me. I need to hide better, sink down more.

Thankfully, after only a few moments of groping blindly, I feel it—a wooden structure, rickety and hard. Somewhere I know won't sink. Carefully, I ease my body across the wooden slats, placing a hand over my mouth to quiet my breathing. My wide, wild eyes stare back towards the path just as Jayden stumbles out of the darkness.

He stops, his angry body slumping a little as he takes in the two tracks. His hands flapping at his sides, thumping his forehead.

'Fuck,' he spits into the reeds. A slice of warm gob lands beside my fingers, and my body shivers. Tilting his head for a moment, he listens. Listens hard. I refuse to make a noise. Closing my eyes, reaching my fingers across the wet wooden structure so I can grip it hard, I anchor myself. It's going to be okay. He can't see me. It's going to be alright. Suddenly, my left hand brushes something soft; an animal? Not an animal. Surely not an animal. Not a rat. No. Please no. Jayden's still there, still listening, waiting hungrily for my one wrong move. Cautiously, I turn my head. I need to know what the creature beside me is. Not knowing is worse.

There's something beside my left hand, something white, shining luminous in the moon. A dead fish? I need to push it out of sight. If Jayden sees it, he'll see me. I press the thing gently. It tilts, rotates, flips around, and I feel bile rise in my throat as I gag. It's a hand. In horror, my eyes follow the line of an arm, a shoulder, a face. Two wide glassy eyes are staring straight at me, shining out into the night—PC Green.

'Fuck,' Leon says, opening the door to the shed and letting me tumble in. 'What the hell?'

'He's here.' I gulp. 'I just...I...' I'm dripping everywhere. So wet and cold that my teeth are chattering.

'Wait, wait. Calm down. Shit.' Leon glances from the mud caked on my boots to my clothes to my body. I'm a mess, but never mind the physical stuff; the emotional is overwhelming.

'My husband, he's...'

'How?'

I shake my head. My words are barely audible; my breathing is so erratic. I'm hardly in control, just wanting to collapse, to cry, to curl up in Leon's over-warm shed and sleep.

'And Green,' I blurt.

'What? You saw PC Green?' There's an excited hope in Leon's eyes.

I stop. How do I deliver this? I feel the warm tears trickling down my cheeks. 'I'm so sorry, Leon.'

I take a shower in Leon's shed. It's caravan style. Despite having first-hand experience living in a trailer, this is the smallest shower I've ever seen in my life. I can barely flex my arms to apply the soap, but I don't care. The mud runs from my body down the sinkhole and away. I wish everything could be sorted this easily. Outside I hear Leon pacing. He's lost interest in the opera. In light of Green's death, I'm not sure he knows what to do with himself. Well, that makes two of us.

When I come out, the shed is empty. The curtain between the bed/bathroom bit has been drawn, and Leon's laid out some clothes at the bottom of his mattress—jeans, a jumper, a fresh hoodie. I glance nervously out of the darkened windows as I dress. Jayden will be after me. He won't have worked out where I am; he doesn't know Leon, but this island isn't big. By tomorrow, he'll have narrowed down the options.

'I got you some things.' The door opens, and Leon comes through carrying a bundle, a sleeping bag, a flask, a torch and a small backpack. 'You can't go back to The Wreckers. That's the first place your ex is going to look, but my place is too easy to break into. I wouldn't feel you were safe if you were staying here.'

'So, where?'

He takes a deep breath as if knowing his answer is going to cause resistance. 'Green Acres.'

'What!' I don't need to see my face reflected in the mirror to know that it's gone a ghostly shade of luminous.

Leon reaches out a gentle hand in an attempt to reassure me. 'I know. I know. But think about it. No one is in there. The bodies have gone.'

'Are you sure?'

'Certain. I watched them load up the last few.'

'The army let you?'

'No. I just watched from the bushes.'

I take a seat on the sofa, sinking into its haphazard cushions. 'What about the virus?'

'Oh, come on.' Leon takes a pew on the coffee table opposite me. 'That's all BS. Whatever they died of, it's got nothing to do with some lightning-fast Covid strain. Something deeper is going on here.'

I bite down on my lip. Does my hunch work? Is this something to do with the military? Could that be why they're being so cagey? 'How about if this thing's happened before. Say the military is involved somehow.'

'Seriously?'

'Maybe the ground is toxic.'

Leon shakes his head. 'Then I'd be dead too or have two heads.'

'Not funny.' We don't have time for jokes.

'I'm not sure. Toxic?' He shakes his head as though dismissing the thought. 'People here live a long time. Normally,' he adds.

'Okay.' Maybe it doesn't fit. But the military has to be involved. 'What about PC Green?'

'What did he look like? Could it be murder?'

I shake my head, unwilling to go there because if it is murder, then my husband is absolutely in the line-up, and why is Jayden here? Me. It all comes back to me.

'Ella?'

'Sorry.' I have to tell Leon what I know. I owe him that much. 'He just looked dead. I don't know how long he'd been in the reeds, but he was covered in mud.'

'Yes, but could it have been a murder or maybe, I don't know, something like a heart attack?'

I glance into his eyes. He's so desperate for answers. Gently, I reach out towards him, taking his hand in mine. 'Leon, I'm so sorry, but I have no idea.'

Leon pulls his hand away. He doesn't want comfort or sympathy. He just wants answers. 'Okay. I'll try and round up Erin. We'll go out and find him. We need to find out what happened.'

'The body was just where the path forks.'

'Yeah. I know it, by the pontoon. Don't worry. You just get yourself to Green Acres, there's snacks and water and everything in the bag, and a sleeping bag so you...'

I know what the missing words mean, *so you won't have to steal a dead person's blanket.* Even so, the thought of going back to the old people's home fills me with dread. 'Are you sure it's the best place?'

'The military is still outside. Your husband's not getting in. Just go the same way we did last time.' Leon stands, letting out a long exhale of air. None of this feels like fun. The relationship that I had been so proud of, the friendship that was blossoming, that's all been hijacked.

'Do you think you should tell Kev? Tell the brigadier?'

Leon shakes his head. 'They don't care, Ell. Nobody cares now but us. Whatever is happening here, I get the feeling the military just wants it over quickly.'

'What do you mean?'

'Let's just say—if we all disappear, there are no questions.'

19

THE SECOND CLUSTER

I break in through the same window we used earlier. The smell of disinfectant is overpowering, hitting my senses in an ammonia rush. Every surface in the kitchen is spookily immaculate. No one has been cooking here for a while. Not even a pot of tea. They've all gone. Out in the hallway, there are a few muddy footprints on the carpet. The only sign that the military came through is the door to the chapel, which has been left standing open, as though insisting that there is nothing to see there. The room beyond the door is empty.

I had been careful not to go around the front of the building towards the car park and the road. I can't afford to be spotted. Leon was right about one thing: Jayden's not getting in here. Once inside, peeping from one of the darkened front bedrooms, Mrs Thompson's—if I'm to believe the small wooden nameplate on the door—I can see the line of armoured vehicles still out front. Two khaki-clad squaddies pace up and down. Their movements exaggerated, like they think no one is watching. One of them, a woman, her dark brown hair fastened in a knot at the nape of her neck, is doing a silly walk. I wish I could do something daft, something extravagant, a gesture which was all about life and fun rather than fear. Do they know what's going on here? Somehow, I doubt it. They're bottom-rung military. They'll be as much in the dark as we all are.

I head for the cupboard, the one where they store the chairs and tables. There's a gap between the furniture. A kind of corridor. It's narrow, just enough space for one person to sit or lie. Laying the sleeping bag down across the floor and stashing my backpack onto a stack of chairs, I pull the cupboard door closed from the inside. If anyone comes in, they won't find me. For tonight, at least, I'm safe.

WHEN I WAKE, I have absolutely no idea where I am. Everything around me feels odd. There's metal pinning me in place, and the air is thick, heavy with my regurgitated breath. Then it all comes back. I'm hiding in the cupboard at Green Acres. Hemmed in by folded plastic tables on one side and neatly stacked towers of chairs on the other. Safe. Only, I can hear something, someone else. Barely audible. A hissing noise.

'Ella. Psst. Psst.'

Leon! I push myself up and throw open the door.

'Seriously?' He laughs.

'You're not the only one who likes small spaces.'

He nods. 'Can I come in?'

We sit on the unrolled sleeping bag. Torch on. Our backs to the wall. We're so close we could practically be one person. I don't care. I want him close; I need something human to hold on to.

'So you found him?'

'Yeah.' Leon glances down at his hands, tumbling his fingers over and over as if searching for some inner beat to help him make sense of this mess. 'Found him right where you said.'

'I'm so sorry.'

He doesn't even try and meet my eyes.

'What did Erin think?'

'She's as confused as we are.'

'The virus?'

He draws in a long, low breath. 'She thinks the virus is a load of baloney. She thinks...' And he fixes me with his deep brown sincere eyes. 'Nah.' He waves a hand dismissively in the air.

'Leon. What? She thinks what?'

'I mean, this is bog standard mad.'

I grab his hand, pumping it between mine as though the action will somehow force the truth out of him. 'It's all mad. You have to tell.'

He sniffs. 'Okay. You asked for it. She thinks it's to do with the pact.'

The air seems to cool a little. I feel caught off balance somehow. 'What do you mean, the pact?'

'So, in the fourteenth century...'

I drag my hand through my hair. 'I know all this. 1350, the villagers make a pact with some kind of mud demon so they wouldn't catch the Black Death. In 1425, the demon comes back and makes their descendants pay.'

He glances at me, surprised. 'Yeah, that's about it.'

'But, Leon, how can that and some mythical demon have any effect on what's happening today?'

'Exactly. Exactly what I said only...'

'Yes?'

'Only Erin told me that all these people, right, they're all keeling over from different causes.'

'Yes?'

'It was Davey, then...'

'Stan and Maggie.' I start to fill in the names.

'Then Doctor Dancey and PC Green, well, he goes missing. They're kind of all in a cluster.'

I don't like where this is going. 'Just because they came into contact with me?'

'No, yes. I'm not sure. I...' He hesitates. 'I don't think you've got anything to do with it.'

'Good. Because I feel fine.'

'Me too, and if you had it, then why aren't I dead? No, it's got to be something more. Do you remember what Terry said?'

I think back to the sweet old deaf guy in the red jumper, to his insistence that we were in danger. 'He thought something was off—the phones were down.'

Leon nods eagerly. 'Not just that. He said that Davey remembered something. He remembered something his parents had said just before they died.'

A shiver passes over me as though someone has just skated over my grave because some of these bits of the jigsaw seem to be coming together. 'Stan said something too, the night I met him. It was odd...'

'What?' Leon flips his position, pulling himself from the wall so he's facing me.

'Stan got spooked. In the pub the night before he died. He started talking about Davey and how he'd been having this...' I glance at Leon. This all sounds so mad.

'Go on.'

'He'd been having this dream. A bad dream.'

Leon looks genuinely puzzled. 'What happened in the dream?'

I shrug. 'He didn't say. I went off to see Doctor Dancey. Stan got left back with Maggie at The Wreckers.'

A light of realisation flickers through Leon's eyes. 'He told Maggie the dream.'

'I'm not sure. She was on the phone when we came in.'

Leon's leaning forward now, eager for every word. 'Who to?'

'Oh, I don't know, Leon. Does it matter?'

'Maybe.'

'Julia. Julia said Maggie called her. It must have been her sister.' Then it dawns on me. 'That's not all. Miley said something odd today, something about a thing being orally toxic.'

Leon looks blank. 'What does that even...'

'Like a curse. Like a spell you pass on through repeating it.'

Leon's getting to his feet. 'Did Stan tell PC Green about this...' He hesitates. 'This dream thing?'

I shake my head. 'I don't think so. No, at least not when I was with him.'

Leon brushes his face with his hands, trying desperately to bring all the information together.

'Wait. Wait.' I can barely contain my excitement. 'The doctor and PC Green.' It's all coming back to me now. 'The night before Doctor Dancey died, he told PC Green that Stan was concerned about something Davey had said.'

'What?'

I shake my head. 'I have no idea. Erin ushered me out of the room. Maybe she knows.'

Leon looks thoughtful. 'I'll ask her.'

'Wait.' Suddenly it hits me. 'I left my phone on, recording. It might be on the phone.'

'Shit.' He cups his hands over his mouth. Excited. 'Well, go on, play it.'

Grabbing my phone out of my pocket eagerly, I glance at the screen. There's just a little battery left on it. I hit play. Doctor Dancey's voice fills the air: *It was just really strange. Stan said he had this dream about...*'

There's a loud electronic ping—a message coming in. Not on my phone, though. I hit the pause button. Leon glances at his screen. 'It's Erin. I've got to take it.'

I nod, and Leon turns away from me, which is a bit daft seeing as we are both in the tiniest space on the island, but I guess he just wants privacy as he hears the news from Erin, a little time to digest whatever it is she has to tell him.

'What!' His voice is shrill.

I can make out a mumbling sound from the other side of the connection. There's a brief pause.

A frown cuts through Leon's forehead. 'All of them?' More mumbling. Again he twists his body away. 'Fuck.'

'Leon?' Anxiously, I move towards him. Desperate to know what's going on, but Leon simply holds one hand up, pushing it towards me as though to silence me.

'Okay.' He nods, still not speaking to me, drawing in a deep breath. 'I'm coming. Have you called the military?'

The voice from the other line mumbles on, although I can't catch the words.

'Right.' Leon looks down anxiously at his shoe, although I'm not sure he's seeing it. His mind is far away. 'Okay.' He nods, decisively. 'Keep it between us. I'm on my way.' He flicks the phone off. 'Ella, I've...'

'Got to go?' I say simply.

He nods. I get the feeling he's avoiding looking at me.

Whatever this is, it's bad. Even his face looks different: drained. Older. The youthful curiosity has gone. Now he's just scared.

'What's happened?' I say, my voice barely above a whisper.

When he looks back at me, I'm surprised, and unnerved, to see tears pricking his eyes. 'Bodies,' he gasps. 'More bodies. In the café.'

'The book club,' I murmur.

'What?' He looks confused.

I draw in a deep breath, willing it to support my words. 'They were meeting tonight. Julia...'

The breath hasn't worked; my words dry as suddenly the thought comes full frontal in both our heads.

'That tape,' he says cautiously. 'Don't listen to it.' He stares at my phone as though the small, slim handset is radioactive. 'Just.'

My hands flit through my hair, as though they have no purpose anymore. Every inch of me feels lost. 'What should we...?'

'Nothing,' Leon says, decisively. 'Not yet anyway. It's still dark. Can you meet me at my place?'

'Sure.'

'An hour.' He hands me his keys. 'In case you get there before me, but the tape...'

'I know,' I nod, 'no listening.'

20

AUDIO FILES

It's four o'clock in the morning by the time I finally get to Leon's. Breaking out is easy. The guards still aren't bothering with the back of the building. Their remit is most likely: guard the entrance, don't let anyone in through the door, bare your teeth and growl if necessary. So far, they're not being put to the test. Not yet. The sleepy community of Attercoppe are still working on trust mode. But it's early days.

Leon's hut is warm and comfortable. The exact opposite of my cupboard. I make myself a cup of hot chocolate. Pull the crocheted rug from the back of the sofa and curl up on the wide cushions of the couch. The upholstery is worn, loved. No doubt relegated from the main house when Leon set up shop here. I imagine Leon and his mum and dad, PC Green even, all sitting, laughing, drinking, seeing in Christmases, and celebrating birthdays. That was all gone now. Although Leon was still lucky, he had his mum, a woman that he loved and one that loved him right back.

So, despite all this, Leon was in a better position than me. Come to think of it, most of the planet was in a better position than me. I slouch back into the arms of the sofa, pulling the crochet rug up and over my head. Hoping Jayden's somewhere sleeping.

About an hour later, I wake with a start, sitting bolt upright as the door clatters open, punching a blast of cold air into the room. For what seems like a solid five minutes, Leon just stands in the doorway, hands across his mouth, a look of pain and hurt flickering over his eyes.

'Leon?'

He comes through the door, closing it behind him on the cold, mist-riddled too-early morning, bringing into the room the smell and feel of a cold, damp frost that's seeped into his clothes. I pull my legs up underneath me. Shawling the blanket around my shoulders, allowing him space to sit. Leon's knees seem to buckle as he sinks heavily onto the couch, plunging his face deep into his hands.

'Well?' I ask, barely able to contain myself.

'Dead,' he mumbles.

This doesn't make sense. Instinctively I find myself pulling the blanket a little tighter across my body. 'The book club?'

'All dead.' His hands drop to his sides, tears staining his cheeks.

My mind spins. 'You notified the military?'

Leon nods. 'Yeah, at least after we'd checked it out ourselves.'

'What did Erin think?' My voice sounds desperate, because the information isn't coming quickly enough. I need more.

'Erin?' Leon asks. His voice way too languid as though he's swallowed a bucketful of Valium. 'Erin's confused. It looks like everyone died of natural causes.'

'What?' It doesn't make sense.

Leon stares into my eyes. 'Yeah, only...' He hesitates. 'Not necessarily the same natural cause.'

I nod, awkwardly. 'So, like the others?'

He echoes my nod, only his is over-slow, exaggerated. 'And then,' a glint of bewildered amusement flashes through his eyes as he pushes himself back into the cushions, 'we're standing there, Erin and me, surrounded by bodies. She's wearing the whole white kit and caboodle, when Miley walks in.'

My eyes narrow. 'The author?'

'Yeah, seriously.' Leon shrugs, bemused. 'He just saunters in. I mean, he pretends to be shocked but...'

'You're not buying it?' I sit forward a little on the couch. 'Leon?' I reach out one hand, touching him gently on the shoulder. Willing him to continue.

He glances awkwardly towards me, placing his elbow on the wing of the sofa, taking a moment to rub his furrowed forehead with his angled arm. 'The guy knew. I can't prove it, but I swear...'

There's a brief pause. I remember earlier in the evening, standing watching Madeline Beaumont's sculpted arm emerging from the waves, Miley at my side. 'He was supposed to be speaking this evening,' I mumble.

Leon turns towards me, his face searching mine.

'At the book club,' I say. 'They had been reading his book.'

'He didn't tell us any of that.' Leon looks puzzled.

'So what did he say?'

Slowly, Leon runs his palm across his top lip, trying to remember the exact sequence of words Miley spilt. 'Okay, so we're standing there. Miley comes in. Kind of says *oh my god*, type stuff.'

I nod. 'And?'

'And...he keeps a safe distance, but he's not reaching for a mask.'

'So,' I say eagerly, 'he doesn't think it's viral.'

'Maybe.' Leon's eyes glint as he places all the pieces together. 'Then he tells us he left his notebook at the café, grabs it and makes a hasty retreat.'

'Notebook?' This seems odd. 'You didn't try and stop him?'

Leon recoils. 'Hey, me and Erin, we're too messed up to care. He could have emptied the till. That wasn't our concern. Anyway, that's not the point.' He shoots me an irritated look. 'The point is, then we hear this groan.'

'Someone was alive?'

'Barely. Have you met Karen Dench?'

I let my mind flit back through all the characters I've come into contact with since I got here. The name doesn't ring a bell. 'Don't think so.'

'Postmistress. Well, turns out she was alive and just itching to speak. She stumbled out of the ladies. I mean, it wasn't pretty. There was blood oozing out of her nose. Erin went to her straight away. Got her into a booth. We kept telling her not to worry, keep calm, but she was so keen to say something. Her eyes...' He shudders at the memory. 'They were tiny, these dark pricks barely visible, and the smell.'

I remembered the odd smell in Stan's car, then again at the home, then at the meeting, and something else—lots of women wearing way too much perfume. 'What did she say?'

'Nothing that made sense. Julia had had a dream.'

'That was what Karen the postmistress told you?'

Leon nods. 'She'd had a dream. Maggie had also had it.

Julia said she was going to write it down.' He stares at me, still confused. Unable to process the events.

'Where is Karen now?'

Leon shudders. 'Dead. That was it. Blood started spurting out of...well, everything.'

For a moment, we say nothing. Leon looks shattered. This is all way too much, but we have to make sense of it. I know that now. If we're going to survive, we need to work out what's going on here, and quick.

'Leon?'

'Yeah?'

'You said Julia was going to write the dream down.'

'That's what she told us.'

'And Miley came back for his book?'

Leon's eyes glitter with life. 'Shit. Julia wrote whatever it was down in the book. The thing that is...what did you say earlier?' He scratches his head. 'The thing that is *orally toxic*.'

'Exactly.'

'This, whatever it is, spreads by word of mouth.'

Leon pulls out his phone, flicking through his texts. The last message from PC Green.

I read it over his shoulder. It's simple. To the point:

– *Need to talk. Out by boat shed around three.*

Leon lets the phone slip from his fingers. 'We have to stop this.'

I couldn't agree more. 'Yes, absolutely, and then I need to get off the island. This, whatever it is, it's not my only problem.'

'Yeah. Did you say your husband was in Malik's shed?'

'That's where I saw him.'

'Wouldn't surprise me. Malik's always up to dodgy deals.'

'He'll kill me if he finds me.'

'Okay, so we need to stop that happening. Hey...' His

eyes light up. 'Say we got this *toxic oral event* to your husband. Delivered it to him. That would get rid of him.'

It might be a good idea, but it's way too complex. 'We'd have to get Miley's book, then surely read it to Jayden. Does it only kill you if you then pass the thing on to someone else?'

Leon looks uncertain. 'I think, maybe initially, it works like that, only this thing feels as if it's gathering speed. The book club, they hadn't passed it on. Maggie told Julia over the phone. She died pretty soon after releasing it. Almost like Maggie was the host, and once it left her, it had no more use for her. Julia must have told everyone at the book club as she wrote it down in Miley's book. But this thing is gathering force now. It doesn't need you to pass it on anymore. It's going to take you anyway. Why not try and use it to do something good before we shut it down?'

There is no way this is going to work. 'Jayden's not going to read Miley's book. He barely reads a newspaper.'

'Not the book.' Leon glances at me, barely able to contain his excitement. 'The recording.'

'What?' I'm not following.

'Your phone. You've got a recording: Doctor Dancey telling PC Green about the dream that Stan related to him. Davey's dream.'

'Which Davey had overheard his parents talking about in the 1950s, but because he was a child, he forgot it.'

Leon nods eagerly. 'Davey was just a kid. Shortly after he overheard the dream, his parents died, and then the military took over the island for a bit. There was so much confusion going on, Davey put it out of his mind.'

'Till he didn't. What woke the memory?'

Leon shrugs. 'Who knows. The point is, it is awake and getting stronger.'

'And you think the same thing happened to the twenty-five; that's why they committed mass suicide?'

'Has to be. They knew they had to stop it.'

I pull myself from the sofa. This is all going too fast. It's crazy, then again... 'You seriously think it would get rid of Jayden if he heard it?'

'It's worth a try.'

I pull my phone out of my pocket and check the recording. 'It's three minutes long. If Jayden were to hear it playing, he'd investigate after the first thirty seconds. He'd probably have smashed the thing in a hissy fit before a minute was up.'

Leon gets to his feet, grabbing the phone from my hand. 'I can isolate the bit where Dancey tells PC Green about the dream.'

'Not without hearing it yourself.'

But Leon's not listening. He's Bluetoothing the audio file to his computer. 'If I separate the audio files, pull Dancey's voice from Green's, I should be able to select just Dancey. I can take out any pauses...' The Bluetooth connects, the file starts to upload. 'Get it working, so I've just got the story.'

'Leon, you can't. This is hopeless. You'd have to listen to the thing.'

He shakes his head, wide, over-exaggerated sweeps. 'Not at all.' He kicks his stool out from under the console and takes up his place. In one sweep of the fingers, he drags my audio file into his editing software. A series of channels fill the screen. 'This is it here.'

The tube-like channel turns green. I can see the waveform—a series of peaks and troughs.

'I know this is going to sound strange,' Doctor Dancey's voice mumbles from beyond the grave courtesy of Leon's speakers.

'You see, that's Dancey.' Leon scoots the cursor down the track.

'*What do you mean? A dream,*' PC Green asks. His voice so open and innocent to listen to it feels painful: a terrible imposition.

'Now it's easy.' Leon pushes his chair back in. His shoulders rounding, cave-like, around the widescreen. 'I identify the voices. Separate them into different tracks. Cut down Dancey's track till I'm pretty sure all I've got on it is the toxic oral event.'

'The dream,' I say, feeling as if my thoughts are being pushed and torn in all directions, and not one of them makes any sense.

Leon flicks his fingers idly over the console. 'Some bloody dream.'

'Then, after taking it to Jayden, you'll destroy it.'

He nods. 'Absolutely. I won't listen to the thing. I'm going to go solely on waveforms, then stick the recording under his door when he's sleeping and leg it.'

'What about Malik?'

'He doesn't sleep there. He should be fine. We'll have to go back later. Destroy the tape.'

I smirk. 'You can't get it to self-destruct all by itself.'

He laughs. 'Nah. Sorry.'

I place my hands on his shoulders, staring at the lines of deathly green audio on the monitor. 'Why are you doing this, Leon? You barely know me.'

He brings his right palm over his shoulder, placing it across my left hand. 'To be honest, with this current shitstorm we've found ourselves in, if we can bundle a bit of something helpful in with all the crap that's going down, it'll help to cope with the bad stuff. You go back to Green Acres. I'll text you when it's done.'

'Do you think he'll just drop dead on the spot?'

'The book club did.'

I can't help it. I feel an unbelievable sense of relief—I'll be safe at last. 'Okay. You know where I am.'

'Sure.' His voice sounds flat, distracted. He's already itching to get on with the work.

21

THE BEGINNING OF THE END

It's still dark as I cut back across the footpath. A heavy mist clinging to the air, making everything grey and soupy. I haven't had enough sleep. My limbs feel weary. The horror of this small place is catching up with me. How can a book club just drop dead? I can easily imagine a different world, one which is sitting on the other side of the causeway. A place in which I have no idea that any of this is happening. If Jayden hadn't taken that wrong turn, where would I be?

Still in danger, I realise ironically.

Jayden and I had been working on borrowed time. All the scams I'd been involved with were dead and tired. Nobody answered the phone anymore. I'd served my purpose. He didn't even try to have sex with me these days. When the sex dried up, that was the point where I knew the clock was ticking on our relationship, and he wasn't the kind of guy to let a woman slip away quietly. There had been someone before me: Irma. Eastern European, I think. Not that he mentioned her. I'd caught her name in snatched conversations sometimes when I'd first moved in.

'No Irma, then?'

'That one's plainer than Irma.'

'I liked Irma better. She knew how to smile.'

That kind of thing. Two weeks later, and the Irma talk died. Initially, I'd thought she'd run off. Now I'm not so sure. I found a bracelet once with her name on it. The kind of thing you can wear every day without taking off. Only it wasn't attached to her wrist anymore. Driving me into the woods that night, did Jayden have any intention of bringing me out?

When I see the blurred lights of the military vehicles, I push up onto the balls of my feet and quiet my breathing as I continue on past, hidden by a strip of field and the foot-path hedge. Sounds from the guards carry towards me in misty wisps. They're talking about what they're going to do at the weekend. They seriously haven't got a clue.

When I ease the kitchen window open and flop my body through onto the cold, hard floor, the smell of bleach hits me again. This place is way too chemically expunged to be healthy for anyone. Never mind bacteria. Human life is going to be struggling. I wander back out into the hallways, which stand strangely empty. The door to the chapel is closed. Someone must have been in. I need to be careful. It'll have to be the cupboard again. Nobody will go looking for anything in there. I curl up in my sleeping back, and instantly, I'm fast asleep.

I wake to a metal chair leg poking into my back. I've somehow wedged my lower body under the pile. I take a while to orientate myself, glancing at my wristwatch. It's 10.00. I can't remember the last time I slept past seven. There's a message on my phone from Leon. It came in at 5.30.

– *Done.*

Done. I feel a wonderful sensation of freedom. I hope it worked quick and that Leon was right—Malik doesn't sleep in that shed overnight. Leon had seemed certain, so it should be okay. It had always been a case of Jayden or me. Only one of us was ever going to walk away from all of this. There's another text:

– Tomorrow, think we need to get out. By boat if necessary. Can't trust the military. Meet me. My place.

This is all music to my ears. I get to my feet, bumping into the chairs, the tables. There's not much room in here. Pushing open the door just a crack, I peer out. The light is so bright. The cupboard isn't set full-on to the windows, but the windows are large, and it is daylight. I can't go out. The military will still be parked up. I'm going to have to lie low until darkness.

Emptying the bag that Leon gave me, I'm pleased to see I'm well prepared. There's food: biscuits, a little bread and cheese, a few bits of fruit. I also have the flask and a bottle of water. A bottle which, at some point, I'm probably going to have to pee into. Never mind. I'm alive. I take a bite of the apple as I flick on my phone. Damn, the battery is flat. I don't have a charger. It's going to be a long day.

By four thirty, the crack in the door informs me it's getting dark outside. Dark enough to move out of my hiding place by five. I've managed to avoid peeing in the bottle, but my first port of call is going to be the toilet. There are two off the entrance. Male and female.

I duck into the ladies, which is, of course, pitch-black. I switch on the torch that Leon had packed for me. That guy thought of everything. Glancing in the mirror, I realise I'm a total mess. I tie my hair back and splash water on my cheeks. There's a glug in the pipe. I'm quick to switch it off. Stupid, how stupid. If someone had been in the building, they would have heard it. I stand for a moment, listening. Then something else. My heart sinks—a flush. I hit the off button on the torch. Once again, I'm in darkness. None of this is good. Someone just pulled a flush.

Somebody is close.

I glance around me. There are only two cubicles. In the darkness, I can see their rectangular shapes. The doors to both of the stalls are standing open. The sound must be coming from the gents. I flatten back into my cubicle. Stand on my seat and wait. Outside, I hear a door swing open and someone shuffling away. I sigh, letting my breathing switch back to normal; one of the patrols must have come in, maybe to check, but more likely, just to relieve themselves. I need to be careful. I peel the door back and peer out. It's empty, all is quiet. Quickly, I cut across the carpeted hallway to the kitchen. Examining the rim of the door before I step through. There are no lights on. I should be safe.

The kitchen is untouched. The army must be taking its food elsewhere. So far, so good. As I move through, I notice an abandoned phone charger, plugged in and waiting. Ten minutes. If I just juice up my mobile a little, I'll get a much better picture of what's happening outside Green Acres. I attach the phone, slink my back down against a cabinet so I'm crouched on the floor and wait. I manage to wait ten minutes before eagerly grabbing the handset.

There's a message from Leon:

10.20 – *Need to talk.*

I'M ABOUT to reply when it hits me. I scan the words once again, this time with a gut wrench of nausea—isn't that how it always starts? People needing to talk. People itching to spread that dream. Leon is in danger. I can't waste any more time. I need to get to him. The charge will have to be enough.

'HERE, LEON,' I say, stating the obvious as I push back the door to his shed. Only the room is empty. The bed made, the throw on the sofa with immaculately tucked corners. The sound desk, however, is a different story. Dirty plates, coffee cups, drained glasses. He must have been up all of last night working on the sound tape. I flick on the computer. I can see three lines of audio. One is labelled: Dancey—Dream. I put the cursor on it and backspace. It's gone. We have to make sure the damn thing doesn't get out. Hopefully, he's already gotten rid of the tape he had taken to Malik's.

If, indeed, he did manage to get there. I go to the recorded file on my phone and remove that, too. This thing has to die. After my brief spurt of action, I realise that I have no idea what to do next. There's no point in wandering all over town. Leon will be back soon. The need to talk could be totally innocent. Perhaps he seriously does have something he needs to tell me. Did he manage to play the tape to Jayden? We do genuinely have things that we need to talk about. I'm jumping to conclusions because I'm on edge. Leon has to be fine. He knows about this thing and how to avoid it. I might as well tidy up the snack detritus. I pick up a mug, its contents long and cold, but as I do, a slip of paper falls to the floor. A note. I bend down and grab it. Placing it on the stack next to his computer, but as I do, I happen to glance at the top: Ella. My name is written there, in bold letters, underlined.

This note's for me.

Sinking down in Leon's swivel chair, I scan through the lines.

ELLA

I'm so sorry. I played the tape into Malik's hut. Didn't need to leave the device, so have deleted. Only then, I was so tired when I got home. I fell asleep at the console, had my Bluetooth head-phones on. Must have accidentally hit play. I know what it is, Ella. I know the dream. It's terrible. It's like an itch. I want to tell you, want to tell Mum. Want to shout it to anyone who'll listen. I've got to get rid of it. We have to make it stop. I'm going to do it in the right way. Hope it works. Get my mum out, Ell. Please, God, get her out before she hears.

SINKING BACK INTO THE CHAIR, tears sting my eyes. I can barely breathe. Not Leon. Surely not Leon. I glance back through the note, the lines blurring as I read again and again. What did he mean—do it in the right way? How can you make this thing stop until there's no one left standing to hear it? Suddenly, it hits me: the twenty-five. Whatever Leon's about to do is somehow connected with them. I run from the shed as if the Devil and all his helpers are on my back. I have to get to the front, to Leon.

As I spring along the front, I see that the water is coming in, lolling in greedy waves around the shore. I run out towards the harbour wall and the café. Its lights are dark. Devoid of all its regulars with their chatter and banter and moans. Instead, now there are strips of yellow police tape over the door.

On any other day, it might hit me as sad that this community hub has sealed up its doors, but today, I don't care about the café. Instead, I step across the path onto the mud, searching the water. There's a boat bobbing recklessly over the waves, abandoned and untethered. I shine my torch out to it, the beam only just reaching the white hull. It's empty. But I can hear something, someone calling. I sweep the torch across the dark water. My eyes catching the haunting sight of Madeline Beaumont's slim arm sticking above the waves, her face held at a hideously proud angle. But that's not the worst thing. There's so much more to come—Leon is clinging fast to the arm. His mouth sinking into the water.

'Leon,' I call, stumbling forwards and looking for a boat. I need to get to him.

'Ella, I have to...' The waves wash into his mouth and splutter.

'A boat, I need a...'

'The dream...' he manages again.

His eyes look manic, and suddenly I step back in horror; there are other people out with him. No, not people. That's wrong. These are dark shadows crawling over the statue. Actually crawling.

'You have to...' Leon splutters again.

I don't know what the shadows are, even though I realise now that I've seen them before. When I got in Stan's car, I thought I'd seen something. Again in the pub that first night. I could have sworn there were people in the shadows. Then again, at Green Acres. Hideous shadows of death. No faces, just skinny arms and legs that trap and stalk.

'Leon,' I sob as his head disappears under the water. I

wait, wait for another word, another clue, unable to pull myself away from this macabre scene. But he doesn't resurface. The water has swallowed him whole. Even the dark shadows seem to have gone, evaporated into the waves. Did I really see them? Now I'm not so sure.

'Eve?' I feel a small tug at my arm and turn to see Charley standing behind me.

She still looks immaculate. However, there's an edge to her now. The confidence she had only yesterday appears to have evaporated. Instead, her face is drawn, pale, haunted.

'You can't do anything,' she says gently as she pulls me away.

'My name's Ella.'

'Fine,' she mumbles, not a whole heap interested, and suddenly I realise how unimportant all of this is. Details have been brushed aside because there's only one thing that's important anymore, the basic thing, the one thing that unites us all—survival.

WHEN WE GET to the museum, I notice that the window has been broken, there's glass all over the floor.

'I have an app on my phone,' Charley tells me as we move through the door, away from the elements. 'It said there was a break-in, so I came to investigate.' I notice it's not just the window; some of the cabinets have been broken into as well. Charley props a piece of hardboard against the broken window causing the elements to quieten down a little.

'What happened?' I ask, my voice sounding far away. Haunted still by the image of my wonderful friend sinking beneath the waves.

'According to the CCTV footage, which I've scanned

back through, Leon broke in. Grabbed the chains from the exhibition.'

'Chains?'

'The ones the twenty-five supposedly used.' She draws her small, immaculately painted nails anxiously through her chignoned hair. 'I mean, Leon, for Christ's sake. And then out in the estuary. What the hell is going on here?'

I say nothing, still trying to fit all the pieces together.

'I've texted PC Green.'

'He's dead,' I say, my voice sounding unnaturally flat.

Charley stares at me in horror. 'What. How?'

I take in a deep breath, not sure where to start or how to tell this. 'Do you have anything to drink? I mean, something seriously strong?'

WE SIT in Charley's office: a storeroom out the back. As it turns out, Charley is a vodka drinker. It tastes like nail varnish to me, but I drink it anyway as I run over the story. I start at the beginning because this whole thing is way too odd to start anywhere else. Davey overheard something as a child. Some kind of virus that's passed in a story about a nightmare. I expect her to gip a little—*virus* and *story* seem like two words which shouldn't be dancing together. Yet, Charley takes it all in her stride, leaning forward a little in her chair so she doesn't miss a beat.

'Anyway,' I say, taking a large breath. 'Davey's parents died shortly after, so he had a lot on his plate. He was just a kid. He put it out of his mind. Only recently, he remembered it, and he told Stan.'

'Then Davey died?' She looks at me curiously, her

forensic mind already trying to piece together the bits I haven't got to.

'That's right. Then Stan had it, the story, or the virus, or whatever it is, and he told Maggie and Doctor Dancey.'

She nods thoughtfully.

'Only now it's going faster. It seems to…' I clear my throat. 'I think it may be able to kill groups of people en masse if they hear it.'

She sits back at this, narrowing her eyes. 'What do you mean?'

'Green Acres, they're all dead, and the book club.'

'Sorry, Green Acres. I thought they had Astrapi?'

'Erin doesn't think so. The military has taken the bodies.'

There's a brief pause.

'And the book club?'

I nod. 'Last night. Leon told me.'

'And now Leon…' She stumbles over her words. 'Leon chained himself to the statue. Hoping to get rid of it?'

'No. I don't know.' Tears force themselves into my eyes yet again. I can't let this happen. I can't become a blubbering mess. To stop them, I grab the vodka bottle and pour myself a hefty slug. The liquid burns my throat. I cough.

'Eve. Sorry, Ella?'

I nod. 'Leon must have heard the story. He…he knew he would have to tell someone; it's like an itch. You can't stop yourself.'

She taps her foot gently against the floor as if the action might rally all the facts into some kind of digestible package.

'What I can't work out…' I say, 'is how it started. How did Davey remember?'

To my surprise, Charley seems to suddenly lose all composure, slumping forward in her chair. 'I wonder…' Her normally cool, sterile voice catches with emotion. 'I was doing this project. Feedback for the…' she waves one extended finger in the air as if encircling the building, 'funders. We've had a lot of lottery funding. They like to have concrete outcomes.' She reaches forward, grabbing the bottle and pouring herself a hefty slug. 'I interviewed Leon about his opera. I don't know if you…?' She glances towards me.

'I've heard it. It's great.'

'Yes, and inspired by the museum, more specifically, the landscape. Leon's equipment was all part of the grant. An attempt to capture a sense of place. Leon spent months recording sounds. They're all built into the music, layered through.'

'Sorry,' I say, shaking my head a little too widely. 'I just cannot see how this fits in.'

Charley glances guiltily at her hands. 'I let Davey hear it. He, he seemed disturbed.'

'You think Leon's music allowed Davey to access the memory?'

She draws in a deep breath, her shoulders swelling. 'Yes.'

I had expected some kind of argument to back it up, some kind of justification. Only Charley left the comment hanging in the air between us.

'I don't see how the music could…'

'Don't you understand? If there is some kind of demon or evil force connected to this place, it's in the air that we breathe, the sounds that we hear. It is the place. Leon distilled that. It wouldn't have mattered normally. The dream, or story, or whatever it is, would have been lost, but Davey had heard it once before. The music woke it back up.'

I'm surprised at Charley. I'd thought she was all science and no imagination; turns out you can have both. Luckily, she's also super organised. I tell her about the shadow people and the smell, two things that I'm pretty sure are connected to anyone who has caught the virus. She promises she'll round up people in the town, at least those she thinks are still "innocent". Bring them back to the museum, then we'll make a case to the military— we need to get off. I've also got a few things to do myself. I left everything back at Green Acres.

Promising Charley I'll grab Leon's mum on the way back, I head out.

Cutting back across the footpath, I find I'm still haunted by the wild look in Leon's eyes. If it hadn't been for me asking him to help get rid of Jayden, Leon would still be alive now. I know I can't afford to wallow in that kind of negativity. Now is not the time. If I live through this, I'll have a lifetime to fill up with guilt. But I promised I'd get his mum out. That has to be my focus now.

Going through the kitchen window at Green Acres is fast becoming normal. I'm even managing to land on the hard-tiled floor without the slightest discomfort. The place is still in darkness. I feel sure questions will have been asked today. Townsfolk will have arrived at the entrance. The army will have fed them a line again, dispersed them, but that can't go on forever.

I move quickly out of the kitchen into the hallway, checking it before I pass the toilets. I know the army is using them. I can't be too careful, but everything is silent, no sound of the pumps singing into action. I'm alone. The front room is all shadows. I cross quickly to the cupboard, swing open the door and see my stuff exactly where I left it. Rolling the sleeping bag back up and collecting what's left of my food, I put everything in my backpack. I'm ready. I turn to go, but the door bangs open, and everything happens way too quickly to even think as my feet are being pushed backwards, and I'm slammed forcefully back against the wall. Large fingers wrap tightly around my neck, my breath being squeezed from my body. Jayden. Bloody Jayden. Why isn't he dead.

'Thought you'd get away with it.'

I can barely breathe.

'Bitch,' he hisses. His slug-like lips coming towards me. His words hissing into my ear. The fingers on my neck tightening, tightening as I grasp and grab, only it's all futile. There is no air left in my body. All I can hear now is my heart beating in my ears. My vision blurs. I'm going to faint. No, I'm going to die. It's all...

Suddenly, Jayden falls away. There's a smash of plaster wheeling through the air. I blink my eyes, throwing a hand across my face for protection as Jayden slumps down at my feet, convulsing, and behind him, I see a small, thin old man in a red jumper.

'Terry?'

He raises his hand again. A knife clutched between his fingers. For one terrible moment, I feel sure he's going to bring the blade down on me.

'Terry! It's me.'

He stops. The hand with the knife lowering slowly, uncertainly, to his side.

'You're alive. I saw the red jumper and...'

Terry waves his arms, dismissing the comment. I get the idea that he's not the only man over seventy who likes red. Instead, he signs—*Are you okay?*

I nod. Running my fingers across my neck. Glancing down at Jayden, his large dying body lying at my feet. He's convulsing. His breathing is off, filled with rattling and splutters. A thin trickle of blood oozes from his ears, his nose, his eyes.

We need to go, Terry signs, and I'm happy to follow.

IT'S late by the time we get back to the museum. I'd expected to see around fifty people. To my utter amazement, it's just a handful. Miley, Rosa, Erin and, to my irritation, Dawn. She even stands back when she sees me as if she's still blaming me for whatever is happening here. I've got two people to add to the mix: Terry and Leon's mum, Bea.

'Is this it?' I ask as we crowd into Charley's office, where the blackout blinds have been pulled.

'I did the test,' she says simply. 'It's just as you said, Ella. Those shadows are creepy. You can spot them even when the lights are on full.'

'And the smell?'

She wrinkles her nose. 'Yeah. Not always, but one or the other; the shadows or the smell, sometimes both, and there's a hard vacant look to the eyes.'

'So what now?' Bea asks. I haven't told her about Leon. It would have slowed her down. 'Where's my son?'

Charley shoots me an irritated look. She doesn't want to deliver the news any more than I do, but she's braver than me. 'He's...gone, Bea. He caught the virus. I'm sorry.'

Leon's mum stumbles slightly. Erin takes her gently into her arms, lowering her to a chair, keeping her eyes held firmly on Charley, encouraging her to go on.

Charley coughs awkwardly, fixing Bea once again with her eyes. 'I don't know if you've been told about the virus. Its MO.'

Bea's crumpled face stares back blankly.

'How it operates,' Charley clarifies.

'A little.' Bea's words are slow, deliberate, as though still running things over in her head and not coming up with any answers. She dabs at the corners of her eyes with her fingers, not even bothering with a tissue to wipe away the tears. 'Through stories?'

'Kind of. Possibly through the retelling of a dream. A bad dream.'

'A nightmare,' I say, as instantly, another piece of the puzzle clicks into place. I turn to Terry, my hands itching to sign—*That's how you avoided it the last time it hit?*

Terry nods. When I turn back, I realise the rest of the group is looking at me intently.

'Terry didn't get it the last time,' I explain, 'because he can't hear.'

Terry signs again.

'What's he saying?' Dawn's voice comes quickly. Full of irritation.

'He says he's not sure if he is totally immune. The lack of hearing seems to help.'

'This is all just stupid,' Dawn blurts. 'It's the virus. Astrapi. We know what it is. That army guy, Brigadier whatsit, he told us.'

Everyone turns sympathetic eyes towards Dawn. She's not totally dim, though. She spots the pity, and it makes her bristle.

'Well, whatever this thing is.' Her voice sounds pinched, hard and insistent. 'I haven't got it. I'm going to walk over the causeway and tell them. They have to take me away from this bloody place. I've had enough. Seriously. They can't keep me here.' She's shaking, not with fear, though, with a kind of repressed rage.

Terry starts to sign. He must have got the gist. Everyone waits politely till he's finished.

'Terry says we shouldn't trust the military,' I translate. 'They'll be wanting whatever it is to die out on the island.'

Bea looks up. Her eyes red with silent crying. 'You mean waiting for us to die out?'

There's an awkward, heavy moment of silence.

'It's the army. The army,' Dawn insists. Throwing her arms down at her sides. 'If you can't trust the army, who can you trust?'

Erin sighs, wearily running her fingers through her greying hair. 'They lied to you once. Everyone at Green Acres is dead.'

Dawn's mouth drops open, then, as though to prove this simply cannot be possible, she stares at Terry.

'Apart from Terry,' I say, 'because of the hearing thing.'

'Well, I'm still going, and you can't stop me.' Stroppily, she gets to her feet and walks towards the door.

'Look,' Charley takes a deep breath, 'maybe Dawn's right. Maybe we should try to go across the causeway. At least test it out.'

Dawn shoots us a satisfied look.

'Only,' Charley continues, 'I'm not sure Dawn is the right person.'

'Seriously!' Dawn's going for full-on righteous indignation.

Charley pinches her lips together, realising she's going to have to tread carefully. 'You're very emotional, Dawn. A little...' she hesitates over her words, 'unpredictable, perhaps under the circumstances. They see you coming across the causeway looking worried, it might just...unsettle them,' Charley says diplomatically.

'I need to get off.' Dawn's speaking through gritted teeth

now, her puffy childish face twisted into that bullish look of determination I'd seen before as she flounces towards the door.

'Wait.' Charley grabs her arm. 'I feel somewhat responsible for this...situation.'

Erin and Bea stare at Charley curiously.

'I think the memory of this thing, well, I may have inadvertently woken it up.'

'You can't seriously...' Erin goes to protest.

Miley, on the other hand, is all ears. 'Woken it up?' He's leaning into our little huddle, suddenly wanting more.

Charley simply raises her hands with the attitude of someone needing quiet. 'It doesn't matter now. But perhaps Dawn's got a point. We should try the simplest course of action first. Why don't we all go to the meeting hall? I can try to walk across the causeway, get them to talk. Then Dawn, as soon as we're convinced they're willing to listen, I'll beckon you over. So I talk, but I promise you, Dawn, you'll be the first to get off the island if they do let us out.'

Dawn thinks it over for a good minute.

'Okay,' she says sullenly. 'But I'm definitely first over the line.'

22

ESCAPE

We walk in groups of two around the causeway side of the island. I don't want to be paired with Leon's mum. I can't even begin to tell her how sorry I am. Terry seems to want to stick with me. Perhaps because he can at least communicate. Although, having said that, he's surprisingly quiet. Then again, we're all apprehensive. The thought of someone shooting out from one of the doorways and wrestling a *story* into our ears is as odd as it is scary. I'm relieved that the rotting smell appears to have gone. Was the smell ever that of dead fish, or was it, in fact, a dying community?

When we arrive at the hall, Charley has all lights off, but the blinds are open. Through the windows behind the podium wall, we can see the causeway; its intermittent lights pooling across the road.

'No trouble?' she asks.

Terry and I were the last ones in. 'We didn't see anyone, and you?'

Charley shakes her head. 'Not a soul.'

We pull enough chairs for our small group off the stacks at the side of the walls and sit huddled in one corner.

'So,' Charley says, clapping her hands together as though bringing the meeting to order, 'I'm going to try and get across. If they're amenable, if they recognise that we're okay, haven't got the, whatever it is, I'll call to the rest of you.'

'Me first,' Dawn jitters.

Not for the first time since I arrived on this island, I find myself wanting to slap her.

'What's the worst that can happen?' Bea says dully with the weary attitude of someone who's already seen the worst. 'If they turn you away, we just stick together till this thing blows over.'

'Exactly.' Charley pushes back her chair. 'Okay. Wish me luck.'

Initially, we watch from the darkened window as Charley steps out onto the causeway, but Charley hasn't walked more than a handful of metres before Dawn has other ideas. She wants to be closer, so we all troop outside and stand on the steps of the meeting hall at the end of the causeway in a line, watching Charley grow smaller with each step. It seems to take forever. Her small but confident frame is about three-quarters of the way across when we hear a megaphone booming out over the water.

'Please return to the island. For your own safety, return to the island.'

Charley holds up one hand as if asking for calm. She glances back over her shoulder. Dawn is chomping at the bit, easing her feet forward onto the tarmac. I'm not sure that Charley can see Dawn properly, but no doubt she'll have an idea of what's happening this side.

'We want to get off,' Dawn shouts, her shrill voice echoing into the watery air.

Out alone on the causeway, Charley gently flaps one arm as though asking for calm and leans forward a little. I think she's saying something to the guys in uniform, but her voice gets caught in the wind and carried away. The words lost. Most likely, she's telling them we're not infected. We know what the threat is. We understand it, but we're not carrying it. She takes another step forward. Again, the megaphone booms out across the ripple of dark corrugated waves.

'Turn around. Turn yourself around now and head back.'

Charley stops, leaning forward once more, gesticulating with her arms as though speaking, before taking another step.

'Stop,' the megaphone booms.

Charley hesitates. Glancing back over her shoulder before looking forward towards the mainland and *freedom*.

It's then that everything goes belly up. I feel it in a cold rush, a premonition of disaster. A sound that, at first, I can't place but I know shouldn't be happening. It's Dawn, her heavy uncoordinated feet hammering down the steps of the meeting hall and across the causeway. Everything about Dawn's hasty exit looks grotesque and desperate. She's waving her arms in wide circles above her head and shouting. Looking ugly, needy and totally unhinged.

'You've got to get me off,' she shouts. Wails. But those are the only words we catch because a rapid fire of guns drowns everything out. On the causeway, Charley's body slumps to the ground. Dawn ducks down, too, as if hiding, but we know she's fine; she's still wailing. Charley, on the other hand, is perfectly and absolutely still.

'My God.' Bea's eyes are wide in horror, her palm clasped over her mouth.

Erin pulls us back behind the shelter of the hall.

'They just…' Miley stumbles, unable to process what he's just seen. 'They shot her? They…In cold blood, they just…'

I glance back out at the causeway. Dawn has gone. She must have run back to the darkness of Attercoppe.

Erin reaches out, grabbing my hand, grabbing Bea's so that we are all standing in a neat but bereft circle. Her eyes are deadly serious, her voice low as she spells out each word.

'We need to be careful. They have no intention of letting us out.'

Miley's breath is sticking in his throat, a look of panic flickering erratically over his hazel eyes. 'We could row. Get a boat.' Between each brief burst of words, he draws in a rasp of breath as though grasping for ideas in the wake of disaster.

Rosa shakes her head. 'The marshes are treacherous, especially at night.'

'And…' Bea wades in, her features heavy with worry and grief. 'These people might be idiots, but they're not amateurs. More's the pity. They'll have lookouts on all the main tributaries.'

Terry moves forward, his hands working through the air. The others look at me expectantly. I turn towards him, focusing on his luminous fingers as they move with an urgency that has us all mesmerised.

'Terry says *he's been rowing the marshes since he was a boy.*'

He nods, then continues.

'He says *there's a channel out to the old military buildings.*' I take a step back. 'Military buildings, seriously?'

He reaches for me. Working his hands once again.

'*Disused,*' I translate. '*Opposite The Wreckers.*'

He must be talking about the crumbling underbite of white buildings I'd seen on the other side of the water. I shake my head. 'I saw a light on over there.'

He looks thoughtful. Then begins again. '*Did it wobble?*'

'A bit.'

He smiles. '*Fishermen,*' he signs. '*They won't bother us.*'

Erin nods, worried but satisfied. At least we have a plan. 'We can take Malik's boat.'

Bea glances out at the causeway, and Charley's body slumped in a lifeless heap on the road. Two men in hard hats are sauntering towards it. 'We need to avoid the outboard.'

'He has oars,' Miley says. 'He took me out once.'

'How about if Malik's there?' I have to ask. I'm not exactly sure what terms Malik and I have left things on.

Erin raises one long, neatly plucked eyebrow. 'If he's not infected, he comes. If he has it...'

Terry picks up the thought, signing into the darkness of the night. '*We wait till he's not a problem anymore. Only...*' Terry glances out of the window. '*We don't have that much time. Five hours and it will be light. Lighter. Light enough to pick us off like sitting ducks.*'

WE SPLIT UP AGAIN. Travelling in small groups is safest. I get to buddy up with Terry. Erin's insistent that she and Bea do a quick sweep of the island. See if they can spot Dawn or anyone else who has slipped through our hasty search. Rosa and Miley are dispatched quickly, so they can check out the boat situation. We agree to meet near Malik's shed. Near enough to see if he's in it and if he's safe.

Terry and I are the last to leave the shelter of the

meeting hall. I glance at the noticeboard as we turn our backs on the building; the list of activities: knitting, sewing, woodwork. Most of them would have triggered hot spots for the virus, ideal conditions for flare-ups. Was Charley right that the landscape itself was the demon? Or was there something more physical lurking in the oozing muddy wash? The thought sends a cold swell of fear through me. It, whatever it is, doesn't bear thinking about.

Hurrying down the low steps that lead to the road, Terry's signing. I glance towards him, but we don't stop. Five hours may seem like a long time to get off the island under cover of darkness, but we've got to get the boat, get us all in and row all the way across that cold, fast-flowing water.

'*Are you alright?*' Terry's asking me, his face full of concern.

'Yeah. In shock, but okay.' Strangely, I don't even feel tired. No doubt the rowing will put paid to that.

He looks thoughtful as if I haven't really answered his question, but instead of pushing it, he simply pulls his anorak tighter around him as if whatever he's got on his mind can wait. We move past The Wreckers. The lights still beaming out onto the street, just as I left them. It would be safe to go back in, to retrieve anything I'd left, but there wasn't much there anyway. A spare set of clothes. If I did get out of this, I could find something somewhere. Clothes are the least of my worries right now.

We push on along the deserted street. Terry beginning to lag; the adrenalin must have seeped out of his body. The full weight of the situation is finally sinking in. I ask him about Green Acres, what happened, and he tells me that at first, he'd tried to get help, then he'd realised there was no point. It was all happening again, just like when he was a kid, only this time, it was happening fast. He went to the church in the village and prayed. He said he couldn't think of anything else to do.

When he saw the armoured vehicles go past, he thought it best to wait. He saw the refrigeration vans go one way, then an hour or so later, he watched them go back, heading towards the causeway. He knew then that there was no way off. The army had the island under a different kind of lockdown than anything most people had ever seen before. That was when he decided to go back to Green Acres. The time I thought I'd heard someone in the cubicle next door that must have been Terry. He'd been hiding out, unaware I was nipping in through the window in the kitchen and hiding in the cupboard.

Being far less nimble, Terry had left Mrs T's French window on the latch. When he heard someone stampeding through the building, he thought it must be the military. But one peek out of his hiding place in the library had shown him something odd: a man buzzing with anger and hate, striding through Green Acres. Terry wasn't going to get involved, but then he heard a woman gasping for breath. Me.

'Bit of a hero,' I say, squeezing his arm thankfully.

He shakes his head, moving his hands slowly in front of him, forming words. *Sometimes you just have to act.*

He hadn't realised it was me being strangled. That was most likely why he had hesitated when holding the knife up high.

'I thought for a moment you were going to get rid of me as well. The look in your eyes.'

Terry turns his face to me, a look of sadness written over every inch of his drawn, wrinkled features.

'Yes,' he signs.

He must have been scared, in defence mode, and just not recognised me.

BY THE TIME we get to the hut, the others are already assembled, and I can't help but feel a lurch of irritation at the sight of Dawn. Why does that woman continually keep cropping up? Couldn't they have just left her? Luckily, she's not whinging.

Rosa is already on the pontoon, kneeling on the wooden slats and unhooking Malik's boat. Erin stands and strides out of Malik's hut, an oar resting over each shoulder.

'Was he in there?'

'No,' Bea says, bent double over a large bag that she's stacking with water bottles and snacks which Miley's bringing out of the café.

'Have they cleared the bodies?' I ask. An involuntary shiver passing over me as I remember those aquarium windows and Julia setting up for a village meeting that would end up killing her.

Miley gives me a blank look.

'The book club, they...'

But of course, he already knows this. I get the feeling that we haven't got the full story on him yet, and something about that worries me.

'There's no one there.' Miley hands me a water, offering me a thin smile.

Personally, I think the provision thing is way over the top; we're not planning on being out there for a week.

'We need to go,' Rosa hisses. She's holding the boat now, her body leaning out over the water from the rickety wooden platform, ready for us to step in.

'Go on,' Erin says kindly to Dawn, who's already pushing her way towards the boat.

'She knows to be quiet, right?' I hiss.

Bea touches my arm. 'It'll be okay.'

I have my doubts. We're an odd bundle of humanity. If you were to choose who you were going to save, I'm not sure our names would even make it through to the reserves list. Maybe Erin, a nurse. Nurses are always useful. Possibly Bea —she's done nothing wrong, the grieving mother and a dab hand on the food prep front. But the rest of us?

Dawn steps into the boat awkwardly. It jerks under her weight, and she loses balance. Gasping as she rocks.

'Careful,' Rosa shouts, holding on to the thing with all her might as the boat continues bobbing erratically.

'Aww!' Dawn stumbles, falling across the wooden seats. Luckily, Erin still has hold of the oars.

'Shh!' Erin whispers from the shore, her arms out and wide, flapping gently in a *keep it down* attitude.

From the low bobbing boat, Dawn stares up at Erin. Wide-eyed, scared and for just a moment, she gets my sympathy. These are extreme conditions.

I brush down the pontoon past Bea, moving quickly towards the back of the boat, dropping to my knees and reaching out over the water from the rickety structure and pulling that up to the wooden dock so that the edge of the thing runs along level with some kind of solid structure. The boat stabilises. The slap, slap, slap of the waves against the prow calm.

From our knees, Rosa and I stare up at the others. We need to get on with this. Dawn adjusts her weight onto the far edge of one bench, and one by one, we all climb in, keeping a gap on either side of the boat for the rowers. Rosa appears to have bagged the job of rower one. There appears to be no question on this, and the way she handles an oar, even without it touching the water, demonstrates she's at ease with the whole thing. I'm surprised when Erin thrusts the other oar into my hand. I thought Miley would go for it, but he's hunkered down at the stern next to Dawn, clutching his coat around him as though he's in danger of freezing to death.

'I'm not much good,' I whisper.

Erin smiles kindly. 'We'll make do.' Without any additional comment, she moves on, handing out black blankets, draping them over us all in the hope that somehow, this added strip of darkness will keep us safe from prying eyes and gun scopes.

'If we can get out past the middle,' Erin says, gazing into the darkness, 'they won't know which side we're coming from. We'll be safe.'

The middle seems like a long way as the cold water snakes around our small boat. It's fast too. We could easily be carried off course. If only we could use the motor. But I know that's not an option, the noise would attract too much attention. I glance over at Rosa. She's seated beside me, our inside shoulders touching, our faces so close. She turns and gives me a nod, indicating to hold my oars higher out of the water. We don't want anything dragging us back around. Both oars raised, Bea gives the pontoon a little push, and our boat slides out into the night.

'They just shot her,' Dawn says. Her voice sounding small and stunned.

'Shh.' Terry holds his finger over his lips before signing.

'*Sound travels over water,*' I whisper.

Dawn pulls the dark blanket up over her ears. Her face a picture of stubborn misery and shock. Half of me wishes I could sink down under a blanket, but I get the feeling we don't have much time. Rosa's oar is already dipping down towards the dark water. I follow suit.

Rosa's stroke is better than mine, more efficient. I have to hold my oar up over the water with every other pull to stop us from turning around in circles. Drips off the raised oar fly back in the wind, and speckle my face. That water is like ice. God forbid we capsize. Terry's at the bow of the boat. His arm pointing out across the water, showing us the way. Bending us expertly through tributaries we wouldn't even know were there. I can't see the crumbling military buildings on the other side of the estuary. Not now.

There are no lights, but at least Terry seems to know where we're going. We cut through the water, none of us making a sound. So it's even eerier when suddenly, we hear a noise. We're only fifty yards from the shore. But something, someone, must be standing on the shore. Calling? I raise my oar, Rosa does the same, and anxiously, we run our eyes along Attercoppe's streets.

'You hear that?' Erin whispers.

Rosa and I nod. But what, what did we hear? Then see it: a door is standing open. A yellow light pouring out. I know that door, that house. It's Jamie's house. The blond kid who I'd seen reading a book with his dad after the meeting.

'Don't stop,' Miley hisses. 'We can be heard from this distance. They could shout at us.'

At first, I think he's got his words muddled. He means *shoot us*. Then I realise he wasn't talking about the military. Miley means that the infected inhabitants of Attercoppe could shout out the dream over the water at us. Sink us with nothing more than their voices.

Dawn instinctively blocks her ears.

Only it's not Jamie's father stumbling out into the night. It's the small, huddled, lost shape of a child. His blond head bobbing above the blanket he's wrapped himself in. His hands clutching a battered brown bear. He stands in the street, watching us silently.

'Damn,' Rosa says, pulling her oar in towards the boat. 'We've got to get him.'

'No.' Dawn's breath comes in a series of loud gasps. 'He could have it.'

'Bound to.' Miley shakes his head sadly. 'If his dad's got it…'

I'd seen how close the father/son unit had been, sitting wrapped together on that peacock-blue sofa, their faces pressed together as if they were joined while they had pored over the open book.

'He can't have it.' There are tears sliding down Bea's cheeks. 'Please, God, no.'

She's kept it together so well under the circumstances, but the thought of one more child dying this evening is just too much.

'We need to go back,' Erin says decisively.

'No. No,' Dawn rasps.

'Shhh,' Terry hisses. His eyes wide.

'I'll go.' Decisively, Rosa lowers her oar into the boat, unzipping her coat. 'If he's infectious, I'll…' The words dry on her lips. She takes in a deep breath. 'Then you lot head off without me.'

'But you're the fastest rower,' Miley says. 'We'll never make it without you.'

Rosa shoots him a look, one eyebrow raised, as though asking—*okay, so you go.*

'I…I…can't swim.' Miley clutches his stomach. I'm not sure why. Perhaps it has something to do with him not being able to swim; even the thought makes him feel nauseous. Maybe that's why he's panicking so much. Being on the water scares him.

'I'll go,' I say.

Terry squeezes my arm gently. A thank you, I think.

Quickly, I pull off my large coat, noting how greedily Dawn eyes it.

'And if he's infectious?' Erin asks.

I glance back at the shoreline to the small solitary figure standing there with his bear. 'Then you are going to have to go on without us.'

Erin nods. There's a moment of silence, and then Terry leans forward towards me, his hands signing quickly but clearly.

'What's he saying?' Miley asks.

'He's telling me to swim downstream slightly. Outside of The Wreckers, it looks like mud, but that's just silt. There are rocks under the mud.'

'Hence the name,' Miley says excitedly.

'I guess.'

Terry continues to sign.

'He says I'll be able to stand on it when I get far enough in. It'll feel like I'm sinking, but I won't be.'

Then Terry taps his watch before glancing out towards the east and the horizon where the sun is still hiding. There's no need for me to translate. Everyone knows what Terry's just said—we are running out of time.

23

THE CHILD

I have to dive off the boat. Any attempt at lowering myself into the water would rock it too much, and Dawn's jittery as hell. It may be a dive, but I'm not convinced the Olympic swimming team would be too impressed. I lower my body so far towards the water. It's more of an eel-like slide than anything which would garner a round of applause. The good thing is that there's not much of a splash. The surfacing, however, is a whole different ball game.

As soon as the icy water comes up over my chest, every corner of breath that I'm carrying in my lungs gets expelled in a violent explosion. The grip of the water is so harsh around my torso, so unforgiving. I surface, gulping and splashing, my arms and legs floundering. Panicked. Sheer raw panic. I shouldn't have done this. I'm not a strong enough swimmer. I can already feel the water whisking me away; it must be on the turn, about to drain out to the sea and keen to take me with it.

I glance at the boat, which is already slipping away. They're all still huddled there, a cluster of sad, broken beings. I could go back to the boat, insist this is too much, make them take me on board again, but when I turn towards the shore and see Jamie standing there on the road. The lights from his house still spilt out into the street, cutting a golden wand across the tarmac. With his sad, lost face looking straight at me, I realise I'm his only chance of safety, and I know I have to try.

It's too difficult to fight against the tide, so I follow Terry's advice. Luckily, the water is dragging me downstream towards The Wreckers, so I let it take me, concentrating only on closing the distance between myself and the shore. No other thoughts of direction. It's a struggle. The initial shock of the ice-cold grip may have gone, but it's still too cold for human life. Stay in this water too long, and I'll catch hypothermia. It hits me as I claw through the dark water that there's no way I can bring the kid out through this, no way. It would kill him. Then I'll have to stay. The boat will have to go on without me. Reaching my hands out through the water, I pull and claw and will myself towards The Wreckers. The distance closing. Jamie getting closer. And as I swim, the lad walks sadly towards the water's edge. I'm not sure I can make it. The tide is pulling at me, wanting to take me far off and away.

'Now,' I hear a voice behind me. A voice I barely know. It's coming from the boat. Terry?

He's taking a risk in using a voice that has all but rusted up. Using it when he knows to speak is dangerous; it could attract attention. He must feel he needs to. I'm exhausted. Now? What can he...then I realise: I'm there. I can put my feet down. Cautiously, I lower my legs. It's a fight against the current, but down they go, and suddenly they hit something, something soft. Terry's right. I'm there. I've made it. I lean back, allowing the weight to sink into my ankles, but my excitement soon changes to panic; the mud is eating me up. Absorbing me. I feel it groping, clawing at my feet. Dragging me down. Panic rises in my chest. I have to get out of this. I can't do it anymore. I...

They've stopped! My feet have stopped sinking. It must be eight inches of mud. Heavy, but not insurmountable, and beneath the mud, I can feel something hard—the rocks of The Wreckers. I stand and start walking through the water, pushing my weight against it till it slips down my body, becoming shallow waves. Jamie is in front of me; I scan the street for dark shadowy clusters. Those shadow people that seem to haunt anyone that's been unlucky enough to hear the dream. Nothing. I sniff the air for a smell. Again, nothing. Pulling my feet one step at a time out of the mud, I step quickly towards the shore. There's resistance: the mud, the water itself trying to hold me back, but with the leverage I'm getting from the rocks underneath my feet, I'm making headway.

'Jamie?' I call out quietly.

He nods his cherub head, his golden hair bouncing forward as he moves closer to me.

'We've got a boat,' I say. Which is a bit obvious. 'We need to go.' I'm not clear yet how I'll get to the others. There must be other boats, though. There has to be.

'Daddy?' Jamie's voice sounds frail, wavering and confused. His face crumpled in a mass of lines.

Perhaps Jamie's dad walked out when he realised what was happening, just like Leon and PC Green and the twenty-five walked out so that others could live.

'Mummy,' I say. Catching hold of an idea. Mummy's not on the island. That's why Jamie's dad was upset. 'I'm going to take you to Mummy. Is that okay?'

He looks at me, standing there in front of him, dripping

wet, a muddy stranger. I think he's going to bolt. Run. Scream. Draw attention, but no. Instead, he reaches out one small pale hand, and I grasp it.

'It's going to be okay,' I say. 'But we've got to find us a boat so we can get to…'

I turn around, gesturing with my arm towards the estuary behind me, and a sense of dread fills every inch of my being—they've gone.

I feel tears stinging my eyes. My arms go limp at my sides, the life washed out of me. They've left me.

'I…I…'

Jamie is looking up at me. His face about to crumble. His mouth moving up and down as if foreshadowing a sob.

'Ella?' There's a voice at my shoulder. I turn to see Rosa.

My arms reach out around her and grab her to me. 'I thought you'd left.'

She holds me tight. 'Some of them wanted to. I insisted. And since I'm rowing…'

Over her shoulder, I can see the boat nestled back at the pontoon.

'You looked like you were struggling in the water. You'd have never got back with the kid.' She pulls away. 'We don't have much time. The tide's starting to turn. We need to get across the main drag of the estuary.' She reaches for Jamie's hand. 'Come on, you two.'

As I ROW BACK out into the estuary, the cold night air nipping at my wet skin, I try not to torment myself with thinking about who would have said it was a good idea to leave me. I'd definitely put Dawn's name on the list. Possibly even Miley. But the others, Terry, Erin, Bea? I just couldn't see it. Rosa was right when she said the tide was turning. I'd felt it a little when I'd swum towards The Wreckers, but this time rowing out even a measly fifty feet, and our oars are proving much less compliant.

Rosa hunkers her shoulders, bringing her oar up decisively so it lies across her body. 'Keep in time, Ella. Do everything I do.'

I copy the exact way Rosa pulls her oar, keeping my head down as we slip into the same rhythm. Over the sound of the wood cutting through the rippling waves, I can hear Bea; she's enveloped Jamie into her arms, tucked him in a blanket, and is telling him stories about his mum—how she's missing him. How she's waiting for him just the other side. How everything will be alright. Within ten minutes, the boy is fast asleep.

When we get closer to the other side, its dark slumbering hills seeming to roll in towards us, Terry points us in the direction of a channel that should avoid any of the mud banks; we can't afford to get grounded. The water gets a little less insistent on its outward rush as we move closer to the shore. I wouldn't say rowing becomes easy, but there's a satisfaction in knowing that the open water part is done. Now we just need to navigate some of the creeks. If the military sees us, they might just assume we had cast out from the mainland. Although, we look an odd bunch, and I'm guessing they must know Erin by sight. We are far from home and dry, and yet the channels of mud and tufts of grass are soon wrapping their arms around us. Hiding us. I glance over at Rosa. She looks exhausted. Jamie, Dawn and Miley are fast asleep. Erin and Bea are too troubled by what they've seen to doze. They sit staring behind us towards Attercoppe.

'What does it mean?' I ask as we row slowly up a muddy, thin channel.

Rosa looks at me blankly.

'The name, Attercoppe.'

She smiles. 'It's the old English word for spider. A poison head spider.'

Knowing this gives me no comfort. Has the place always been cursed? Staring back over the estuary, I can still see the lights from Jamie's house, as well as a soft glow from The Wreckers. The buildings sitting there as though waiting, caught in a web.

'Yeah.' Rosa sighs. Pulling up her oar, resting it for one moment on her thighs and rubbing her palms. 'Can you believe what happened?' she whispers, mindful of waking the others, more than concerned about being caught.

I shake my head.

Bea's voice breaks the cold, still air. 'I knew it.' It comes loud and clear. So loud it makes us all jump. Instantly, there's an air of panic. The boat rocks. She's moving forward towards Miley. The slap, slap, slap of hungry water outside this small wooden boat suddenly terrifying.

'Careful,' Erin shouts, but there's no stopping Bea. She pulls away from Miley, clutching something in her hand. At first, it makes no sense. I can't make out what it is. Then I realise it's Miley's notebook.

'It's in here, isn't it?' Bea eyes him with a burning, intense anger that seems to have erupted from nowhere.

Miley looks bemused, rubbing his eyes innocently, waking up uncertain where he even is. Then he notices the book clutched carelessly between Bea's fingers, dangling out over the water.

'That's mine.' Before the words are out of his mouth, he's moving forward too fast, too heavy.

'Miley!' Rosa gasps.

The boat lurches ungainly and out of control in the dark expanse. Jamie's awake and crying.

'Stop,' Erin shouts, but Bea's not listening. She's holding the book out further now across the dark lapping waves.

Dawn pulls Miley back. 'Idiot. Stop it. Stop it.'

He swats her away.

'You sit there,' Bea says, loud, clear and decisive. Although there's something odd. Something manic about her expression, her eyes burning.

My God, it hits me. Has she got it? She's acting like a mad woman. Has she heard the dream? But no, that can't be right.

Angrily, Bea flicks at the pages of the book; its white leaves flapping in the cold morning air. 'One more rock of this boat, and this goes in.'

Miley leans back. Elbowing Dawn deliberately in the ribs as he does. 'It's my notebook,' he says, trying to sound calm. 'My work. Just my next novel.'

'Leon told me,' Bea says slowly. 'My son told me that the night of the book club, you came back for your notebook.'

'I...' Miley blusters. 'I left it by mistake.'

Bea looks at him in disgust. 'Someone, Julia? Wrote this cursed dream, or whatever this thing is, she wrote it in your book.' Bea waves the thing again, flapping the pages like a raft of bird's wings.

Miley attempts to sit forward once more. This time Dawn gives him a sharp jab in his own ribs. He ignores it, his eyes remaining focused on the book.

'No. What are you ranting about?' he says dismissively, introducing a small, strained laugh as if Bea's mad.

But we're all looking at him now. Because what Bea's saying fits exactly with the facts.

'You asked Julia to write it down?' Rosa's voice contains a sneer of disgust.

'What?' He laughs. 'I mean, it's just silly. It's just a nightmare. Not real.'

'Did you ask her to read it to the others as she wrote it?' I can't keep the horror out of my voice.

'No, I mean. I didn't say not to. I just...'

In one full long sweep, Bea brings back her arm.

Miley reaches both hands forward, his mouth dropping open, his brow raising as Bea jettisons the book, long and hard, out into the marshes. We all watch, transfixed, the thing flying through the air, expecting at any moment to hear it hit the water. But no, the thing comes down slowly, landing on a clump of grass and mud like a tired bird after a long flight.

'You can't!' Miley's up on his feet. 'All my work.'

The boat's rocking again. This time it's worse. Lurching angrily in the water. Jamie's shrieking. Dawn's grabbing at Miley's trousers, trying to force him down.

'Too much!' he shouts indignantly and dives from the boat.

'Miley, don't be stupid,' Rosa calls after him.

He surfaces, gasping after the cold rush of water that must have squeezed tight into his lungs.

'Can he swim?' I move to the edge of the boat as Miley continues gasping and spluttering. 'He said he couldn't...'

But the water is calming around him. The initial impact hastily forgotten.

'It's my work,' he cries bitterly, his arms reaching out in a crawl towards the book.

'If you touch it,' Bea calls after him, 'I swear I'll kill you myself.'

'You wouldn't understand,' he snarls back at us as he swims.

Swims. What a liar. Even so, I call out over the dark water. 'Miley, don't be stupid,' I shout, not sure that it's safe out there, even if a person can swim.

But he doesn't answer. Perhaps he doesn't hear me, or maybe he doesn't want to. Meanwhile, Terry is signing; it's difficult to keep up, to translate, to absorb the signs and change them into words when my head is all panic.

I turn back to the water, to the rapidly receding Miley.

'You need to be careful, Miley,' I shout. 'Terry said the mud is deep over here.'

We watch as he continues pulling through the water anxiously towards the clump of grass and the book.

'I swear if he touches that thing...' Bea mutters.

'Hush.' Erin takes her hand.

The book is still resting on a mud flat. I can't see very well, but I get the feeling it's lying open. The moon just catching its pale pages. Miley's arm reaches out towards it.

'Got it,' he calls back, his fingers clutching the binding. Curving around it, drawing it close. Taking a moment to glance back at us triumphantly before turning to look at the ghostly cursed pages.

It's then that things get strange. Even stranger. It starts with an uncomfortable feeling. Each person in that boat feels it. Instinctively we pull our coats tighter, sink slightly into our bodies and the black blankets for warmth and protection we can't seem to find. The wind shifts. Its direction changing, bringing with it a subtle icy blast and a strange howling.

'Miley, you need to get back in the boat,' Rosa calls anxiously.

But he looks transfixed, his face angled at the open

pages. His eyes running anxiously across the moonlit sheets of paper.

'Oh my God,' he mutters.

Terry pulls at my arm. He's pointing to his ears, indicating with his fingers.

'Cover your ears,' I shout.

In the water, Miley's foot slips. The bank he must have been standing on suddenly melting into mud.

'It says...' He turns back towards us. Bea is covering Jamie's ears with her hands and singing a gospel song. Singing it loud and clear. The sound of the words growing with each bar that comes out of her mouth.

'*As I went down to the river to pray, studying about the good ol' way.*'

I look over at Miley. He's fighting to speak, unable to see what's happening. The genuine horror of his situation because, all around him, the mud is full of shapes oozing towards him. Yet still, he wants to tell us something: he's desperate to tell us the dream.

I start to sing too. Loud. '*And who shall wear the Robe and Crown, good Lord, tell me who.*'

Even above the singing, I can just make out the most hideous gargling sound as mud feeds into Miley's open, constantly moving mouth.

'*O Sisters, let's go down.*' Rosa is singing as well. She draws her oar into the boat, turns her face away and sings.

We run through the whole thing. Then go for Amazing Grace and Jerusalem. We sing way past the moment when Miley has slipped under the water clutching his precious book. We sing till the shadow people leave, till the smell returns to only that of marsh and salt, till we have barely any breath left in our bodies.

.   .   .

WHEN WE ARRIVE at the far bank, with the crumbling military outbuildings, we are still singing, although there is very little joy in the process.

The others all get out, staggering up the shore as I help Rosa drag the boat up onto the bank and hide it under dead branches. In the morning, they may be looking for us. We can't afford to leave any trails.

The buildings are old, dilapidated, but the four walls and partial roofing will at least give us some cover. Rosa manages to get a fire going. And we're glad of the food Bea brought along. Terry hands me a bottle of water, and I drink. No one talks, though. No one mentions what we've just seen. Tomorrow we will have to make a plan, but we need to get a little shut-eye before we can move on. I unroll my sleeping bag and give it to Jamie and Bea. There are tears in Bea's eyes as she takes it; it's Leon's. The thing must remind her of home. She holds it sadly to her face, inhaling the familiar smells.

'Still smells of my boy.' Her voice is barely audible.

I say nothing. Not sure what you can say. Instead, I sink down by a wall, pull the hood of my hoodie as far up as it will stretch and despite the hard concrete ground beneath me, sleep.

24

———

LONG GOODBYES

When I wake, everything feels...odd. The light too bright. The noise of the day far too still, the ground impossibly hard and nothing about anything is feeling remotely morning fresh. My head is foggy. Despite the piercing intensity of the new day, the images surrounding me appear blurred and clouded. I try to get up but soon realise I can't. It's not just that I feel unsteady, which I do, but my hands won't function. Looking down, I see they're tied, bound with multiple rounds of gaffer tape.

Something here is very wrong. When I attempt to move my legs, I discover that's not possible either; they're wrapped up just as tightly. A hard slug of cold air sinks through my throat, bringing panic with it. Could the military have found us? It must be them, although that doesn't quite fit—would they use gaffer tape? Surely they'd have rope and men with guns, and where is everyone anyway? My people, the people I escaped with, where are they? Edging my body away from the sharp grit of the wall that I'm propped against, I attempt to get a clearer picture of what's happened, starting with how we got here in the first place, because nothing is clear. I remember that we'd escaped in a boat over the marshes. Terry had been guiding us. We'd had to go back to get a kid, Jamie, but there are worse things in my head. Things that came before the escape. Images of Leon cloud my brain as a wave of sickness rises through my body. In my mind's eye I can still picture Leon drowning in the estuary, tied for eternity to Madeline and the twenty-five as the tide rose, and the horror doesn't stop there. Charley. I remember Charley standing on the causeway, trying to talk to the authorities. I can almost hear the ricochet of bullets from the past. They'd shot her down. Executed her in cold blood. These people were ruthless. No way were they going to let us escape. Pulling at the gaffer tape wrapped around my wrist, using my teeth in an attempt to cut into the gluey black strips, I know I have to get myself free. The military must have found us, seen us sloping off over the water. Bided their time till we were sleeping, then swooped in. We should have split up last night, moved on. Had someone stayed awake watching. Only...Why is everything so quiet? Where are the others?

I edge my body down the wall, rolling onto my back, hoping with my body on a flat surface I might be able to pull the binding on my legs apart, but as I roll onto the floor my body bumps into a water bottle. It must be mine—the one I'd set beside me before I lay down for the night. It topples, spilling to the floor. Glancing through the clear plastic base, I notice something curious—a powdery residue seems to be trapped in the bottom. Floating cloud-like in the clear liquid, disturbed from the fall. It's then that I realise my mouth is a little too dry, a little powdery. My tongue feels heavy and dead inside my mouth. Could there have been something in my water? The dry mouth, the fact

I'd fallen asleep so quickly despite the hard unforgiving concrete. Could someone, one of our own group perhaps, have drugged me? But why would they do that? It didn't make sense. Not someone from our group at least. We were all on the same page, all fighting the same battle. They must be close by, in the same predicament. Maybe. I glance around me. Somewhere a bird calls over the marshes. There's no sign of anyone. For one single moment, I feel entirely bereft. This world with all its horrors seeming so very big. Bigger, now that my "friends" have vanished. I shake my head, irritated. Drawing myself a thick slug of mineral-laden, watery air. I'm not sure what's going on here and maybe it doesn't even matter. The point is—I need to get free. If only they hadn't bound me so tight. I try to ease my legs apart once again, but there's no give. No hope. Exhausted, I feel panic rising through my body. All is lost when suddenly, the panic subsides, replaced by curiosity. There's a gentle tap, tapping on my shoulder. So gentle, so thoughtful. I turn, blinking up into the light to see Terry standing over me. His kind face, his sweet eyes, and my panic turns to relief. Terry's not tied. He's not bound. He can help—get me out. We're safe. Free. Moments from freedom.

'Terry,' I pant. 'I've been tied up.' I hold up my arms. 'Can you get these off?' I whimper expecting him to move forward, to start to cut the gaffer with a stone, or a knife, or even his teeth, yet curiously he makes no attempt to release me. Instead, Terry takes a step back.

'*Sorry*,' he signs.

Panicking, I glance around me, unsure what's happening or why he's not helping. Nothing about this is making any sense. 'Where is everyone?' I gasp, switching my body around on the floor, struggling, trying to free myself, yet with every twist and turn the binding seems to tighten.

'What's happened?' My voice sounds like somebody else's, some hurt, scared creature, and my mouth is still so dry. I feel tears of frustration sting my eyes. Terry reaches for me again, placing a hand on my shoulder and signing for me to slow down: speak slower. Since my hands are bound, he's having to lip-read and struggling. I manage to still my body, frustrated, but knowing that I need to find out what's going on and Terry holds the key. I need to speak slowly, one word at a time. Calm is the only way we'll get out of this situation.

'Where is everyone?' I say, mouthing each word.

Terry sighs. Gently, he moves closer, supporting my shoulders as he helps me prop my body against the nearest wall until I'm sitting. Curiously, I feel a little less vulnerable. Terry smiles at me sadly, before nimbly crouching down opposite and beginning to move his old hands steadily, slowly, in explanation.

'*I'm sorry,*' he signs. '*They've all gone on. They will be safe though—lie low for a while. I told them I'd stay with you.*'

'But I don't understand?' I say, breathlessly. 'Was it the military?'

Terry shakes his head.

'Then what?' Frustration forces me to clamp my jaw. Why isn't he telling me what's happened? I don't understand. 'Terry, please?'

He smiles at me sadly but doesn't reply. Instead, he pulls his bag towards him and takes out a clatter of small, brown pill bottles. Letting them spill onto the hard floor between us.

'Why?' They're not even his. Is he feeling sick? It doesn't make any sense. 'What are you doing, Terry?' I bluster.

There's such a sad look on his face, resigned, but totally bereft as slowly, methodically, he begins to unlock the bottles, pushing the safety catches down on each one before giving them a twist till each bottle is standing mouth wide open in front of him.

'Terry? Please. What are you doing?' I continue, a note of panic rising in my voice.

Still, Terry doesn't reply. Instead, he picks up one bottle and pours some pills into his hand, pushing them into the well of his palm before swallowing them. Swallowing them all.

'What. Terry!' I don't know what the pills are, but there's one thing for sure—he's taking way too many. I want to knock them out of his hands, slap his back, tell him not to be so stupid, but I can't move, the wound gaffer tape is on too tight.

'Terry please,' I sob, 'tell me what's happening.'

He smiles at me sadly before emptying yet another bottle into his hand.

'What are you doing?' I shout.

'*I know, Ella,*' he signs. Letting his watery-blue cataract eyes rest on me sadly for a moment. '*That man, your husband,*' Terry signs. '*I know that he told you the dream.*'

I feel a cold rush of panic wash over me. There's a pause. A pause in which Terry helps himself to yet another handful of tablets, munching down on the dry hard pills, swilling them with a gulp of water, before continuing.

'*I saw the look in your eyes, Ella, when I hit him, when he fell away. He must have whispered the nightmare to you only moments before.*'

My God, I realise. Terry really had been going to kill me when he'd taken out Jayden. It wasn't a case of mistaken identity. He knew I was contagious. 'But you didn't get rid of me. You knew, but you didn't kill me?' I say, a desperate note of pleading in my voice.

He shakes his head slowly. Stopping for a moment in his

pill consumption to toy idly with three of the empty brown bottles, before starting to sign once more. '*I know it doesn't always work straight away—the curse. I know it's an odd one, but there was something about you...I couldn't smell it on you or see the dead people.*'

Dead people? I guess he must mean the shadow people, the ones that haunted the places where the dream virus had passed through. 'So,' I gasp. 'Maybe I'm alright?' My voice sounds a little too desperate, even in my own ears, but I continue anyway. 'If I don't have that rotting smell, if the shadow people aren't all over me, maybe it doesn't always work, this dream.' I clutch hold of this tiny thread of hope like a drowning man. 'Maybe Jayden said it all wrong?' I plead.

Terry looks up at me sadly, before starting to sign once more. '*You can't be alright. It gets everyone eventually.*' He takes another pill, this time using just his thumb and forefinger as if treating himself to an exotic delicacy.

An uncomfortable thought suddenly hits me. 'Did you tell the others to leave me when I went back for Jamie?'

He nods. '*Sorry. But...*' He continues moving his hands. '*Rosa and Erin wouldn't. I didn't tell them why I felt it was best to leave you, not at the time. They thought I was scared.*'

He fixes me with his cold blue eyes.

'*I didn't tell them the real reason then. I did that this morning.*'

I don't want to die. I've been through so much, and all for what? Yes, Jayden had whispered the dream to me. Whispered it as his fat slug lips brushed against my face. Yes, I know the horror or most of it. Enough perhaps. Yet, I haven't got the symptoms—no shadow people closing in on me. If I inhale, there's no smell of rot, and there's no desire to start blurting all the gory hideous details that my husband spilt into my ear. Isn't that what happens? The dream is like an itch. People have to tell, but I haven't got that, any of it. 'Please believe me, Terry. I feel fine,' I say.

Instead of answering, Terry takes another pill, before cutting the binding on my hands. I'm not sure what he intends to do. I know he doesn't believe that I'm fine. I know he thinks it's just a matter of time before the smell kicks in, the shadow people arrive, and I start spouting out the dream like a human fountain. Only I have no idea what happens next? Will he turn me in? The authorities don't want anyone who's been touched by the nightmare. They've made that clear. Will Terry kill me? It seems unlikely. Rubbing my wrists, I realise that even having my hands free makes me appear more human. Terry doesn't have it in him to kill anyone in cold blood. Then it dawns on me...my water bottle. What did he put in it? I hold it up. 'Did you poison me?'

Terry shakes his head, vaguely amused, before he starts to sign once again.

'*No. Just drugged. No need to kill you, Ella. You're carrying the poison yourself.*'

'The curse?'

'*Yes.*' Slowly, and with great effort, Terry pulls the rolled-up sleeping bag towards him and settles himself back against the wall. '*Now,*' he signs, '*Ella, tell me about the dream you had last night. You tell me, you die, and I'm...*' he rattles the bottle beside him, '*not going to tell anyone. This thing stops with us.*'

It's then that it dawns on me, with an incredible sense of euphoria: I'm not dying. 'I didn't dream last night,' I say, every inch of my body tingling with elation.

Terry shoots me a disbelieving look, his eyes weary, already dropping from the drugs.

'No, Terry.' I grab his thick papery hands between my own. 'I swear, I don't dream. It can't get me.'

The words of my mother come flooding back. *'A grumpy old dwarf of a thing shouldn't have dreams.'* She didn't actually say *shouldn't*. I've changed that in my head over the years, making the memory of her even crueller. She actually said *doesn't*. I had been asking her why I didn't have dreams. It was curious. Everyone else I knew had them, but not me. She'd said I was too ugly, too grumpy. She was like that— never one for giving out compliments. When I was older, I figured it out. Most people have dreams. Some people just don't remember them, but I'm not convinced I've ever had them. I certainly didn't have one last night. Whatever curious chemistry has to take place in the brain to get you to the land of nod, I swear to God, I just don't have it. Perhaps it was because my life had been stunted, or maybe...I look around me at our curious camp, think about our strange escape. Maybe I don't dream because fate had other plans for me.

'Seriously, Terry, I don't dream. That's why there's no smell, no dead people. I can hear the dream, but it doesn't sink in. Not fully. You need to be able to dream. That must be how the horror gets in and destroys a person. I'm immune. I could maybe tell you the dream, what Jayden told me at least, but because I haven't dreamt it myself, it wouldn't have any force.'

And Terry, bless him, does the sweetest thing: he laughs, a joyous sound, a sound that is laced with pure delight at the fact that somehow, our oddball band of escapees finally got the better of this curse.

~

I STAY with Terry until he dies. It's peaceful—like falling asleep after a long hard day. If you know there are no night-mares lurking in the shadows for you, sweet dreams are a possibility. I prop Terry's wafer-light body against the wall and tuck him in using Leon's sleeping bag, abandoning the empty pill bottles around his legs. I can telephone the police when I put a bit of distance between us. They'll pick him up, do the right thing.

When I start packing up our makeshift camp, I manage to find a little food that the others must have left for Terry. I don't think they knew what he was intending. Rosa would have tried to stop him if he'd told her. I wish I'd managed to do that, but this world is far from perfect, and maybe it wasn't such a bad way to go—knowing you'd stopped some-thing so evil from erupting across the face of the globe.

Pushing an energy bar into my pocket, my hand brushes against something else stuffed deep inside the dark folds of material. I pull it out, peering at the thin strip of card. For a moment it doesn't seem to make any sense. Then I remember—it's the card I'd taken from Maggie's flowers:

A joy to all who knew her.

I smile to myself, running my fingers over the words—something to aim for. Helping myself to a bottle of water, I survey the camp one last time. I know we've all got to keep under the radar for a bit. With Jayden gone, that shouldn't be a problem for me. I've decided to try to find Grant. His world had been the only place where I'd managed to find a little happiness and stability. Maybe he's married now with kids of his own; maybe that's not even important. Grant was the kind of character who had love in abundance. Besides, I'd like to pay him back for whatever it was my mum had taken all those years ago, and now with Jayden's USB, his contacts, his scams, I could easily pull my weight financially.

Right now, I need to get on with living, carve out a life for myself and leave the horrors of the past where they belong —behind me. Whatever my future looks like, it's going to be better than before.

The End

A NOTE FROM THE PUBLISHER

Thank you for reading this book. If you enjoyed it please do consider leaving a review on Amazon.

We hate typos. If you find any, let the team know and we can get it amended. publishedwithpassion@aol.com

MORE BY THIS AUTHOR

The Insect House - Bloodhound Books

Helen and Gareth grew up in a world where absolute freedom was the norm, but the arrival of a predatory priest saw their childhood paradise turn rotten. A murder was committed. Gareth went A.W.O.L, and Helen put her life on hold. Twenty-five years later, Gareth is back.

"An Outstanding piece of new writing." James Holloway. The Cut.

"Loved this. Well constructed plot with a twist at the end." (amazon uk review)

"Fresh Original writing. A gripping tale with great characters, and a twist." Rob Backhouse. Mustard.

"From start to finish, not a word wasted." Alan Huckle. Eyes Write.

ALSO AVAILABLE

Reap What You Sow - Bloodhound Books

Struggling journalist Sophie can't believe her luck when she lands the job of a lifetime—writing the personal history of renowned geneticist Tim Henderson, from his idyllic Greek island. But the island, and Henderson, turn out to be hiding much more than Sophie bargained for.
5 out of 5 stars

"A compelling psychological thriller that is always one step ahead of the reader, a great read." (Amazon Review.)

"Totally gripping. I loved this book. Couldn't put it down and read it more or less in one sitting." (Amazon Review.)

"Greek mythology expertly woven into a creepy psychological thriller... what's not to love!" (Amazon Review)

SIGN UP FOR THE NEWSLETTER

The newsletter comes out once a month.
I'll be reviewing what to watch and read.
Unsubscribe anytime.

ACKNOWLEDGMENTS

With special thanks to Breck for beta reading. Isla for alpha reading. Maryssa for editing, Louise McGuinness for proof-reading and Katarina for the cover design.